SUSPECTS IN T

"Tell me what you
put a half-eaten coo
his pen. He took notes w
looked up. "How is he paid for his work? Does he get a percent of the sales or is he on salary?"

"No idea." Val made a mental note to ask Clancy that question. "Clancy needs money to take care of his brother's medical bills. If sales of Usher's books declined because of rumors about his health and Clancy's compensation is tied to those sales, he'd want to make sure the rumors didn't resurface. Maybe he found out Emmett was behind them."

The chief flicked his wrist. "*Ifs* and *maybes.*"

Val moved toward more solid ground. "The person at the Usher house with the most obvious reason to get rid of Emmett is Madison Fox-Norton, known as Maddie Norton in the theater group. Gunnar overheard Emmett blackmailing her. She had the opportunity to add meds to Emmett's burrito during the rehearsal. Did she and the other people at the Usher house have access to blood pressure meds?"

"We have no probable cause to search the Usher house for meds, if that's what you're hoping. To get a court order for a search, we need compelling evidence tying someone to a crime."

Val was disappointed, but not surprised. "Granddad and I will be at the house this evening. Maybe we can find out something that will give you a reason to conduct a search."

The chief threw up his hands in an I-give-up gesture. "You just tried to convince me that someone in that house is a murderer. If you're right, it could be dangerous for both of you. Stay away from there . . ."

Books by Maya Corrigan

BY COOK OR BY CROOK

SCAM CHOWDER

FINAL FONDUE

THE TELL-TALE TARTE

Published by Kensington Publishing Corporation

The Tell-Tale Tarte

Maya Corrigan

KENSINGTON PUBLISHING CORP.
http://www.kensingtonbooks.com

KENSINGTON BOOKS are published by

Kensington Publishing Corp.
119 West 40th Street
New York, NY 10018

All Kensington Titles, Imprints, and Distributed Lines are available at special quantity discounts for bulk purchases for sales promotions, premiums, fund-raising, and educational or institutional use. Special book excerpts or customized printings can also be created to fit specific needs. For details, write or phone the office of the Kensington special sales manager: Kensington Publishing Corp., 119 West 40th Street, New York, NY 10018, attn: Special Sales Department, Phone: 1-800-221-2647.

ISBN-13: 978-1-4967-0917-2
ISBN-10: 1-4967-0917-9
First Kensington Mass Market Edition: July 2017

eISBN-13: 978-1-4967-0918-9
eISBN-10: 1-4967-0918-7
First Kensington Electronic Edition: July 2017

10 9 8 7 6 5 4 3 2 1

Printed in the United States of America

What was it that so unnerved me in the contemplation of the House of Usher? It was a mystery all insoluble.

—"The Fall of the House of Usher"
by Edgar Allan Poe

The thousand injuries of Fortunato I had borne as best I could, but when he ventured upon insult I vowed revenge.

—"The Cask of Amontillado"
by Edgar Allan Poe

I was never kinder to the old man than during the whole week before I killed him.

—"The Tell-Tale Heart"
by Edgar Allan Poe

Chapter 1

Why would a man in his seventies change his appearance overnight? Val Deniston stared at her grandfather, her spoon motionless in the skillet of sizzling onions.

Framed in the doorway to the kitchen, Granddad looked as if he belonged in a fountain-of-youth drug ad, not at all like the man who'd welcomed her as a housemate a year ago. Only yesterday he'd resembled Santa Claus, with a fluffy beard, white curls fringing his head, and wire-framed bifocals slipping down his nose. Now he had shorter hair, a trimmed beard, rimless glasses with tinted lenses, and a tweed driver's cap covering his bald spot on top.

Val pointed her wooden spoon at him. "Who are you, and what did you do with the real Don Myer?"

"I got a new style for the New Year. What do you think?" He sauntered across the kitchen as if on a runway in a fashion show. Then he shed his black wool car coat, hung it over his chair at the breakfast table, and showed her his shirt and pants—black, hip, and expensive.

"You look . . . fantastic, Granddad." Something other than the New Year must explain his makeover and possibly also his long absences from the house the last few days . . . something or someone. Six months ago, he'd spruced up his appearance, though less radically, to charm an attractive widow, but he'd soon reverted to his plaid shirts and well-worn pants.

He patted his jaw. "How do you like my whiskers?"

"A big improvement." He'd grown a full beard to play Santa, arriving by boat at the town dock to kick off Bayport's holiday fest. Instead of shaving off the beard after the fest, he'd hacked at it for weeks. "Your barber gave you an elegant beard, but he took off too much hair above it. I liked the curls around your ears."

He snorted. "Barber! I went to a stylist in Annapolis. You should go too. You're starting to look like that poodle across the street."

She feigned horror. "The apricot poodle? No way. My hair's darker, like cinnamon." She fingered her unruly curls. "And if it needs a trim, Bayport has plenty of stylists. Why'd you go all the way to Annapolis?"

He pointed to his tweed cap. "I bought it at Hats in the Belfry. You can't buy anything like this in Bayport."

True. The hats sold in this town appealed to the tourists who flocked to Maryland's Eastern Shore for boating on the Chesapeake Bay, duck hunting, and golfing. Before now Granddad had never worn a driving cap. He'd bought few new clothes since Grandma died almost seven years ago, except maybe underwear. He could count on receiving socks, shirts, sweaters, and pajamas for birthday and Christmas gifts. "What are you doing that requires a stylish wardrobe?"

"Work for a new client. I'm finally attracting the right type of business. No more tracking down runaway tabbies or stolen garden gnomes."

"With a business card that identifies you as a problem solver and sleuth, you have to be prepared for any challenge. Mrs. Smith was very grateful you found her cat."

"She wasn't grateful enough to pay me with cash, just cookies. I want to earn back some of the money I forked over for that online private-eye course. My client is paying my expenses and even gave me an advance." He adjusted the angle of his driver's cap.

Val turned the burner down as she digested Granddad's words. With that dubious online training and a minor role in solving a murder or two, what could he be doing to merit up-front payment? Did his client want him to go where a younger person wouldn't fit in? Maybe he'd exaggerated his undercover snooping in a retirement community last summer. She only hoped he wasn't getting in over his head. "What kind of work does your client want you to do?"

"That's confidential." He pointed to the pan on the stove. "Looks like you're making enough onions for the whole town." He sniffed. "I smell beef and bacon too. What's the occasion? You don't usually cook good stuff like that for me."

At her mother's insistence and despite his grumbling, Val kept him on a low-cholesterol diet. "The French onion soup and the daube Provençal are for a dinner party I'm catering tomorrow. The flavors have to blend for a day."

"You didn't tell me you had another catering job."

"I just got it three days ago, and I've barely seen you since then." She wouldn't let him get away with changing the subject from his gig to hers. "When did you start working for your new client?"

"This week." Granddad picked up her recipe card from the counter and held it at arm's length. "I can't read it with these tinted glasses. I need my bifocals. Can we use this soup recipe in the cookbook?"

"Sorry. It doesn't meet your exacting standards. *If an old codger like me can cook, anyone can. Five ingredients is all you need.*"

He frowned. "When did I say that?"

"In your first interview, after you submitted my recipes as your own and won the job of food columnist." Having fooled local newspaper readers into believing he could cook, he now wanted to take his Codger Cook ruse to a larger audience by publishing a cookbook.

"I think of them as family recipes. Your grandmother taught you to cook right here." His sweeping gesture encompassed the cheerful kitchen and the butler's pantry in the old house.

Val still felt Grandma's calming spirit in the kitchen and changed the subject rather than argue with Granddad over his right to the recipes. "By the way, I'm going out to dinner tonight with Gunnar. There are some leftovers in the fridge."

"Don't need 'em. Got plans of my own tonight." He went to the sink for a glass of water. "Gunnar hasn't been around lately. I was afraid you two broke up."

A few months ago, Granddad would have been thrilled if her romance with Gunnar turned sour. "He's working on a big forensic accounting contract and rehearsing for the Treadwell Players' next production." Val had seen less of him lately than at any time since he moved to Bayport last summer.

"With Gunnar so busy, you have more time to test recipes for the cookbook."

She put down the wooden spoon and turned toward him, her hands on her hips. "In the fall, when you came up with this cookbook idea, you agreed to test the recipes for it. Unless you do that, you don't get to use *my* recipes in *The Codger's Cookbook* and put Don Myer on the cover along with Val Deniston."

"Don't get in a snit about it. I'll do my part when I'm not tied up with a client, but we gotta move fast on the cookbook. I'm lining up an agent."

Val stared at him, incredulous. Unless publishing had become far less competitive in the year since she left her job as a cookbook publicist, he couldn't have snagged a reputable agent with so little of the book finished. He must have fallen for a scam. "Where did you get this agent?"

"Never mind. Just test some recipes and get 'em on paper. You got a couple hours now, before you go to dinner, and you can work on it tomorrow if Bethany manages the café for you."

"This afternoon I'm going to help her pick out a dress for a wedding. She worked today at the café. I can't ask her to do it again tomorrow. After teaching first graders all week long, she needs at least one day off." Bethany would also work at the café on Monday, the Martin Luther King Day holiday, so Val could sleep in after catering the night before.

Granddad stroked his neat white beard. "If I find someone to help you at the café, do you think you can finish the cookbook in the next six weeks?"

She stirred the onions vigorously. Six weeks from now she might not have a café to manage. Based on the rumor she'd heard today, the space occupied by her café at the athletic club would turn into a sportswear boutique. She'd hold off on telling Granddad until she confirmed the rumor. "I can't work every day for the next six weeks on the cookbook. Do you know what happens in the middle of next month?"

"Middle of February? Hmm. Your birthday." He shrugged. "You're gonna be thirty-three, so it's not a big birthday. That shouldn't keep you from finishing the cookbook."

"My birthday is also Valentine's Day. I'd like to take some time off to spend with my valentine." Gunnar had talked about the two of them making a trip to New York then, her first visit back there since leaving her fiancé and her cookbook-publicist job. Val tried to ignore her grandfather's dejected expression. "I can finish three chapters by the beginning of March, but only if you test the recipes.

Three chapters will be enough for an agent to send to a publisher."

"Okay." He took the black car coat from the back of the kitchen chair. "I'm going to run some errands." He left the kitchen.

His new look and his secrecy about what his client wanted him to do struck her as fishy, but as long as the work didn't land him in hot water, it wasn't all bad. The job had pulled him out of the post-Christmas doldrums he'd suffered ever since her brother's family had gone home to California. Granddad had really enjoyed his great-grandsons over the holidays and missed them.

The café contract occupied Val's thoughts as she caramelized the onions. If she lost the contract, she'd need another job fast to help Granddad with the household expenses. Without her income, he'd have to sell the large Victorian where he'd spent most of his life. And she'd have to admit failure, that sickening feeling she'd had after her career and her engagement ended. She had six weeks to prove she wasn't a failure at the café.

Val drove into the parking lot at the Queenstown outlet mall. At three on a Saturday afternoon, with the post-holiday sales in full swing, the mall was swarming with shoppers. She pulled into a space and read the text Bethany had sent with the name of the shop where they should meet. Unfortunately, she didn't say in which of the outdoor mall's four sprawling buildings the shop was located. With parking lots around and between the buildings, Val could have a long chilly walk.

She got out of the car, scanned the longest building in the complex, and counted herself lucky to see the shop nearby.

When she went into it, she immediately spotted Bethany's ginger hair and neon yellow parka. Val joined her at a circular rack of dresses. "Sorry I'm late. Buying and prepping the food for the book club dinner took longer than I expected. I have to serve a meal related to the book under discussion."

"What are they reading?"

"Rick Usher's recent best seller. I'm making a French dinner because the story's set in Paris."

Bethany moved the hangers along the rack, studying one brightly colored dress after another. "I've read every one of Usher's horror books. I didn't know he had a new one. What's it called?"

"*The Murders in the Rue Cler*, but it's not horror. I looked it up online. It's about a French detective, Gaston Vulpin."

"Usher models his writing on Edgar Allan Poe's. He publishes one eerie book and one murder mystery each year. I don't know how he manages to write so much. He's getting kind of old."

"He has help. There's another name on the book cover, under his." If Granddad had his way, his name would appear first on *The Codger's Cookbook* and the person who actually came up with the recipes would get second billing in smaller type.

Bethany pulled a hanger off the rack. "I picked out a couple of dresses I liked. Everyone says sideways stripes make you look fat, but up-and-down ones should be okay. What do you think of this?" She showed Val a boxy sheath with multi-hued vertical stripes.

The colors reminded Val of a set of jumbo crayons. "Narrow vertical stripes might be slimming, but those wide stripes would make even a runway model look chunky."

"No matter how much I diet, I'll never be thin enough for a runway." Bethany put the dress back and unhooked another one from the rack. "This is my second choice."

She held up a full-skirted dress cinched at the waist by a wide black belt. Above and below the waist were amorphous blobs of red, pink, and white, with bits of green interspersed, like a field of poppies viewed by someone nearsighted.

Val couldn't decide whether the flower riot would look better or worse than the crayon box on Bethany. Neither would flatter her. "That dress would be fine in the spring," and on someone half Bethany's size. "A January wedding calls for something else. Let's try another store."

A frigid wind whipped around them when they left the shop. Val spotted a bearded man in a black coat and a driver's cap sauntering through the parking lot. Granddad in his new clothes. Maybe this visit to the mall was related to the job he was keeping secret from her. Could someone have hired him to be a mystery shopper?

Val pointed toward the farthest lane of the parking lot. "There's my grandfather over there."

Bethany squinted at him. "That doesn't look like him."

"He got a makeover since the last time you saw him." Val stopped at a window display. "Look, this shop has forty percent off." She pulled the door handle.

"Wait, Val. Your grandfather's walking funny. Weaving and—" Bethany broke off as a car horn sounded from the far end of the lot.

Val watched a car creep toward Granddad. He paid no attention to it. He staggered. Then he disappeared as if a trap door in a stage had swallowed him. The car jerked to a stop.

Her heart raced. Granddad had fallen, or the car had knocked him down.

She dashed across the lanes of the parking lot, evading drivers cruising for empty spaces. A pickup truck backing out of a space nearly hit her. By the time she reached the place where she'd last seen Granddad, a crowd had gathered.

A middle-aged woman on the fringe of the group wrung her hands. "He just dropped on the ground in front of my car. I called 911."

As Val edged her way into the crowd, she spotted a tweed driving cap and tinted glasses on the pavement. Granddad's new purchases. Her eyes burned with tears.

Three people bent over him, blocking her view of his face. She saw only his dark trousers and shoes. Black loafers with metal hardware.

Granddad never wore loafers! And those shoes would be way too small for him.

Dizzy with relief, she wiped away her tears, craned her neck, and glimpsed the face of the man on the ground.

A day ago she wouldn't have seen any resemblance between him and her grandfather. But now, after an extreme makeover, Granddad had a similar haircut and beard, as well as the identical hat and glasses.

A burly teenager bending over the stricken man said, "I can't feel his pulse."

Val shivered, chilled to the core. Granddad was a dead ringer for a dead man.

Chapter 2

Val's heart pounded as she peered at the ashen face of the man now receiving CPR. Where was her grandfather while his double lay motionless on the ground? If she knew, she would rush to him and hug him tightly enough to feel his heart pulsing.

Bethany sidled up next to her. "I couldn't keep up with you in these." She pointed toward her boots with chunky high heels. Then she peered over Val's shoulder at the man on the ground. "Poor guy. He reminds me of someone, but not your grandfather."

"Granddad just got his hair and beard trimmed exactly like that man's."

"Your grandfather cut his hair? I loved his white curls." Bethany sounded shocked and hurt, like a freshman returning from college to find her room at home redecorated.

The burly young man giving CPR looked up, beads of sweat on his forehead. "I don't know if I'm doing this right. Anyone else want to try?"

The teenager looked distraught. Like Val, he'd

probably done chest compressions only on a dummy. Her recent CPR refresher gave her confidence. "I can spell you."

She switched places with him as sirens sounded. Mouthing the words to "Stayin' Alive," the recommended song to set the beat for CPR, Val kept up the compressions until the EMTs arrived and took over.

How long had it been since the man collapsed? She'd lost all sense of time. Chest compressions alone had a minute chance of reviving him, but CPR plus defibrillation within five minutes of cardiac arrest would give him a better chance of survival.

Val joined Bethany on the sidelines. "I hope he makes it."

"You did all you could," Bethany said. "When did you learn CPR?"

"I took a training course after I moved in with Granddad. I'd never forgive myself if he had a heart attack and I stood by helplessly." Val reached into her shoulder bag for her phone. "I'm calling him." She'd feel calmer once she heard his voice.

He didn't answer the landline or his cell phone. She was disappointed, but not alarmed. He must have gone out without his cell phone or forgotten to recharge it.

She marched toward the row of stores lining the parking lot. "Let's go find you a dress."

Bethany limped behind her. "Slow down. I think I got a blister from trying to run in these boots.

You flew off in a panic just because you saw a man with a coat and hat like your grandfather's."

Val shifted her pace from fast forward to slow-mo. "Not only the clothes, his hair and beard too. Granddad just got those trimmed this morning."

"Simple explanation. When he went for a haircut, he saw that man in the shop and asked the stylist to trim his hair and beard the same way. He could have bought a similar hat and coat because he liked the guy's style."

"You can explain away the hair and the clothes, but not Granddad's new eyeglasses. They were like the ones on the ground where that man fell—rimless with tinted lenses." Val stood aside for a family of shoppers strolling abreast on the sidewalk. With the family past them, she and Bethany resumed walking. "You can buy sunglasses and reading glasses from a rack in a drugstore, but where do you find glasses like that on the spur of the moment?"

"That does sound eerie, like a horror story—the Stepford grandfathers."

Val laughed. "I can't imagine Granddad as docile as a Stepford wife." But he'd submit to a makeover if a client stroked his ego and paid him enough.

They went into the shop with the forty-percent-off sign.

Bethany zeroed in on a ribbon-trimmed lilac dress with puffy sleeves and a tiered skirt. "Do you think this will work on me?"

Maybe for a square dance. "You'd look more sophisticated in a simpler style."

Bethany checked the label. "Uh-oh. A size too

small. I could probably squeeze into it if I began dieting today, but I can't. I have to start my new diet when the moon is full, and I just missed it for this month."

Val rolled her eyes. Her friend's latest fad diet sounded even wackier than the others she'd tried. "What does the moon have to do with your diet?"

"It's the werewolf diet. You fast on the first day of the full moon. There are other rules too."

"Like running around the woods and howling?"

"Not funny, Val." Bethany hung up the lilac dress.

"Give me a heads-up when you go on the vampire diet so I stay away from you after sundown." Val had an idea how to get Bethany to try on something that would flatter her more than her usual outfits. "You asked for my advice about a dress. Will you let me pick one out for you?"

"As long as I get a veto."

Giving her veto power would just prolong this shopping jaunt. Val wanted to get home in time to catch Granddad before he left for the evening. "How about if I pick out two dresses and you choose between them?"

Bethany folded her arms. "I'll do it, if you let me pick out a dress for you."

"You're the one going to a wedding, not me. I don't need a dress."

"Duh. You don't need a wedding to wear a new dress. For a change, put on something with more pizzazz."

Val suppressed a laugh. Until now she hadn't realized her tastes in clothes offended Bethany. Ironic that they were both trying to give each other's wardrobes a makeover. "I wear comfortable clothes in classic styles."

"You mean slacks and sweaters in navy, black, and tan. The next time you go out with Gunnar, wear something clingy and edgy in a bright color. It might add a spark to your stalled romance."

"People burned by previous romances are wary of sparks." Val went over to the sales rack and sorted through dresses in Bethany's size. "And *stalled* is the wrong word. We're still moving along."

"Slowly."

"We both have a lot going on. He's working on the Treadwell Players' upcoming play. I'm busy with the three Cs—café, catering, and cookbook."

"Be careful you don't drift apart." Bethany studied the dresses in Val's size. "The same rules apply for both of us. I select two dresses for you. You buy the one you like best."

Or disliked the least. Val rejected the fire engine red dress Bethany chose and agreed to buy a clingy electric blue dress. The color worked well with her hair. Bethany rejected a cream-colored dress as dull, and then hemmed and hawed over a teal dress. Yes, the princess cut flattered her curves without emphasizing them, but wasn't the dress too plain for a wedding? Val solved the problem by finding a multicolor scarf to jazz it up.

Back at home, she was disappointed not to find Granddad. She called his cell phone and heard it ring in the front hall where he'd left it to charge. Her check of online local news gave her no information about the man who'd left the mall parking lot on a stretcher.

She decided against wearing her new dress to dinner with Gunnar. She would save it for when she could give him her undivided attention. Tonight, she'd have a hard time thinking about anything except the man in the mall and his similarity to Granddad.

Gunnar also had something on his mind. He arrived uncharacteristically late to pick her up and without the smile that usually turned his face from less than handsome to almost attractive.

Once they were seated at the restaurant, he talked about the travails of installing new software on his computer, which had taken him most of the day.

She sympathized. "I can see how that would make you cranky."

He didn't object to being called cranky. She wasn't even sure he'd heard her. He barely looked at the menu.

She pored over it. "I'm going to order the seafood risotto. The last time I tried it here, it tasted good but the portion was small. I see they've added grilled scallops to it. That should make it more filling."

"I'll have the same and a green salad."

Val opted for a more exotic salad with fennel, Belgian endive, and watercress. Once they ordered, she tackled the issue of his mood head on. "You seem preoccupied. Is everything okay?"

"When I was about to leave the house to pick you up, I got a text message." He ran his fingers through his thick dark hair. "One of the guys in our theater group died suddenly."

"I'm sorry to hear that." The death explained his somber mood. Since joining the Treadwell Players, he'd spent so much time with the troupe that they were like the Chesapeake Bay branch of his family. Val wondered if the dead man could be the one who'd collapsed at the mall this afternoon. "How did he die?"

"The message didn't say. I called a few people but no one had any details."

The actor's name wouldn't mean anything to her, but she might have seen him on stage. "Was he in the Noel Coward play the Treadwell Players put on last fall?"

Gunnar nodded. "*Private Lives*. He was the male lead."

Val remembered the debonair man with dark, wavy hair. Definitely not the old guy she'd given CPR this afternoon. "I thought he was a good actor."

Gunnar fiddled with a breadstick. "A good actor. That sums up Emmett Flint."

The tone of his comment verged on speaking ill of the dead, but what did Gunnar mean by it? That Emmett Flint could have been a great actor, but was merely a good one? That he had no other skills besides his acting ability? That he was always performing, not just on the stage? "You didn't like him."

"And the feeling was mutual." Gunnar snapped his breadstick in half.

The waiter arrived with the wine. While he went through the ritual of displaying the label, opening the bottle, and filling their glasses, Val's curiosity about Emmett Flint increased. What could have provoked the hostility between him and Gunnar? She'd never seen Gunnar pick a fight, though he'd come close three months ago, when her former fiancé showed up in Bayport.

"What was the issue between you and Emmett?" she said when the waiter left.

"Talking about that guy is a sure way to ruin dinner." Gunnar drummed his fingers on the table. "Are you all set for your catering gig tomorrow?"

"I made the onion soup and braised the beef for the daube Provençal. Tomorrow I'll add the vegetables. While I was frying the onions, Granddad walked in, totally transformed." She described her grandfather's altered appearance. "He has a client for his new business who footed the bill for the makeover. Granddad wouldn't tell me what kind of work he's doing or who the client is."

"Here's to your grandfather." Gunnar raised his wineglass and clinked it with hers. "When I'm his age, I hope I can reinvent myself every six months . . . and have a granddaughter who backs me up."

He wanted a granddaughter? He'd never before mentioned a desire for children, something they should discuss . . . but not tonight.

While they ate their salads, she told him about the man in the mall parking lot and his resemblance to Granddad.

Gunnar sat up straighter and seemed, for the first time this evening, to listen intently. "Did anything else strike you about the man besides his resemblance to your grandfather?"

"His small feet. He wore shoes Granddad would

never wear. Loafers, expensive leather, with horsebit buckles."

"Ferragamo shoes, as the man with the small feet once told me. You performed CPR on Emmett Flint."

Val shook her head, her wineglass halfway between the table and her mouth. "The man in the parking lot was older than the actor in *Private Lives* and mostly bald with a gray beard."

"Emmett was mostly bald. He wore a wig in that play. He shaved off his beard for the role and grew it again once the show was over. His natural hair color was more pepper than salt, but he knew how to turn it gray or white. If you want to look older, you apply a temporary dye to your hair with a toothbrush."

Val speared salad with her fork. "How old was he really?" Surely nowhere near Granddad's age.

"Late fifties. He could have added decades to his face by using a wrinkle stipple on it."

"An actor would do that to play a role. Why would he age himself to go to a mall?" A disturbing thought hit her. "Maybe the same person who paid for Granddad's makeover paid Emmett to make himself look older and dress in a similar way. Does that sound farfetched?"

"It sounds remotely possible. Emmett wouldn't have done anything unless he benefited somehow from it." Gunnar fiddled with his salad fork. "In a way, I benefit from his death. I'm the understudy for the role he had in our upcoming production."

Her jaw dropped. Why had he kept this news to himself until now? Maybe because stepping into the shoes of a dead man made him uncomfortable. "That's great. Is it a big part, like the one he had in the last show, or a minor role?"

"There aren't any minor roles in *The Glass Mendacity*. It's an ensemble comedy, a mash-up of three Tennessee Williams plays, with characters from *The Glass Menagerie, A Streetcar Named Desire,* and *Cat on a Hot Tin Roof.* I play Big Daddy from *Cat,* the patriarch who's dying. I'll wear stage makeup and padding to look three decades older."

She expected him to be more pumped about snagging a major role. Maybe he was having a touch of stage fright. "Are you worried about your debut? Or does it bother you that your break is the result of someone's death?"

"A little of both." Gunnar gulped his wine as if it were much-needed liquid courage. "Something else is bothering me, though I think you would have mentioned it if it was an issue. When you saw Emmett in the mall, did it occur to you he might not have died of natural causes?"

Chapter 3

Val stared at Gunnar across a table as their dinners arrived. He must have a reason to think his fellow actor met a violent end. An image of the stricken man sprang into her mind.

When the waiter left, she said, "Emmett's clothes didn't have any obvious bullet holes. He wasn't bleeding that I could see. His head had a scrape on it, possibly from when he fell over." She couldn't tell from Gunnar's impassive expression if he welcomed this news. He had a poker face that a card shark would die for. "Did you ask that question because of my talent for attracting murder victims?"

A ghost of a smile enlivened Gunnar's grim face. "No, I asked it because of Emmett's talent for making enemies. I heard he squeezed his wife financially when she wanted a divorce. He demanded a neighbor remove a bush that encroached on his property. A few days ago, I caught him harassing a woman in the cast."

Val speared a scallop. "Why did the Treadwell Players keep giving him roles, if he was so obnoxious?"

"He hid his malice behind a charming façade . . . most of the time. And he had acting talent." Gunnar took a bite of risotto.

Though he didn't look as if he was enjoying his food, Val took a moment to savor her scallop. It was cooked to perfection and went well with the creamy risotto. "Did Emmett have a day job?"

"He got occasional roles on stage, did audio recordings, and even tried writing plays. He created a successful one-man show, portraying Edgar Allan Poe. One of the other cast members told me that a lot of actors dress up as Poe and give dramatic readings of his works. Emmett called his play *Après Poe.*"

"You may not know this, coming from the Midwest, but Poe is very big around here, especially in Baltimore. Granddad recently went on a tour with a senior group to the Poe house and grave there. Was Emmett originally from this part of Maryland?"

Gunnar shrugged. "He inherited a house in Bayport. He's in a theater group in Easton and the one in Treadwell. I don't know anything else about him."

Val took that as an end to the conversation about the dead actor. "You don't have much time to memorize your lines before the show opens."

"I know them pretty well from watching the rehearsals. My Southern drawl might need a lot of work."

"Let me hear you say something in Southern."

He recited a few lines from the play. "What do you think?"

"Sounds good to me, but what do I know? I grew up on naval bases and spent a decade in New York City."

With him anxious to go over the role he'd inherited and Val determined to talk to her grandfather, they didn't linger over dinner. When Gunnar dropped her off, she saw Granddad's Buick at the curb and hurried into the house. He'd left the hall light on for her. The snoring she heard from his bedroom at the back of the downstairs hall meant she'd have to wait until tomorrow to tell him about his look-alike.

The next morning, she put off leaving for the café for as long as possible, but when he still hadn't emerged from his bedroom by seven, she gave up. The café at the Bayport Racket and Fitness Club opened at eight, but before then, she had to bake muffins and make breakfast energy bars. The early birds who started exercising at seven would be anxious to replenish the calories they'd just worked off. She left her grandfather a note on the kitchen table, asking him to stop by the café because she had important news for him.

Business was brisk at the Cool Down Café until ten thirty. Twice during the morning, Val was thrilled to see every seat filled at the café's eating bar and handful of bistro tables. The café was generating more profits than it had six months ago, when she'd feared that her initial half-year contract to manage it wouldn't be renewed. The club manager had renewed her contract after all, but only for another half year, which would end in March. Now the club had a new manager, who might not be satisfied with the revenue from the café. How could he imagine the alcove off the reception area would generate more money from clothes than food?

Granddad walked into the café during the lull between breakfast and lunch, took off his parka, and hung it over the back of a stool. He sat down at the eating bar. "I don't know why you couldn't tell me your news over the phone."

His red parka, gold-rimmed bifocals, and low-level grumbling told her he was back to his old self, despite his recent makeover. "I wanted to tell you the news while you were eating a pecan muffin and drinking fresh coffee."

He pursed his lips, like a kid wary that medicine would follow the spoonful of sugar. "Okay. That's better than the stuff you usually want me to have for breakfast—twigs and seeds with nonfat yogurt."

After putting a muffin and coffee in front of him, she went around the counter and sat on the stool next to his. "When I was at the mall yesterday, a man collapsed in the parking lot. A teenager and I gave him CPR until the ambulance came. He died later."

"That's what you wanted to tell me?" Granddad patted her arm. "You did all you could, so don't fret about it."

He attacked his muffin with gusto, apparently no longer anticipating bitter medicine to follow it.

His relief surprised her. "What news did you expect me to give you?"

"Yesterday you talked about going away with Gunnar for Valentine's Day and you spent the evening with him. I figured you two might be making things between you more . . . uh, official."

Official as in getting engaged? "Nothing's changed between us."

"Good. With your track record, you don't want to rush into anything."

"One rotten fiancé does not a track record make," Val muttered, but this wasn't the time to remind him that her love life was her own business. "The man in the parking lot looked like you. That's why I rushed to help him."

As she described the man, Granddad put his muffin down. Deep furrows appeared in his brow. "Nothing unusual about a man with a beard like mine and a black coat. But the same kind of hat and glasses . . . that's sorta strange. You know his name?"

"Emmett Flint. He was in Gunnar's theater group." Val watched her grandfather's face for a reaction to the actor's name. She saw none. "I figured he was your client and got you to wear the same kind of clothes he planned to wear yesterday."

"You're wrong about that."

Val wasn't ready to give up. "Emmett could have used a different name and changed his appearance when he hired you. He often wore hairpieces that made him look younger. Yesterday he made himself look older by graying his hair and beard."

Granddad brushed crumbs from his plaid shirt. "My client never had a beard and never will have one."

Finally. A crumb of information about the person who'd paid him an advance. "So your client's a woman. Maybe she knew Emmett Flint and hired you to dress like him."

Granddad looked rattled as he set his cup down. "Thanks for the muffin and coffee. Good luck with your catering tonight."

Val waved to a trio in yoga outfits who came into the café. "Take a seat, I'll be right with you." She turned back to Granddad. "If your client dictated how your beard and hair should be cut and what clothes you should wear yesterday, you need to be on your guard. Emmett Flint had the same hair and clothes as you. He was a nasty character. Whatever this woman is paying you isn't worth getting involved in something shady."

He climbed off the counter stool. "You're jumping to conclusions . . . as usual."

The fact that some of her past conclusions had been wrong didn't mean this one was. "If you'd give me more information about your client, I wouldn't have to guess what's going on. I could do some research."

"I can do my own research. Just remember which of us took an investigation course." He patted her on the shoulder. "It's better if you stay out of it."

Better for her, but maybe not for him.

Between serving lunch at the café and preparing the food for the book club dinner party, Val had little time to dwell on Granddad's situation, though it gnawed at the back of her mind for the rest of the day.

* * *

At four o'clock Val carried the food for the book club dinner party to her car—a pot of onion soup, a Dutch oven holding the beef daube, bags with the ingredients for the salad and the dessert.

A bare inch of snow had fallen while she was home preparing the food. Perfect snow, enough to coat the trees and bushes, not enough to cover the roads. It took her twenty minutes to drive from Bayport to the larger town of Treadwell, where the book club dinner would be held.

Judith Humbolt threw open the door of her two-story brick colonial before Val had a chance to ring the bell. "I'm so relieved you're here. I was worried that you would have an accident because of the snow, and then what would I do? Order pizza? That would have been just terrible."

Val resisted the urge to say that an accident would have been no fun for her either. "I'm here now. You can relax."

Judith fingered her blunt-cut silver hair. "I've had the dining room table set since Friday. I'm hosting the book club for the first time, so I need to make a good impression."

She led the way to the kitchen. Val set down the first load of food and went back for the rest.

Judith watched as Val removed a cast-iron pan from a bag. "Why did you bring that?"

"To make the tarte Tatin."

"I thought you'd have the dessert ready." A note of hysteria crept into Judith's voice. "And that pan isn't big enough. We're having eight at the table and then two more guests for dessert."

"Tarte Tatin is best served fresh. I brought the

ingredients for two of them." Val would make one right away and the other while the guests ate the main course.

"But I didn't allow any time for making dessert in the schedule. Here, I printed a copy for you." She thrust a sheet of paper into Val's hand.

"I'll have plenty of time." Val glanced at the agenda. *5:45—Set out appetizers in the living room.* What appetizers? Now she was the flustered one. "I thought you wanted onion soup as the appetizer."

"Soup is the first course at the table. Before we sit down, though, we'll have raw vegetables and cheese in the living room. Instead of appetizers, I should call them *crudités* and *fromage* in keeping with our French theme. I'll put those out while you get the hot dishes ready."

Relieved, Val checked the rest of the timetable.

6:00 to 6:15—Book club gathers in the living room.

6:45—Val puts soup at each place and bread on the table. Then Judith invites everyone to the table.

7:00—Val clears away soup bowls and brings the salad and main dish.

What did Judith do in her former life? Orchestrate dinners at Downton Abbey? Val pointed to the schedule. "Do you want the salad served as a separate course?"

"No, no." Judith waved her hand back and forth like a windshield wiper. "That might take too long. By a quarter to eight, at the latest, everyone has to leave the table and move into the living room. You'll set the coffee and teapots on the tray table there and serve the dessert when the *special guest* joins us."

"Who's your special guest?"

"It's a surprise. I don't want anyone to know in case my arrangements fall through." With that, Judith left Val in the kitchen.

By six o'clock, the daube was simmering on the stove and perfuming the air with a heady mix of beef, wine, garlic, and onions. Val had just put the first tarte Tatin into the oven when the book club members began arriving.

With the dining room as the buffer between the living room and the kitchen, she couldn't hear what the women were saying. Their occasional laughter suggested they were discussing something other than a grim crime novel.

When Judith took her into the living room to meet the club members, a woman with an authoritative voice was speaking to the group. Judith waited for thirty seconds and then interrupted her. "Excuse me, Simone. I'd like everyone to say hello to Val Deniston. She's the caterer who's making tonight's Parisian dinner."

The women in the club ranged in age from early forties to late sixties. Judith introduced them so quickly that Val had trouble attaching names to faces, with one exception. In a room full of women wearing sensible shoes, pants, and sweaters, the fiftyish Simone stood out in suede high-heeled boots, a narrow black skirt, and a blood-red blouse. Her thick hair, the color of dark roast coffee, hung down to her shoulders.

Once the women moved into the dining room for the first course, Val could hear their conversation as she worked in the kitchen. Judith opened the discussion by asking what the others liked best about *The Murders in the Rue Cler.* Simone, the voice of authority, said she liked nothing about it. It was the worst book Rick Usher had ever written, and she should know because she'd read them all.

Another woman countered that it was her favorite Usher book. She loved the descriptions of the food at the Rue Cler markets. Simone pointed out that the focus on food was highly unusual in an Usher book and speculated that the Usher protégé whose name appeared in small type on the cover had written those passages and much of the rest of the book.

When Judith said she found the book's emphasis on revenge disturbing, Simone insisted the revenge theme was the book's only strong point. Citing examples of vengeance in revolutions and wars between countries, she called it a basic human impulse. Judith called it a base human impulse. The others jumped into the fray, taking sides on the merit of revenge in the book and in life.

Once Val served the main dish, she was too busy making the second tarte Tatin to pay attention to the table talk.

At seven fifty, five minutes behind schedule, Judith herded her guests into the living room and brought in two chairs from the dining room for extra seating. Val cleared the table.

She was back in the kitchen when the doorbell rang and easily overheard the conversation in the hall when Judith's special guest arrived.

"Thank you both so much for coming on this cold night," Judith said. "I'll take your coats."

A man with a low raspy voice said something Val couldn't catch.

"I'll have to speak for him tonight," a man with a mellow voice said. "It's painful for him to talk with a sore throat."

"I'm sure our book club members will have lots to say to both of you. Come into the living room and meet everyone."

Immediately after that, Val heard excited female voices, but couldn't distinguish any words. After she cut the tarte Tatin and put slices of it on dessert plates, she looked up to see a man in the doorway between the dining room and the kitchen.

"Sorry to interrupt," he said. "I'm Clancy Curren."

The special guest with the functioning voice. His name sounded familiar, but Val knew she'd never seen him before. Shorter than average, he wore jeans and a light blue sweater that matched his eyes. The dirty-blond hair curling onto his forehead and down his neck gave him a youthful appearance, though he was probably pushing forty.

"Hi, Clancy. I'm Val Deniston."

"The ladies were raving about your dinner." He walked to the stove and pointed to the Dutch oven. "Is that the beef you made?"

Val lifted the lid. "It's daube Provençal."

Clancy leaned down and sniffed appreciatively, his hands behind his back, like a kid told to look, but not touch. "I haven't eaten anything that smelled this good in a long time."

"There's plenty left over. Would you like some?"

"Just a taste. We were only invited for dessert." He took the forkful of beef she gave him and savored it with his eyes closed. "Mmm. Fantastic. Do you often cook at other people's houses?"

"I sometimes cater small dinner parties."

"Small dinner parties. Good. Would you consider making lunch and dinner every day for a group of four?"

For a moment, Val was too startled to speak. "I'm flattered, but that wouldn't work. I make breakfast and lunch every day at the café I manage."

Clancy's face lit up. "Then you can cook dinner for us."

"I'm sorry. I'm really busy at the moment. A few months from now, I may have time to cater dinner a few times a week. Certainly not every day."

He pouted. "But we need you now. It wouldn't be a long-term job. Our personal chef left for the Philippines ten days ago to deal with a family problem. She's due back in February at the latest. None of us can cook. We're tired of frozen meals and desperate enough to pay well."

Val cut into the second tarte that sat on the counter. "If money's not an issue, why not arrange for a restaurant to deliver meals or go pick them up?"

"We're miles away from any decent restaurants and they don't offer takeout. The only restaurants near us with takeout are fast food places."

She put a tarte slice on a dessert plate. "Where exactly do you live?"

He leaned toward her. "At the house of Usher."

Val waggled a finger at him. "I've read Poe. Nothing would tempt me inside a place called the house of Usher."

"It's not the mansion in Poe's story. The house

belongs to Rick Usher, the novelist. I'm working on a book with him."

Val now realized why Clancy's name had sounded familiar. She'd seen it on the cover of *The Murders in the Rue Cler* when she looked up the book online. "You're Rick Usher's coauthor?"

"I like the sound of coauthor. That's more than most people give me credit for."

Clancy was the mouthpiece for the man with the sore throat, Judith's surprise guest. That man had to be the famous author himself. "So Rick Usher's in the living room?"

"Go see for yourself."

Judith whooshed into the kitchen. "I'm sure you'd rather spend your time with a pretty woman, Clancy, but aren't you here to be Rick's voice? He's so hoarse, we can barely hear him."

"I'm sorry. Talk to you later, Val." Clancy scuttled out of the kitchen.

Judith picked up the first tray of desserts Val had filled. "I'll serve these. You bring the second tray."

Val filled the second tray and went past the dining table toward the living room. Judith stood in the far corner. She hovered over the guest of honor, offering him dessert, and blocked Val's view of him. Val handed the desserts to the women sitting closest to the dining room.

Simone peered at the plate Val had just given her. "This is a tarte Tatin, isn't it? Made with *apples.*" She emphasized the final word as if warning Adam against eating the fruit Eve offered him.

The young woman next to Simone turned her hands palm up. "Duh. Traditionally, you make it with apples."

Simone rolled her eyes. "I know that, but you can also use pears." As she spoke, she focused on the corner of the room, where Rick Usher was sitting.

Val gave out the last dessert on the tray and turned around for her first look at the celebrity author, who was forking a piece of tarte into his mouth. His shirt and pants were black. He wore his driver's cap low over his forehead, just above his tinted glasses.

She blinked in disbelief. That wasn't a famous author. It was Granddad!

Chapter 4

Val clutched the tray with shaking hands and stared in disbelief at her grandfather. He froze with a fork halfway back to his plate, doubtless as shocked to see her as she was to see him. He must not have noticed her car parked on the street near Judith's house. He put his fork down and tapped his lips with his index finger. Val got the message: *Say nothing*. Fine, she would keep his secret, as long as she didn't have to pretend he was a famous writer.

She wheeled around and went back to the kitchen.

Judith followed her. "Don't you want to meet Rick Usher?"

Val shook her head. "I'm feeling a bit lightheaded." That was even true.

"Sit down." Her hostess took her by the elbow and steered her to a kitchen chair. "Put your head between your knees."

Next best thing to burying her head in the sand. Val leaned down as far as she could without falling over. “Please go back to your guests. I got a little warm. I’ll be fine in a minute.”

Judith filled a glass at the refrigerator’s water dispenser and plunked it down on the table in front of Val. “Drink this. I’ll check on you in a bit.” She slipped out of the kitchen.

Val raised her head and guzzled water cold enough to give her brain freeze. After Granddad used her recipes to win the job of a food columnist, she’d gone along with the deception rather than expose him as a fraud. Now he’d taken deceit to a new level by impersonating someone famous. Where was the real Rick Usher? And why couldn’t Granddad talk tonight? This morning his voice had worked fine. Maybe his laryngitis was essential to the ruse. If he had a voice, he might have to answer questions about Rick Usher’s book. Better to let another man speak for him—Usher’s coauthor.

Clancy strode into the kitchen, as if her brain waves had cued him to make an entrance.

“Hey, Val. The tarte Tatin was amazing.” He eyed the slice she’d saved for herself on the table.

“I’m glad you enjoyed it.” Earlier she’d found his cheeriness appealing, even infectious. Now it struck her as forced. She moved the plate with the dessert to the counter, farther from his greedy eyes. “Who are the four people who need a cook at the Usher house?”

Clancy looked like a tyke on Christmas morning, ready to pounce on the gifts under the tree. “You’ll act as our temporary chef? That’s fantastic.”

“I didn’t say that, but perhaps I dismissed the

idea too quickly." Now she had a reason to probe what was going on at the house.

"You'd cook for Rick Usher, his wife, her assistant, who's also Rick's publicist, and me." Clancy reached into his back pocket for his wallet, extracted a business card, and gave it to Val. "Call me tomorrow afternoon and we can talk more about it. That'll give me time to run the idea by Rick and his wife."

Val seized the opening he'd given her. She pointed to the living room. "Couldn't you run the idea by Rick right now?"

Clancy took a moment to answer. "Rosana, his wife, is in charge of the household. She wouldn't like it if I talked to him first."

Val scraped a dinner plate and put it in the dishwasher. "You're Rick Usher's voice tonight. Did you sign books for him too?"

"The ladies didn't bring books to be signed. I think most of them read a library copy or the e-book of *Rue Cler*. We brought signed books as gifts for them."

If someone had brought a book to be signed, Granddad probably would have faked a hand injury that made it impossible for him to hold a pen. "Does Rick Usher always wear a hat, even indoors? Most men his age remove their hats when they go into someone's house."

"He took up wearing a cap when he started going bald. The hat and the black clothing are part of his brand."

The tinted glasses must be part of his brand too.

Yesterday Emmett Flint had worn those signature items, maybe to impersonate Rick Usher.

Judith bustled into the kitchen. "You must be feeling better, Val. You're not as pale." She turned to Clancy. "It was good of Rick to come even though his throat is bothering him. We don't want to wear him out."

"Rick always enjoys meeting his fans, but you're right, it's time for us to go."

As Judith and Clancy left the kitchen, Val fingered his business card. The black lettering on the plain white card read *Clancy Curren, Author.* The card included his phone number and e-mail address, but nothing about any books he'd written either with Rick Usher or on his own.

The book club members stayed only a short time after the authors left. While Val cleaned up the kitchen, she could hear the women talking in the hall, thanking Judith profusely for the wonderful food and the amazing experience of meeting Rick Usher.

When the last one left, Judith returned to the kitchen, glowing. "That was such a thrill to have Rick Usher here."

Val slowed down her kitchen cleanup so she could ask Judith some questions. "How did you arrange for him to come tonight?"

"The last time the club met, when we chose the book for this meeting, I found out the Ushers lived around here. Rosana and I were sorority sisters. I contacted her, met her for lunch, and mentioned my book club would discuss her husband's latest book at the next meeting. Then I asked if she could prevail on him to stop by the meeting. Rosana said she'd try. I was surprised she succeeded."

"Why is that?"

"I'd heard he might be in poor health. I expected Rosana to come with him, but Clancy came instead, which was fine. He was quite charming."

Charming and deceitful. Val put the last dirty plate into the dishwasher. "That takes care of the kitchen."

"I hope it's the first of many dinners you make for the book club. I'll lobby the others in the club to hire you for upcoming meetings. They all cook the dinners themselves, but their food isn't as good as yours. I would have made tonight's dinner, but then my husband was called out of town, and I couldn't do everything myself. That's why I contacted you at the last minute."

"Thank you. I'm glad you did."

"I still owe you money. I'll go get my checkbook."

Val packed up her pots and pans. Granddad's client was probably Usher's wife. She must have suspected her ailing husband would balk at the last minute and had backups in the wings. Amazing how far she'd gone to deceive rather than disappoint her sorority sister. There had to be more to this story.

Judith gave Val a check and a copy of *Poe Revisited.* "This is a collection of Rick Usher stories. Clancy left it for you as a souvenir to remember this evening."

"I'm sure I'll never forget tonight." Even without a souvenir.

Val drove home with her hands tense on the wheel. Granddad shouldn't have impersonated another man, even with the blessing of the man's wife. At least the wife hadn't gone as far as standing next to an imposter and introducing him as her husband. No wonder she'd sent Clancy to take her place.

Val reviewed the conversation she'd had with Usher's coauthor. Strictly speaking, Clancy hadn't lied, but he'd chosen his words carefully in order to mislead her.

What was the upshot of tonight's deceit? Granddad earned some money. Judith impressed her book club. The club members were thrilled to meet a famous author. Yet Val couldn't convince herself that no harm would come from the ruse. Tonight, Granddad looked and dressed like Rick Usher. Yesterday Emmett Flint had looked and dressed like Rick Usher. Then he died suddenly. A bad omen. Val wouldn't be able to shake her anxiety until Granddad was safely home and she convinced him to shed his new look.

Granddad's Buick wasn't out front when Val arrived home and parked in the driveway. She hoped he wouldn't have too long a drive home. He didn't see as well as he used to at night, and the strain of impersonating someone had probably tired him out.

After being on her feet since daybreak, she was tired too, but she'd wait up for him. She got ready for bed, wrapped herself in a warm robe her mother had left in a closet, and went to the nook off the upstairs hall. With her cell phone beside her in case

Granddad called, she lounged in the window seat. From there she had a view of the street and could hear him when he opened the heavy front door.

As a child visiting her grandparents, she'd spent many hours in the window seat reading, watching what was going on outside, and listening to the voices that drifted up from below. The nook and upstairs hall, both open to the stairwell, had allowed her to eavesdrop on the grown-ups talking downstairs. What had she overheard? Nothing earthshaking, nothing she remembered now.

She curled up in the window seat with her new book, *Poe Revisited,* and studied the author's picture on the back cover. The bearded Rick Usher in a driver's cap and tinted glasses looked younger than Granddad, but the publicity photo could have been taken years ago. That photo might have served as the model for Emmett Flint as he used the tools of his trade to age himself. No wonder he'd reminded Bethany of someone as she looked down at him on the ground. As a Rick Usher fan, she must have seen the author's photo on his books.

Val opened to the table of contents and was surprised to see that Edgar Allan Poe had written half the book. Each Poe story had a Rick Usher counterpart. "The Fall of the House of Usher" was paired with "The Rise of the House of Usher." The Rick Usher riff on the "The Tell-Tale Heart" was titled "The Tall-Tale Heart."

Val read "The Fall of the House of Usher." Poe's story of Roderick Usher, tortured by the fear that he'd buried his sister Madeline alive, was as creepy as she remembered it. She had just finished the story when her phone chimed.

She fumbled to locate it between the seat cushions and read the caller ID. "Hey, Gunnar. How did your rehearsals go today?"

"Okay. I went over my lines with the director this afternoon. After tonight's full-cast rehearsal, he said I did a good job. He thinks I'll nail it by the dress rehearsal."

She picked up on the discrepancy between his upbeat words and his tone. "You sound a little down."

"One of the other actors told us some disturbing news about Emmett's death. The police have ordered an autopsy."

Val shot up from the window seat. An autopsy meant suspected murder, at least in her recent experience. But not always, she reminded herself. Maybe an autopsy was needed only to clarify the cause of death. Through the window she saw Granddad's car pull up at the curb. Relieved, she sat back down.

"Val? Are you there?" Gunnar said.

"Yes. Is there any question about what killed Emmett?"

"One of the cast members talked to his sister. The doctors told her he died from cardiac arrhythmia. She was at Emmett's house when the police searched it for prescription drugs."

"Maybe he overdosed on a drug that affected his heart." She watched Granddad emerge from the car and walk up the path to the front porch. What would he say when he heard about the autopsy?

"Emmett lived in Bayport, so the town police may know about this. Could you ask Chief Yardley what's going on? Since he's your grandfather's buddy and owes you a favor, you might get more out of him than I would."

"I'll try." She glanced out the window and noticed a car that hadn't been there earlier parked behind the Buick. As the front door opened with a familiar squeak, a shadowy figure darted up the path to the house. Val's heart leapt into her throat. "Gotta go. Talk to you tomorrow."

She tossed the phone on the window seat and headed for the stairs.

"Why did you pretend to be Rick Usher?" A woman's voice carried up from the hall below. "Who put you up to it?"

Chapter 5

Val recognized the emphatic voice of the woman challenging Granddad. It belonged to Simone, the book club member who'd read all of Usher's books. Obviously an Usher fan, she must have seen him in person in the past and realized Granddad wasn't who he claimed to be. Why hadn't she exposed him as a fraud in front of everyone?

"Please come in," Granddad said. "Don't stand out in the cold."

A polite invitation, meant to calm Simone down, though judging by the tremor Val detected in his voice, he was none too calm himself.

"Okay, but I'm not staying long. You got your voice back fast."

Val hesitated at the top of the stairs. She could go down and tip the odds in Granddad's favor, by making it a two-against-one skirmish. Or she could stay put and find out what Granddad might not tell her. As long as he didn't need help, she had no reason to move. If she went down, Simone would probably accuse her of being his partner in crime.

Granddad coughed, possibly to suggest his voice would fade. "What brings you here?"

"I followed Clancy's car from Judith's house to the strip mall where your car was parked. Then I followed you."

Ha. Granddad, the super sleuth, hadn't even noticed her tailing him.

"Would you like to take off your coat? We can talk in the sitting room." Granddad's voice still sounded shaky.

"I'm not here to schmooze," Simone snapped. "Now I know why you faked laryngitis. You don't sound anything like Rick. The other imposter did."

Val's pulse kicked up a notch. The *other imposter* might have been Emmett Flint. As an actor, he could imitate a voice better than most people. The similarity between him and Granddad made sense if both were impersonating Rick Usher.

"You didn't hear my voice at the book club," Granddad said. "How did you figure out I wasn't Usher?"

"You gobbled up the dessert. Rick bit into a worm inside an apple when he was a kid and couldn't stand apples after that."

Poor Granddad. Betrayed by a tell-tale tarte Tatin. Val stifled a laugh.

"How come you know so much about Usher?" Granddad's voice sounded stronger as he switched from defense to offense.

"None of your business. Who are you and how dare you pose as Rick Usher?"

Val wouldn't blame Granddad for saying *None of your business* in return. But placating Simone would make more sense because she could make trouble for him.

"My name is Don Myer. I was hired to take Usher's place at the book club. There's nothing illegal about it. I have a contract to represent him."

"What does that mean? Who signed that contract?"

"Rick Usher's signature is on it."

"How do you know he signed it? Did you watch him?"

Val was getting the hang of Simone's interrogation method. Don't stop after one question when you can pile on more.

"No, I didn't watch him sign it," Granddad said.

"Did you ever actually speak to Rick Usher? Or even see him?"

"We talked on Friday."

Val was amazed at how patiently Granddad was answering questions.

"How do you know you talked to the real Rick Usher?" Simone said. "Would you know the difference between him and an imposter?"

Her grandfather took his time answering her. "I met Rick Usher at his family home. Why would an impersonator be there instead of the man who lives in the house?"

A momentary silence suggested that Granddad had stumped Simone with that question or that she was weighing whether to answer it.

"Rick Usher might be dead." Her voice sounded tight as if she was forcing it through a narrowed throat. "And the people who profit from his writing could be covering it up."

Whoa! Val hadn't foreseen that turn. Behind Simone's abrasive façade beat the heart of a conspiracy nut. Like most conspiracy theories, this one didn't convince Val.

"What gave you that idea?" Granddad's voice betrayed no skepticism.

"After Rick Usher moved here, he kept writing books, but he changed his other habits. He stopped giving interviews and speeches. No more signings at bookstores either. Last summer I read that he was ailing and close to death," Simone said softly. Her voice had lost its angry edge. "Recently, I found out he'd be doing some book signings for the first time in years. Only it wasn't the real Rick Usher at those signings, and nobody noticed except me."

"I can see why you're upset," Granddad said. "You obviously know the real Rick. Why don't you go to the Ushers' house and ask to see him?"

"I'd be turned away at the door." Simone spat out the words as if they were bitter pills.

Why would she be turned away? Val expected Granddad to ask that obvious question.

After a long silence, he said, "What do you want from me?" His voice was quiet and soothing, as if he were placating a child who'd just had a tantrum.

"Stop pretending you're Rick Usher." Simone stressed each syllable. "If you ever do it again, I'll expose you as an imposter."

The front door squeaked and then slammed shut. Val hurried back to the window seat and watched until Simone drive off.

Whew. So she wasn't going to make trouble over what Granddad had done tonight. What's more, her threat to reveal him as an imposter might even keep him from repeating his performance. Val couldn't have hoped for a better outcome.

She went downstairs as Granddad hung up his new car coat in the hall closet. He turned and eyed her with suspicion through his bifocals. "I thought you'd gone to bed. You were lurking up there listening, weren't you?"

"I couldn't help overhearing. I was in the window seat when Simone pounced on you."

"So that's her name. And pounced is the right word. I don't like it when you eavesdrop, but I'm glad you didn't come downstairs while she was here." His hand trembled as he scratched his head, suggesting the encounter with Simone had unnerved him. "It threw me for a loop to see you at the book club tonight. At least you were smart enough not to let on you knew me."

"Let's go to the kitchen, Granddad. You look like you could use a hot toddy." Grandma's favorite tranquilizer. Val wanted him calm before telling him about Emmett Flint's suspicious death.

"Just give me plain old tea," he said on the way to the kitchen. "I need a clear head to decide on my next step."

"Tea with lemon and honey will make your sore throat feel better." She grinned at him.

He laughed. While she made the tea, he sat at the breakfast table where they ate most of their meals. He propped his elbow on the table and rested his chin on his fist. She left him in peace to ponder what she hoped were second thoughts about posing as a famous author.

He looked up as she set the teapot and mugs on the table. "A bunch of coincidences added up to a lot of bad luck for me tonight. You cooking for the book club. You making a dessert with apples. Then a Rick Usher fanatic catching me out for eating it."

"Coincidence? Not for those last two. I proposed crème caramel for dessert. Judith switched to tarte Tatin at the request of one club member. She didn't tell me who asked for an apple dessert, but we can make a good guess."

"Simone. She set a trap. And here I was feeling sorry for her. Clancy should have told me about Usher's apple hang-up."

"He probably didn't know." The tea had steeped long enough. Val filled their mugs. "Usher's aversion to apples goes back to when he was a child. Maybe the subject never came up in his conversations with Clancy, who's around forty years younger."

Granddad stirred sugar into his tea. "Simone knew. She's got to be thirty years younger than Usher."

"She's a fan. She could have read about the apples in an interview he gave a long time ago. Or she might have had a personal relationship with him." Val squeezed lemon juice into her tea. "Cheer up. Simone did you a favor and didn't tell everyone at the book club that you weren't Usher. You're safe as long as you don't stand in for him again."

"I agreed to do it next weekend. A bunch of authors with books related to Poe were invited to a bookstore in Baltimore."

"Circumstances have changed. You have a good reason to back out. Once you tell your client what Simone said—"

Granddad ran his hand over his head as if he had hair to sweep back. "Why would I do that? I don't want to lose a job that pays well. I'd rather take a chance that Simone doesn't know about this shindig in Baltimore. The publicity for it mentions a couple of writers who'll be there, but not Rick Usher by name."

Uh-oh. Granddad wasn't going to give up his gig without a fight. Val sipped her tea, wondering how to sway him. "If Simone shows up there, she'll have a large audience when she outs you as a fraud."

"I'll have my contract with me and prove I have a legal right to be Usher's proxy."

"Your legal right won't spare you or your client from the wrath of Usher fans." Val had put up long enough with the secrecy about his client. "I figured out who hired you, based on what Clancy and Judith told me tonight. You have to warn Usher's wife that she can't get away with using stand-ins for her famous husband. She's the person paying you, and you owe her the truth."

Granddad put his mug down and crossed his arms. "She owes me the truth too. She didn't tell me she got another man to stand in for Usher before she hired me. That actor who just died must have been the impersonator Simone saw. What did you say his name was?"

"Emmett Flint. What makes you think he was your predecessor?"

"I spent a couple of days boning up on Usher and his books. Clancy said it would take me another week to get up to speed. All of a sudden this afternoon, I heard about the book club visit and got a contract. After that actor died, they needed a substitute fast. You know what that means?" He paused, but not long enough for her to answer. "Simone might be right about Rick Usher being dead. The man I met at the Usher house could have been a phony."

Val sighed. "Three people live in that house besides Rick Usher. It's crazy to think they've conspired to cover up his death."

"They all profit from his books. Once he's gone, they don't make as much money."

"They'd profit even if he were dead. Pretending he's alive is a lot of trouble and doesn't necessarily get them more money."

Granddad frowned. "How do you figure that?"

"I was the publicist for Chef Torquil's cookbooks. He was working on his third one when he dropped dead. The publisher got someone unknown to finish it and promoted it as Chef Torquil's final cookbook. It sold way more copies than his others." Val moved the egg-shaped infuser to a plate, where it fell sideways next to a lemon slice. "Usher's final book would do the same."

"Yeah, but then it's over. By saying he's alive, the Usher gang can keep books in the pipeline and the money flowing."

"It's not over, Granddad. When the final book drops off the best-seller list, lo and behold, Usher's wife finds the first draft of a manuscript among his papers. His coauthor, Clancy, cleans up the manuscript. Then that book also hits number one. When sales go down again, an early unpublished manuscript turns up in a bank vault."

Granddad shook his head. "They can't keep going to that well forever."

"And they can't keep up the ruse that he's alive forever. What then? They need a body to get a death certificate. Usher's body won't do if he's been dead awhile."

He dismissed this problem with a wave of his hand. "All they have to do is go boating on the Chesapeake and say he fell overboard. Bodies don't always wash up."

Val sighed. In arguing against his farfetched theory, she'd lost sight of her goal—convincing him not to pose as someone else. She glanced at his nearly empty mug. "You'll need something stronger than tea when you hear what Gunnar told me tonight. Emmett Flint might not have died from natural causes. An autopsy is pending."

Granddad's head snapped back. "Holy smoke. You said that actor was a nasty character. Maybe he was nasty to the wrong person."

"Or he made the mistake of pretending to be Rick Usher. Please don't make the same mistake."

"Hmm." Granddad stroked his newly trimmed beard and looked down in apparent surprise when it stopped short of where it had been for the last six weeks. "Let's not jump to that conclusion."

Val's head throbbed. Nothing she'd said had

convinced him to stop posing as Usher. She'd tried appealing to his self-interest, a strategy that usually worked, but not this time. He'd dismissed the danger of being caught and, even more troubling, the chance of ending up like Emmett Flint. She had one more argument—an appeal to his conscience.

She took a deep breath. "Granddad, would you ever want anyone to pretend to be you, a total stranger claiming he was Don Myer, the Codger Cook?"

"Of course not." He looked askance at her. "I see where you're going with this. Rick Usher wouldn't want that either. So he must be dead."

"Not necessarily. He wouldn't be the first author induced to sign a paper he didn't understand by people supposedly looking after his interests."

Granddad's eyes blazed. He sat up straighter, as if anger had stiffened his spine. "You mean he's not as sharp as he used to be and they're exploiting him?"

"That's far more likely than that he's dead. But even if he was of sound mind and agreed to the impersonation scheme, they're exploiting *you.* They paid you to hoodwink people. You made fools of the women who fawned over you at the book club. Do you think that's right? Do you really want to do that again?" Val had picked up Simone's double-whammy method of questioning.

Granddad studied the inside of his mug as if looking for guidance there. All the tea leaves were inside the infuser, though, not where he could read them. He switched his gaze from the mug to the wall and a photo of himself and Grandma, taken shortly before she died. They'd been married long enough that he could guess what kind of advice she'd give if she were here.

"I thought it would be fun to act like a famous writer, but I felt bad about it tonight." He pinched the skin at his throat, a habit when something troubled him. "Okay, I won't pretend to be Usher again, but I'm not letting those folks at the Usher house know that yet. I want to string them along, go to the house a few more times, and see what they're up to."

"Tonight you tricked the book club ladies. You know it was wrong and won't do it again. Next you're going to trick your client?" Val pointed to the framed photo on the wall. "I remember Grandma saying two wrongs don't make a right."

"This time a second wrong could be the lesser of two evils and make something right. By standing in for Usher, I upset one woman a lot. You didn't see Simone's face when she said Usher must be dead. She was distraught. I'd like to be able to tell her that Rick Usher is alive."

"How will you prove that?"

"Rosana expects me at the house on Tuesday to prepare for next weekend. I'll ask to talk to her husband. If he's the same man I met last week at the house, then I didn't meet that actor we think impersonated Usher."

Val doubted Simone would accept that as proof that Usher was alive. "What if you don't get to talk to him?"

"I'll ask to see him the next day, and the day

after. If I never get to talk to him again, Simone could be right that I met an impersonator at the Usher house last Friday."

Val shook her head. "Rick Usher may be busy writing with no time to talk to you or go to book signings. Why can't you just accept that and forget going back there?"

"If I prove Usher's dead or mentally incapacitated and being exploited, that's big news. The publicity will show I have detective chops. Then I'll get meaty cases to investigate. But I need your help digging up information."

No stopping him now. Without her help, he'd go sleuthing on his own, as he'd done in the past. She might be able to rein him in by acting as his ally. Besides, she was curious herself about the Rick Usher scheme. The urge to snoop ran in the family.

it through a jungle of greenery. Weeping figs and arching palms grew from huge planters on the floor in front of the windows. The plants created a living wall against the outside world.

A woman in her sixties swept into the room with Clancy tagging after her. She wore a pink pantsuit accented with a flowered scarf, a colorful though off-key note in the drab house. Her chin-length hair, mostly silver with a few blond strands, hung like drapes on either side of her elongated face.

She held out her hand to Val. "Welcome to our home, Val. I'm Rosana. Clancy has told me so much about you," she said in a soft Southern drawl.

Val glanced at him as she shook hands. How could he have said much about her when he knew virtually nothing? She suspected her hostess preferred social correctness over literal truth.

"I never expected to find a caterer willing to make dinners for us on such short notice. Clancy has done us a real service in setting this up." Rosana flashed him a fond look. "I'm sure you're anxious to see the kitchen, Val. Come right this way."

She continued to gush as she conducted them up the steps and through the foyer to the kitchen. She was the archetype of a gracious belle, sugary as a treacle tart. Val recalled the recipe for that tart. Its sweetness masked an ingredient that some people didn't taste on their first bite—lemon juice, the sour beneath the syrup.

Rosana showed her around the well-equipped kitchen as Clancy stood by. The room's four walls had two openings. One door led to the foyer and the other to the dining room. Though not small, the kitchen made Val feel slightly claustrophobic. Its one window had a driveway view partially hidden by plants on the sill.

Ivy, ferns, and spider plants cascaded downward from hanging pots over the work island. No dust or cobwebs in the room, but Val would have to watch for dead leaves falling into the food. "Does anyone in the house have food allergies or dietary restrictions?"

"I'm not aware of any allergies. Are you, Clancy?" When he shook his head, Rosana continued, "Please go light on the salt. It's on the table for those who want to add it."

In cooking for Granddad, Val usually halved the amount of salt in every recipe. Rosana's request suggested that, like him, someone in the house had high blood pressure. "What time do you usually eat dinner?"

Rosana tapped her gold watch. "At *exactly* seven thirty. The tossed salad should be on the dining room table when we sit down. I'd like the entrée dished up in the kitchen. Be sure to warm the plates so the food stays hot."

Fine with Val. She could dish up straight from the pots and pans. "So you want me to serve the meal restaurant style, not family style."

"Certainly." Rosana reached up to remove a rusty frond from a fern. "We view our evening meal as a business dinner, not a family gathering."

An odd comment. Maybe calling it a business dinner made Val's services deductible. "Will I have a chance to meet Mr. Usher this morning?"

"I hate to interrupt him when he's writing." Rosana looked pointedly at her husband's coauthor. "It's so nice of you, Clancy, to take time off your work to welcome Val to the house."

The treacle tart version of *get back on the job, you loafer.* Val watched Clancy to see if he'd tasted the lemon with the sugar.

He smiled without showing any teeth. "I have a lot to do this morning, if you two will excuse me. I hope to see you back here soon, Val." He left the kitchen by the door to the foyer.

Yes, he'd tasted the lemon, but it didn't surprise him. He must be used to it.

Rosana took a step toward the other door in the kitchen. "Now I'll show you where we eat."

Val followed her. Like the other rooms Val had seen, the dining room was a box from which no other room was visible except through a narrow doorway. The only striking feature of the nondescript room was a collection of antique dinner bells, the kind used to summon servants to the table. Made of silver, brass, and ceramic, they rested on the mahogany sideboard that matched the eight-person table.

Rosana rang a little silver bell. "I'd like you to meet my assistant. She eats dinner with us during the week. Madison helps me with the publicity side of my husband's career." She crossed her arms and watched the entrance to the dining room expectantly. When no one appeared after ten seconds, she picked up a big brass bell and clanged it.

Val's ears were still ringing when a woman with

sleek brown hair pulled back from her face appeared in the doorway. Younger than Val by a few years and several inches taller, she resembled a model on a runway in a well-tailored black jacket and matching wool slacks. Her face was as blank as a model's until she found out that Val might make dinners at the house.

Her eyes brightened. "Terrific. We need you here. We're running out of the food the chef froze for us before she went away."

"She made a list of the meals she left for us," Rosana said. "I'd like you to show it to Val so she doesn't make any of the same dishes. I couldn't find it in the kitchen."

"I've never seen it, but I can tell Val what to avoid—casseroles."

Val reached into her tote bag for her catering menus. "Here are some dinners I propose. Do you want to talk about the options now?"

Rosana squinted at the page Val gave her. "I'll study this in more detail later." She turned toward her assistant. "Did you finish making the changes I suggested?"

"I was just working on that when you rang for me," Madison said in a saccharine tone that matched Rosana's. "I'll get back to it if you'll excuse me." She whirled around, her long braid swinging behind her, and walked stiffly away.

The young woman did a good job of hiding any resentment she felt at being summoned by a bell and reminded to do her work. If Val ended up cooking for the Ushers, she wouldn't respond to tinkling or even clanging bells. Rosana would have to find another way to get her attention.

She conducted Val to the foyer. "Thank you so much for coming. I'll go over the menus and prices and let you know about the catering."

Before Val climbed into the car, she looked back at the house. A gloomy place, inside and out. She suspected the greatest peril Granddad faced by going back there was falling into depression. She couldn't rule out other dangers if he found proof that Rick Usher was dead. Though a conspiracy to cover up a man's death struck Val as farfetched, she knew the Usher household was involved in an elaborate deceit. Rosana had hired Granddad to impersonate her husband, and Clancy had facilitated that ruse. Despite her mistrust of Rosana, Val was tempted to cook at the Usher house. If she lost the café contract, she could use the extra money to tide her over while she looked for another job.

After relieving Bethany in the café at eleven, Val got a head start on making lunches. She had just set out the vegetables to chop for salads when a tall sixtyish woman approached the eating bar. Irene Pritchard rarely visited the café she'd hoped to manage, at least not since Val beat her out for the café contract last year.

Val pasted on a smile. "Hi, Irene. I haven't seen you lately." *And haven't missed you a bit.*

Irene's stiff-lipped attempt at a smile suggested pain rather than pleasure. "Good morning, Val."

She unbuttoned her charcoal wool coat, an outer layer of dark gray over an ash gray sweater and slacks. Her clothes matched the dreary weather, the color of her rigidly waved hair, and her grim personality.

"Can I get you something to drink?"

Irene slid onto a stool at the eating bar. "Decaf coffee, if it's fresh." Her tone suggested it wasn't.

Val eyed the coffee in the decaf pot on the warmer. She'd brewed it half an hour ago. It probably wouldn't meet this customer's exacting standards. On a previous visit here, Irene had scorned tea made from bags instead of leaves. She had prepared a proper brew in the tea shop she'd run until it went bankrupt.

Val dumped out the old coffee and made a fresh pot. "Something to eat?" She would have offered anyone else the scones she'd made this morning, but Irene might expect clotted cream to go with them. "A muffin or yogurt parfait?"

Irene shook her head. "Thank you. Your grandfather said you were looking for someone to work here part-time. I wanted to let you know I'm available."

Val was too stunned to speak. She couldn't believe Granddad would have told Irene to apply for a café job, not after she'd spread rumors last summer that his dinner guest had succumbed to food poisoning. Maybe she'd heard about the café assistant job through the Bayport grapevine.

A middle-aged man hustled into the café and

slapped some bills on the granite counter. "Black coffee and a blueberry muffin to go, please."

"Excuse me, Irene," Val said.

Filling the man's order gave her a chance to collect her thoughts. Amazing that the proud Irene had come here looking for a job. She must have money problems. Val was tempted to hire her and say nothing about the rumored closing of the café. Irene's food-handling experience meant she could start immediately with minimal training, leaving Val free to help her grandfather with *The Codger's Cookbook* and the impersonation mess.

But Val's conscience wouldn't let her exploit anyone, not even a woman she disliked.

She set a mug with Irene's decaf on the eating bar. "I *was* looking for an assistant, but I found out a few days ago that the club has other plans for this space when my contract ends in March." Val read skepticism in Irene's narrowed eyes. They had a history of not believing each other. Irene probably assumed Val was making up an excuse not to hire her.

Irene reached for the creamer. "That means the club's losing money on the café." Behind Irene's toneless voice and deadpan face lurked an accusation of failure.

Val's teeth clenched. She picked up a knife and hacked at a celery stalk. "Profits from the café have grown steadily."

"Profits would have grown more if you kept the café open longer instead of closing at two o'clock.

Of course, you'd have to either stay on your feet for twelve hours a day or hire an assistant manager."

Val coughed to cover up a laugh. Five minutes ago, Irene had inquired about part-time work. Now she was lobbying to be assistant manager. Maybe she could talk her way into that role in a clothing shop. "The club expects to generate more revenue per square foot by turning this alcove into a sportswear boutique."

"That's crazy. Who's going to drive out here to buy clothes? There's nothing but corn fields all around this building. No stores. No foot traffic. You've got the same problem with a café here." Irene sipped her coffee. "Does your contract restrict you to serving food to club members in this building?"

Val couldn't remember any such wording. The contract dealt mainly with financial arrangements. "No, but practically speaking, the people who come here to exercise are my only customers."

"You need to expand your limited base to make more money. If the customers don't come to you, take the food to them. Your location works in your favor. You're situated between Bayport and Treadwell. You can deliver lunches to businesses in both places."

True, but to do it, Val would need a delivery person. Someone like Irene's son, Jeremy, who used to deliver food from the diner in town. So that's why the proud woman had come here. Val had to give her former rival credit. Irene had concocted a responsible position for herself at the café and a job for her son.

Val looked up from chopping celery. "Not a bad idea, Irene, but it takes time to publicize a delivery service. With only six weeks to go before the contract—"

"Where's the harm in giving it a try? If you come up with a flyer about the café's delivery service, Jeremy can drop it off at the businesses in both towns tomorrow."

Val liked Jeremy. The young man, now in his twenties, had struggled in school, but worked hard at any task that suited his skills. "He doesn't have a job?"

"He works as a busboy at the crab house for dinner, but he has plenty of time during the day. I'm ready to start work too."

Val went back to chopping celery, feeling as if she'd climbed on a runaway roller coaster. How could she put the brakes on Irene's scheme? "Give me time to think about it."

"Of course. I'm sure you'll see it as a win-win proposition. I'll stay here through the lunch hour and get a feel for how you do things."

The woman's persistence grated on Val.

For the next hour Irene sat at the eating bar and made none of the negative comments she'd made on previous visits to the café. A step in the right direction, but not enough to convince Val to hire her on the spot. Before she made a decision about Irene's proposal, she had to find out if replacing the Cool Down Café with a clothing boutique was anything except a rumor. She'd stop by the manager's office and ask him about his plans after she closed the café for the day.

At two o'clock, she hurriedly cleaned the surfaces in the café and went into the enclosed area behind the work counter to store the day's leftovers. The walk-in pantry with a refrigerator was so small that she never pulled the door shut when she was in it because of her mild claustrophobia. She'd just put away the last of the leftovers when she heard voices in the café. With the door cracked open, she could make out what a man and a woman were saying, though she couldn't see them. She recognized the man's voice as the club manager's.

"Will this give you enough room?" he said.

"You'll have to rip out that food prep counter and the bar. That would give me more floor space for the clothes, though not as much as I'd like." The woman spoke fast in a voice that carried. "You'll need to add a low checkout counter by the entrance and a fitting room. What's behind that door?"

The only visible door was the one hiding Val from view. Should she pop out or wait to be discovered?

"Shelves and cabinets for supplies, and a refrigerator," the manager said.

"The fridge has got to go to make room for spare stock. People can use the club's locker rooms to try on clothes. I assume I can put racks of clothes in the reception area to entice buyers in here."

Val couldn't catch any more of their conversation

as their voices faded. No need to visit the manager in his office. What she'd overheard confirmed the rumors about the café's future. She caught a glimpse of a pony-tailed blonde talking to the manager in the reception area.

On the way out of the café, Val turned to look back at the granite eating bar, the wrought-iron bistro tables, and the table in the corner with its cushioned settee. The Cool Down Café had been her second home for nearly a year. Here she'd created delicious, healthy breakfasts, lunches, and snacks for the club members. She'd made new friends among the women who played on the club's tennis team and the other café regulars. And she'd earned enough to help Granddad keep the house he never wanted to leave.

Nothing short of a minor miracle could save the café, and the only miracle on the horizon required an alliance with Irene. If her strategy for increasing the café's profits succeeded and the club renewed the café contract, Irene would make sure the manager knew who'd initiated the changes that led to more revenue. Val risked ending up jobless or the assistant to her former rival. She sighed.

She might as well hedge her bets, hire Irene, and start looking for a new job in whatever free time she could find. She would call Irene later. Now she had to cross off the items on her to-do list. First stop, the Bayport Police Department.

Even if Chief Yardley wouldn't share any information with her, she would tell him that Emmett might have impersonated Rick Usher. The police could then investigate if posing as a famous author had anything to do with the actor's death. The trick would be to tell the chief about Emmett's possible connection to the Ushers without revealing Granddad's connection to them.

Chapter 7

Val took a familiar spot in the police chief's office, on the metal visitor's chair. Earl Yardley, a barrel-chested man in his late fifties, sat on the other side of a desk littered with folders and papers.

He slid the papers to the side and leaned back in his padded desk chair. "Your granddaddy doing okay?" At her nod, he continued, "You don't make social calls here. What's on your mind?"

"Can you tell me anything about the death of Emmett Flint? I was at the outlet mall Saturday afternoon when he keeled over."

The chief reached for a memo pad and pen. "What time was it when you saw him in the mall?"

"It must have been around three. I was with Bethany O'Shay. We'd been to a women's clothing store and were heading to another one when we saw him. He was walking between two rows of parked cars, moving erratically like someone who'd drunk too much. Suddenly, he disappeared. I thought he'd fallen. Bethany and I ran toward him."

Chief Yardley jotted on the pad. "And you recognized him?"

"I didn't know who he was until Gunnar told me an actor in his theater group had just died. I'd seen Emmett Flint in the group's last production, but he looked quite a bit older on Saturday than he did on the stage."

"What did Gunnar tell you about him?"

"That he had a talent for making enemies. He had trouble getting along with his neighbor, his ex-wife, and some members of the theater group."

Chief Yardley twirled his pen. "Why didn't Gunnar get along with him?"

Val heard a change in his voice that made her wary. "I only know they disliked each other." She chewed her lip. "Is there something else I should know?"

The chief said nothing at first. Then he put his pen down and pushed the memo pad away. "Let's say a man died under suspicious circumstances, and I had the same type of relationship with him as Gunnar had with Flint. You know what I'd do? Talk to a lawyer."

Val's ears buzzed, as if the blood in her head had turned into a raging stream. "Gunnar's a suspect?"

"If that shocks you—and it looks like it does—he hasn't told you everything about his dealings with Emmett Flint."

Chief Yardley's words echoed in Val's head and chilled her to the core. This wasn't the first time

Gunnar had been less than forthright with her. "Are *you* going to tell me about their dealings, Chief?"

He folded his hands, creating a steeple with his index fingers. "Ask Gunnar."

But would Gunnar tell her? He'd passed up a chance to do that on Saturday night. "Chief, you know he's not the kind of person who'd kill anyone."

"I didn't say he was. It won't hurt anything but his wallet to talk to a lawyer."

"Do you have the autopsy results yet?" The state crime lab in Baltimore, where autopsies were conducted, often had a backlog. A delayed autopsy would give Gunnar more time to find a lawyer.

"We lucked out and got preliminary results faster than usual. Normally, we wouldn't release those findings, but we're getting pressure to make an announcement. Emmett Flint's sister is a real publicity hound, an actress. She went on local TV, questioning the competence of the emergency medical services, the hospital, and the police."

"On what basis?"

"The EMTs got his heart going, but his blood pressure kept sinking. His sister didn't believe it. She said he had high blood pressure and took medicine to lower it."

Val could tell the chief wasn't going to give her the autopsy results until the public announcement, but he might correct her assumptions. "He could have taken too much of his medicine."

"Death from an overdose of meds can be an accident, suicide, or murder. Often older folks accidentally overdose. They confuse the dosage of different drugs or forget they've already taken the prescribed amount and take more. With a younger person who doesn't have memory problems, suicide is more likely."

"Suicide would bother his sister."

"Right. She suggested that someone with access to those types of meds slipped them into her brother's food or drink." The chief shifted the papers back to the center of his desk.

Val read the paper shuffling as a sign that he wanted to return to work. She'd just as soon leave and talk to Gunnar, but she had information about Emmett Flint that the police probably wouldn't hear from anyone else. "In the mall parking lot, Bethany said Emmett Flint reminded her of someone, but she didn't know who. She's a great fan of a best-selling author who lives on the Eastern Shore, Rick Usher."

"I've heard of him. And?"

"Yesterday, when I saw a photo of him, I realized that Emmett Flint resembled him, but only after Emmett made himself look older with gray hair and lines in his face. And he had on the same type of clothes and glasses that Rick Usher wears in his publicity photos."

"I saw the clothes the victim wore. Ordinary winter clothes." The chief glanced at the papers on his desk.

They obviously interested him more than a possible similarity between the dead actor and the famous author. Val was tempted to tell him she'd overheard that a man had impersonated Rick Usher, but she had no proof that Emmett had been the impersonator. Even the fact that Granddad had been hired to impersonate Usher would prove nothing about Emmett Flint. As she knew from her previous experience with the chief, he would ignore her theories unless the facts supported them. On her next visit here, she'd come better armed with facts.

Before she left, though, she wanted to know whether her nemesis would be assigned to the case. "One more question, Chief. Is the sheriff's department involved in the investigation into Emmett's death?"

"If that's another way of asking if Deputy Holtzman will be on the case, the answer is yes. The case crosses jurisdictions. The county sheriff, the state police, and our department are all working on it."

She groaned inwardly and stood up. "I won't keep you from your work any longer, Chief. Thanks for taking the time to see me."

"Give my regards to your granddaddy."

She hurried from the building to the parking area. Once inside her Saturn, she whipped out her phone and called Gunnar. She reached his voice mail and left a message, suggesting they meet in town for dinner.

Next she scrolled through her contacts to find Judith's number and called it. When the book club hostess answered, Val identified herself and said, "I wanted to thank you for the chance to make dinner for your book club. I'd like to send everyone in the club the recipe for the onion soup. Could you give me their names and contact information?"

"What a nice idea! We always communicate by e-mail. Send me the recipe and I'll forward it to them."

Not what Val wanted. Moving on to plan B, she would get what information she could about Simone, but in a way that wouldn't make her interest in the woman too obvious. "Thank you. While I was in the kitchen last night, I couldn't help overhearing the book discussion. Which of the women was talking about the scenes in the Rue Cler market and the descriptions of the food there?"

"That was Mary Ellen. She's quite a cook herself. The dinner she made for our last meeting was fantastic, almost as good as yours."

"Thanks for the compliment. What was the name of the woman who knew Rick Usher's books inside out? I figured she must be a librarian."

"You're talking about Simone. She's not a librarian. She teaches in the English Department at Chesapeake College."

Better than a librarian for Val's purposes. College Web sites usually included the names and academic credentials of faculty, a good starting point for her research on Simone. "Was she the one who picked out Rick Usher's book for discussion?"

"We all decide together on the book for the next meeting. I can't remember who proposed it first, but it was Simone's idea to invite Rick Usher. At the December meeting I'd talked about knowing his wife, Rosana. A few days later, Simone called to suggest I invite him to the book club."

"Having an author come makes it special." Simone had the manipulations skills of a puppet master. "Nice talking to you, Judith. I hope I get the chance to cook for your book club again."

Val hung up, drove home, and parked as usual in the driveway. As soon as she went into the house, she smelled burnt sugar. Fortunately, she didn't smell smoke. Granddad no longer burned food as often as he used to, but he still had the occasional cooking disaster. She went into the kitchen and found him grating cheese.

"What are you making, Granddad?"

"I decided on a Super Bowl party theme for my column this week. I'm making bean dip and guacamole. Your recipes had five or six ingredients. I cut them to three ingredients each."

In the last six months, he'd pared down many of her recipes to five ingredients for his newspaper column. Now, starting with a recipe that already had five ingredients, he still couldn't resist throwing out a few of them. "Why don't you just follow my recipes?" Maybe he wanted to put his personal stamp on them to justify using them.

"Because both of those called for fresh chopped tomatoes. In the winter the supermarket sells things that look like tomatoes, but they sure don't taste like them. I'm using salsa from a jar. The tomatoes, onions, and peppers are in there already, so I don't have to chop anything."

A salsa jar, a can of refried beans, lemons, and

avocados sat on the island counter. None of those could have produced the burnt sugar smell. Val opened the oven door. The smell was stronger there. "Did you bur—I mean, bake—a cake?"

"Not a cake, the same dessert you served last night. Just because a recipe has only five ingredients doesn't mean it's easy." He added grated cheese to a bowl containing refried beans and salsa.

Val glanced into the sink and recoiled. Something resembling charcoal was sticking to her cast iron pan. "What happened to the tarte Tatin?"

"The recipe said to cook the sugar until it was a rich golden brown. Well, one second it wasn't golden enough, and the next second it was real brown."

More than a second had elapsed between one stage and the other. "Caramelizing sugar is tricky. When it cooks too long, you just have to dump it out and start all over."

"I had the apples all cut up. I thought the juice from them would loosen the gooey stuff at the bottom of the pan when I put it in the oven. Instead, everything except the crust turned black in the oven." He pointed to the pan. "You think we should toss that out?"

They wouldn't have many pots and pans left in the kitchen if they got rid of the ones Granddad had blackened. "It's Grandma's pan. Even charred food comes off cast iron if you clean it right, but it takes time."

"I can't do it now." He put the bowl with the bean dip in the microwave to warm it. "I'm on a tight schedule today. After I turn in my column for this week, I'm meeting Ned for pizza."

"You can clean the pan tomorrow." He probably expected her to clean up, as she usually did after his failed cooking experiments. He'd have to deal with this mess himself. Maybe the next time, he wouldn't take his eye off the sugar that was caramelizing. "How did you get hired to impersonate Rick Usher?"

"Rosana contacted me. She'd read about me in the newspaper, the article that talked up my business." Granddad pushed the start button on the microwave. "We got together at a coffee shop in Treadwell on Wednesday. She asked if it would bother me to pretend to be someone else. I had no problem with that. I thought she wanted me to work undercover and spy on somebody."

"What else did she say about the job you were supposed to do?"

"Not much. She said I'd have to learn some things first. She'd pay while I got trained up. She gave me directions to her house and told me to show up there Thursday after lunch." The microwave beeped. Granddad took the bean dip out. "First thing I had to do, when I went there, was memorize a bunch of facts about someone, just like spies learn their cover stories. Birthdate, schools, jobs, travel, that sort of thing."

"Facts about Rick Usher."

"I didn't know that then. Once I proved I could remember all that stuff, she introduced me to Clancy." Granddad stirred the bean mix. "Ned's invited a couple of people at the retirement village for happy hour before we go for pizza. I'm going to bring the dips. You want to try this one?"

Val loaded some onto a chip and crunched down on it. The flavors of tomatoes, beans, and cheese blended well. "I like it." Sometimes Granddad's cooking experiments turned out well.

Her cell phone rang. She fished it out of her shoulder bag. Gunnar was calling, saying he had a rehearsal that evening. He could meet her for a quick meal at five. She suggested the Bugeye Tavern and told him she'd walk there. She could use the exercise.

Granddad had left the kitchen by then and gone into the study. He was sitting in front of her computer, pecking at keys.

He looked up from the keyboard as she joined him in the study. "Don't ask me any more questions. I gotta finish typing my column for this week."

His typos always slowed him down. He caught them on the page, but never noticed them on the screen.

"I'll type your column," she said. "I'm not making a habit of this. It's a onetime deal because I want to hear more about the Ushers and get on the computer to research Simone."

"Here, have a seat." He gave her the desk chair and sat on the sofa across the room. "I'll dictate the rest of the introduction and say something about each recipe. I jotted the ingredients and instructions on those papers I left on the desk."

Val typed what he dictated and the recipes. She printed a copy for him to proofread. Then they exchanged seats so he could e-mail the column to the editor at the *Treadwell Gazette.*

Once he'd done that, he told her more about the days he'd spent at the Usher house. On Friday, he found out he might be called upon to represent Rick Usher if the author wasn't feeling up to going out. Clancy introduced him to Rick, who was working in his study. It was a brief meeting with no mention of Granddad's role. Then Clancy filled him in on the author's career and gave him a list of book titles to memorize. On Saturday morning Clancy quizzed him on Usher's bio. Then he explained what kind of clothes to buy and where to get them. He also gave Granddad the money for them and a pair of glasses Rick Usher no longer wore. They had tinted, nonprescription lenses.

"They work okay for me," Granddad said, "because I have good distance vision, but I can't read with them."

"So Clancy was your mentor, Granddad." Had Usher's protégé also mentored the other impersonator? Probably. "What's your impression of him?"

"Friendly, easygoing, a cheerful fellow on the surface. I don't think he's happy inside. Now and then he stares into the distance as if something out there is haunting him."

"It's not the ghost of Rick Usher. That's a figment of your imagination. Don't project it on Clancy."

"I don't know what's eating him, but something is."

She was about to tell him she'd visited the Usher

house that morning when her phone rang. She pulled it out of her pocket. The caller ID read Clancy Curren. Speak of the devil.

Granddad stood up and went to the door. "I'm going to Ned's place."

Chapter 8

Clancy didn't sound as upbeat on the phone as he had in person, or maybe Val only imagined that because of Granddad's comments about him.

"If you'll be at your café tomorrow morning," Clancy said, "I'd like to bring you a contract for catering. Is there a time when you can get away for a break?"

"I don't get any breaks, but it's less hectic between ten and eleven." She'd like to talk to him too. Coaxing information from him about the impersonations might take a while, and she'd prefer no audience for it. "I'll be free after two. If we talked then, we wouldn't be interrupted."

"Morning's the only time I can get away. I'll arrive at the café at ten thirty. What's the address?"

Val knew what he'd be doing in the afternoon—working with Granddad at the Usher house, grooming him for his next appearance as Rick Usher. "The café is in the Bayport Racket and Fitness Club. It's on a country road between Bayport and Treadwell." She gave him directions.

"Thanks. See you tomorrow." He hung up.

Val cradled the phone in her hand. If she could get him to confirm that Emmett Flint had impersonated Rick Usher, the investigation into Emmett's death would widen to include his dealings with the Ushers. Of course, Clancy would be reluctant to admit any connection between himself and a man who'd died under suspicious circumstances. Possibly Simone could confirm the identity of Granddad's predecessor. If she'd followed him home, as she had Granddad after he appeared as Rick Usher, she'd know where the previous impersonator lived.

Val put away her phone and turned to the computer. She opened a browser window, navigated to the Web site for Chesapeake College, and found Simone Wingard among the English Department faculty. Simone had a master's degree in comparative literature and a Ph.D. in English from Boston University. A brief online bio revealed Simone had written her dissertation about Poe's influence on French literature. She had previously taught at Northern Virginia Community College.

Val typed Simone's full name into a Google search box. Up popped references to articles she'd written about Poe for scholarly journals. Val added Rick Usher to the search box. No sites came up that mentioned both Simone's and his name. Val would love to know why the scholar was so interested in Usher. She could call Simone in her office at the college, but she'd rather see her in person. It's easier to hang up than close a door on someone.

Val navigated to the White Pages site and entered *S Wingard* in the name box and *Maryland* in the location box. Bingo. Simone lived in Treadwell. No telephone number was listed. Val jotted down the address. She'd need a good chunk of time to drive to Treadwell, talk to Simone, and drive back to Bayport.

Val penciled in a Simone hunt on her mental calendar for tomorrow and checked her watch. She had just enough time to walk to the Bugeye Tavern to meet Gunnar.

With the sun going down, the air had turned frigid. She put up the hood on her parka and walked briskly toward Main Street. In winter Bayport resembled a sleepy town. But from March through October, cars clogged the streets and tourists the sidewalks. This evening, by tuning out the purring of the occasional car motor, Val could imagine what life must have been like two centuries ago when Main Street's narrow wood buildings housed the families of shipbuilders. Now antique stores, gift shops, and small restaurants occupied those buildings.

A gust of wind blew her hood back off her head. She shivered as she approached the Bugeye Tavern. Named for the two-masted sailboat used to dredge oysters in the nineteenth century, the tavern had served beer and whiskey to the watermen who gathered there when they returned to port. Now it catered more to tourists than to the dwindling number of men and women who made their living from the bay.

Once inside, Val walked past the tavern's polished wood bar and through the archway leading to the back room. Six wooden booths lined the sides of the narrow room. She paused, amazed at the room's transformation. A couple of months ago, the place had looked as if it hadn't changed for a century, with the odor of beer spilled long ago wafting up from the floorboards. Whatever the tavern owners had done in the interim to turn the floor shiny had sealed in the odor. The room also appeared twice as big, thanks to a mirror on the far wall. Ceiling mirrors between the wood beams and plush red cushions on the benches in the booths completed the retro bordello décor.

This early in the evening on a winter Monday, only two of the dozen booths in the room were occupied, one by a pair of older men drinking beer. Val walked past them toward Gunnar. He was studying a menu in a booth halfway between the entrance and the far end of the room.

He jumped up to help her out of her parka. She didn't see the dazzling smile he usually gave her, but at least she got a big hug.

She was sorry when he released her. "You're nice and warm. It'll take me a while to thaw out." She slid into the booth across from him.

"I'd keep you warm from now until tomorrow morning if I didn't have a rehearsal starting in an hour." He handed her a menu.

She skimmed it. "What are you going to order?"

"Beef sliders with fries and a side salad."

She wasn't hungry enough to eat that or any of the dinner platters. "A Caesar salad with grilled salmon sounds perfect for me." She closed the menu. "I visited the chief today. He hinted that Emmett may have OD'd on prescription meds, possibly ones that lowered blood pressure." Val repeated what the chief had said about Emmett's sister.

Gunnar grimaced. "She was right to rule out suicide. Emmett wasn't the type to take his own life."

The waiter arrived at the booth and delivered water. "Can I get you folks something to drink besides water?"

Val eyed the ice in the glasses. Her hands still hadn't warmed up after her walk here. "Hot cider, please."

"Same for me. And we'd like to order the food too." After the waiter took their order and left, Gunnar said, "What else did the chief tell you?"

"Not much." Val poked around her ice water with a straw. What the chief hadn't told her bothered her more than what he had. "He was surprised at how little I knew about what he called *your dealings with Emmett Flint.* What went on between the two of you?"

Gunnar gulped some water before he answered. "He and I had a fight at the theater after our rehearsal Thursday evening."

For a moment Val was too surprised to speak. That must have been a heck of a fight if Chief Yardley knew about it. "The police were there?"

"No, but Emmett filed a complaint with them and threatened to sue me for assaulting him. I was only trying to protect myself. He also demanded the director bar me from the theater group."

And then he was murdered. A pang of fear shot through Val. Gunnar not only had a grudge against Emmett but also benefited from his death. Now that Gunnar's accuser couldn't testify against him, the lawsuit would go away, but a murder charge might replace it.

Val tamped down her growing anxiety. "Tell me what happened from the beginning. How did the fight start?"

"The understudies sit in the audience and watch rehearsals so we know what to do if we have to fill in. I stayed behind after Thursday night's rehearsal ended to make notes on Emmett's performance. As I was leaving I saw him in the hall with Maddie. She plays the part of Laura in *The Glass Mendacity*. She's one of the characters plucked from *The Glass Menagerie* by Tennessee Williams."

Val had seen the Williams play off-Broadway. "Laura's the introvert who daydreams and polishes her glass animals all day."

"And lies. Maddie has that in common with the character she's playing. Thursday night Emmett grabbed her arm and said something like *I'm calling the shots now. Do what I say unless you want your secret to get out.* I told him to let her go. He told me to shut up and mind my own business."

Val knew him well enough to guess what happened next. "You tried to help her."

He nodded. "No good deed goes unpunished. I went up to her and asked if she wanted me to walk her to her car. Emmett shouted, 'Get your ugly mug out of here.' He swung at me. I ducked. Then he came at me again. I hit him in self-defense."

Val would have run or yelled for help instead of swinging back, as most women would.

The waiter arrived with their ciders, giving her a

chance to collect her thoughts about Gunnar's actions Thursday night. The *ugly mug* comment had riled him. No one would call him handsome. He looked like a hit man, according to Granddad. Would Gunnar have ducked a second time rather than fought back if Emmett hadn't insulted him? Maybe, but that's not what had happened. The person who landed a punch looked like the aggressor, not the person whose punch missed its mark.

When the waiter left, she said, "Did you have to hit him? Couldn't other people have kept him away from you?"

"Maddie was the only other person there."

"Then you have her as a witness that you were provoked and hit Emmett in self-defense."

He shook his head. "She lied about it. She told the police she turned away and didn't see him go for me. The only thing she saw was me knocking him down."

Val wrapped her hands around a mug of warm cider. Her fingers would warm up quickly, but the chill inside her would be harder to get rid of. "If she lied about what happened, she was probably afraid of him. He can't hurt her now. Maybe she'll retract what she said."

"I asked her to do that. She stuck by her statement to the police. I have a scene with her where I accuse her of lying. Tonight, when we rehearse that scene, I'll bellow 'Mendacity! Nothing but mendacity!' with more feeling than I ever have before." He spoke the line as if he hailed from the Deep South.

"Has she lied about other things?" When he shrugged, Val tried to figure out why the actress wouldn't change her statement after Emmett's death. Either she really hadn't seen Emmett go after Gunnar, or she couldn't afford to admit lying to the police. "He obviously had something on her, what he called her secret. Maybe she doesn't want the police to know he was blackmailing her because that gives her a motive to kill him."

"She says that I misunderstood his words and that he was acting out a scene from a play. That's nonsense."

"She's hiding the truth to protect herself." And make Gunnar look guilty. "What does she do when she isn't rehearsing a play?"

"P.R. work, mostly social media. She handles publicity for the Treadwell Players. She says she's worked for various clients, but doesn't say who they are. I looked her up online, but couldn't find a Maddie or a Madeleine Norton in this area who's the right age."

"I've seen Madeleine spelled lots of ways. After the first three letters, you can have an E or an A. The name could end in L-E-I-N-E, L-I-N-E, or L-Y-N."

Gunnar threw up his hands. "I don't even know for sure that her name is Madeline. It could be Madonna or Medea."

Or Madison, like Rosana's assistant. "What does Maddie look like?"

"Around thirty or a little younger. Thin, on the tall side, with brown hair down to her waist."

Val's pulse sped up. "She sounds like a woman I met today named Madison. I don't know her last name, but I'll find out."

Before Val visited the chief again, she would verify that the woman Emmett had threatened worked for the Ushers. The waiter put a basket of sliced cornbread on the table. "Your dinners will be ready shortly."

Val and Gunnar reached for the bread at the same moment, their fingers brushing.

She felt a warmth spread through her, not just because of his touch. For the first time since he told her about his fight with Emmett Flint, she saw a way of deflecting suspicion away from Gunnar. "Your fight with Emmett happened Thursday night. Did you see him with Maddie after that?"

"We had a rehearsal Saturday morning. I didn't see them together except when they were acting in a scene."

"Did he have anything to eat or drink that she could have gotten near?"

Gunnar spread butter on his cornbread. "We take turns bringing a box of doughnuts for our mid-morning break. Emmett never ate sweets. He left the theater, picked up a breakfast burrito from the café down the street, and brought it back with him. He got to eat half of it before the rehearsal started again. The rest of his burrito sat on the table in the back hall for the rest of the morning, where anyone could get to it. You have to go through the hall to go to the bathrooms and the dressing rooms."

Good news. "Maddie could have mashed something into the burrito."

"She could have. I could have too." He picked

up his cider and eyed it as if he wished the cup contained something stronger. "Don't jump to the conclusion that Emmett's breakfast burrito contained whatever killed him. He might have eaten lunch before he collapsed in the parking lot."

"How long did Saturday's rehearsal last?"

"Until noon. Emmett wasn't in the last scene that was rehearsed. He could have left earlier."

An image of Emmett in the parking lot, looking like Granddad, flashed into Val's mind. "Would you ask the other cast members if they saw him made up like an old man before he left or if he told them where he was going after the rehearsal. I'd like to know when and where he donned his disguise." Without mentioning her grandfather, Val told Gunnar what she'd said to the chief earlier about Emmett's possible impersonation of Rick Usher.

Gunnar looked almost as skeptical as the chief had. "Even if Emmett impersonated an author, what did that have to do with his death?"

"Possibly nothing, but I'd like to rule out any connection between the impersonation and his death." To make sure Granddad hadn't put himself in danger by following in Emmett's footsteps.

walk up the steps to the covered porch. She lifted the heavy knocker on the front door, but before she had a chance to release it, Clancy flung the door open and greeted her with a toothy smile.

The heavy sweet scent from an elaborate arrangement of lilies made the foyer smell like a funeral parlor.

Clancy took her coat, hung it in the closet near the door, and led her through the foyer. He pointed out the entrance to the kitchen and the spiral staircase leading to his room above the kitchen and dining room. The foyer ended in a passageway that opened to a step-down living room with a high ceiling.

He oriented her to the house's layout. "To the left along this passageway is the Ushers' private space, including Rick's study."

Val pointed to a massive raised hearth on the right side of the living room. "The dining room's on the other side of the fireplace wall?"

"Yes. Rosana's office and a guest room are beyond the dining room. This passageway takes you to those rooms and to her assistant's room over the garage." Clancy gestured with an open palm toward a Victorian claw-foot sofa in the living room. "Make yourself comfortable. I'll let Rosana know you're here."

Val stepped down into the living room. With its lofty ceiling and large windows, the room should have felt open and airy, but an excess of heavy antique furniture weighed it down and dark walls hemmed it in. The windows at the back of the house faced a broad river, but Val could barely see

"You're busy? What about me?" She ticked off all the things she was supposed to do on her fingers. "I'm supposed to research Simone, go full speed ahead on *The Codger's Cookbook*, and wangle details about Emmett Flint's death from the police chief. That's in addition to spending most of the day doing my job in the café."

"That reminds me." He set the dry teapot on the counter. "This morning I went to church after I left you in the café. When the service was over, I got to talking with folks about how you needed help in the café. I think you'll hear from someone who's interested in part-time work there."

"Thanks, but that's no help in the short term. I'd have to put in extra time to train a newbie." With the café contract in jeopardy, Val couldn't justify hiring an assistant, who'd have to look for another job before long. But Granddad had plenty to worry about tonight without her burdening him with the bad news about the café contract.

She kissed him good night, went up to her room, and took out Clancy's business card. She hadn't expected to use it when he gave it to her this evening, but now, after hearing Granddad planned to snoop at the Usher house, she was uneasy. Maybe she was overreacting. Only one way to know—check out the place herself.

She called Clancy. "Hey, there. It's Val. I was thinking about your idea of my catering dinners at the Usher house."

"Great! I talked to Rosana, and she's okay with it. But she wants to meet you first."

Chapter 9

The waiter arrived with their dinners. Val tested the salmon sitting on top of her salad. Well seasoned, not overcooked. After a few bites, she pushed the lettuce around her plate. She was tempted to let Gunnar know what her grandfather had done. But if Granddad found out she'd blabbed, he might not tell her anything else about his dealings with the Ushers.

Gunnar had apparently lost his usual hearty appetite, leaving one of his sliders untouched. "Even if the police determine that Emmett OD'd on meds after he left the rehearsal, I'm not off the hook. I went home from the rehearsal and worked on the forensic accounting contract all afternoon. Nobody in the neighborhood saw me. Nobody talked to me on the phone until the director called to tell me Emmett was dead. I have no alibi." He drank down half a glass of water. "I'd better talk to a lawyer."

"Good idea." She didn't want to tell him that Chief Yardley agreed. Something had been gnawing at the back of her mind ever since she talked to the chief. She might as well put it on the table. "Why didn't you tell me last night about the fight you had with Emmett?"

He took a deep breath and released it. "I wasn't sure how you'd react and didn't see any reason to spoil the evening."

Did that mean he didn't trust her to stick with him when he was in trouble? How many other things had he kept from her? A lot when they first met, but he'd justified it then because his job demanded it. He couldn't use that excuse now. If they couldn't confide in and depend on each other, they didn't have a bright future together. A subject for another day. Right now, Gunnar needed support and she'd give it.

She reached across the table and squeezed his hand. "Don't worry about your fight with Emmett. As you said, he picked fights with a lot of people. The police will find more likely suspects than you to accuse. Maddie is—" She broke off as a woman's voice drifted toward her from the entrance to the back room.

She didn't need to look behind her to know who the woman was—the fast talker who'd scoped out the café, planning to transform it into a sportswear boutique.

"Why don't we sit in the last booth?" the woman said. "More privacy."

She and her male companion passed the booth, too engrossed in each other to notice Val and Gunnar. Val could see only the backs of their heads, but she'd wager her tarte Tatin pan that the man was the club manager.

She crunched down on a romaine leaf and looked at the mirror on the far wall. It reflected the blonde and the man with her. Sure enough, the manager. They slid into the booth in the corner. Would they come to the tavern to talk about transforming the café into a clothing boutique? Hardly. They could easily do that in the manager's office at the club.

She cut off a larger piece of salmon, forked it into her mouth, and checked the ceiling mirror above the corner booth. The manager and the blonde were holding hands across the table. They wouldn't want to do that at the club, where his wife and teenage children often came to exercise.

Obviously, something besides the prospect of increased revenue was motivating the manager to swap out the café for a boutique. Even if Val hired Irene and doubled the café's revenues, it still might close. What could she do to save it?

"Earth to Val," Gunnar said. "I can see the wheels turning in your head. What's on your mind?"

"Blackmail." She speared a piece of red pepper with her fork. "I was tempted to try it, but there are a lot of reasons not to. A marriage could break up over it. I probably wouldn't get what I want anyway. And if I did, I'd have trouble living with myself."

"Also you might not live long. Blackmailers have a lower than average life expectancy. Who was your victim going to be?"

"The club manager." She told Gunnar about the manager's plans for the café and about his arrival in the tavern with the woman who'd take over the space to sell sportswear. "I'd hoped to change his mind by proving the café could bring in more money, but now I know something besides money may decide the issue."

"Blackmail occurred to you because the manager's married?" At Val's nod, Gunnar continued, "Don't look so glum. He may have personal reasons for pushing a clothing boutique, but the club owners probably have final say. You can go over his head and plead your case if you can show the café can make more money than a clothing concession. How are you going to wring more money from the café before the contract is up?"

"Irene Pritchard suggested delivering lunches in town and keeping the café open longer hours." Val gave him the details of Irene's proposal.

"You talked about hiring an assistant to free up your time. To help your grandfather with his cookbook. To go away with me for Valentine's Day. Irene's plan doesn't give you that. Why don't you make her a counteroffer that gives you what you want? More revenue from the café and free time for yourself. Figure out how she can help you get that and how you can help her do what she wants."

Gunnar always suggested compromises. Val liked that trait, especially in someone she might someday live with. But was compromise possible with Irene? "Our goals aren't compatible. Irene wants to take over the café from me. She's always held it against me that I got the contract to manage it a year ago when she assumed she'd win it. And she expected to be the *Treadwell Gazette* recipe columnist until

Granddad edged her out for that. Hiring her is like inviting the fox into the chicken coop."

"Didn't she give you information that helped solve the murder last summer?"

"Eventually. But first she insinuated that Granddad was the killer."

Gunnar drank up his water. "If someone else went to you with the same proposal Irene had, would you accept it?"

Easy question. "I'd jump at the chance to hire anybody with her background."

"Structure the deal so she has a vested interest in your success. The first step is to figure out what she really wants. What motivated her to approach you after all the bad blood between you?"

Val cradled her mug of cider, reviewing what Irene had said today and in previous conversations when she'd shown a softer side. Today she had led up to what mattered most. "I think she wants a job for her son, Jeremy."

"Then she'll make concessions in what she asked for herself to get what she wants for him." Gunnar looked at his watch and motioned to the waiter for a check. "I don't mean to rush you, but if you finish eating in the next five minutes, I'll have time to drive you home before heading to the rehearsal."

She put her fork down. "I'm done. Would you mind running me by Bethany's house instead? I'd like to hear her take on Irene's proposal."

Val phoned Bethany from Gunnar's car to make sure she was home and then called her grandfather. Still at the pizza restaurant with his friend, he said he'd pick her up at Bethany's house on his way back home.

Ringing Bethany's doorbell touched off excited barks from inside the tiny bungalow. Val was surprised to hear barking at two different pitches, like a duet between Bethany's spaniel, the alto, and another dog, the baritone. Odd that Bethany hadn't mentioned getting a companion for Muffin, the spoiled spaniel.

Bethany opened the door, holding a Labrador retriever by the collar. A beautiful dog. The Lab's coloring reminded Val of vanilla ice cream with caramel topping. Bethany's reddish-blond cocker spaniel swished his tail furiously and leapt for joy at the sight of a visitor. The bigger dog's tail barely twitched.

Val eyed him. "Hey, Bethany. You have a new addition to your household?"

"I'm dog-sitting for the neighbor across the street. Come on in. He won't bite you."

Val took off her gloves and bent down to pet the spaniel. "Hiya, Muffin. Are you feeling neglected now that you aren't an only child?"

"She is. Poor Muffin doesn't know this is only temporary. I hope she forgives me when Styx goes back home. Lie down, Styx." Bethany pointed to the floor.

The Lab complied, after selecting a spot near the heating vent.

Val hung her parka on the clothes tree near the

door. "Is that his name because he chewed on sticks when he was a puppy?"

"It's spelled S-T-Y-X, like the mythological river the soul crosses when it dies. My neighbor trained him to be a human remains detection dog, so the name fits."

"I never met a cadaver dog before." Val forged a path through a cramped living room that screamed "soft and round" from its pouf valences to its floor pillows. Muffin leaped onto the overstuffed emerald sofa decorated with wisps of light hair. No telling who'd left them behind since Muffin's hair and Bethany's matched so well. If Val sat on the sofa, she'd take home a collection of hair on her black slacks. She perched instead on a spherical leather hassock. "Does Styx have a steady job?"

"He's on a volunteer list, along with my neighbor Lisa. She's his handler. If the police or sheriffs suspect a body is hidden or buried, Lisa takes Styx to the area so he can sniff around. He can tell the difference between an animal carcass and a human one." Bethany plopped on the sofa. "Hey, maybe you should get a dog and put him through the training course. With your habit of running into dead bodies, a dog like that would come in handy."

"I don't expect to find any more bodies." Val crossed her legs, which made the hassock start tipping. She uncrossed them and kept both feet on the floor. "I came here to tell you what's going on with the café."

Bethany reacted with indignation to the news that the café might close to make room for a boutique. "The club members want to eat and drink when they finish exercising, not buy clothes. The manager's crazy."

Crazy in love maybe. "Irene Pritchard wants me to hire her. She gave me some ideas for making the café more profitable." Val explained them to Bethany and asked for her opinion.

"I'm not sure you'd make much on delivering lunches, but keeping the café open in the evening might work, especially if Irene made ready-to-go meals for the members to take with them. Then they wouldn't have to stop at the supermarket on their way home."

Val sat forward on the hassock. "That's a really good idea. We could offer food that's easy to transport and reheat."

"When Irene ran the tea shop in Bayport, she made delicious meat pies and pastries with cheese and vegetables. Add a salad and a dessert to those, and you'd have a good dinner."

The doorbell rang, and both dogs went into a barking chorus.

Val stood up. "It's probably my grandfather, here to drive me home."

"You get the door." Bethany went over to the Labrador retriever. "I'll hold Styx so he doesn't escape and run back to his own house."

"Don't mention the café contract to Granddad. I don't want him to worry about it." Val opened the door to her grandfather. "Come in while I put on my coat."

"Hi, Mr. Myer." Bethany held the Lab firmly.

"Good to see you, Bethany." He bent down to pet

Muffin. "I remember this spaniel. That big fella's new, isn't he?"

"New to my house. I'm dog-sitting him. His name is Styx."

Granddad went over to the Lab and petted him. Bethany told him about the dog's training. Judging by the number of questions he asked, the subject of human remains detection fascinated him. Val hustled him out when he ran out of questions.

As he pulled his Buick away from the curb, she said, "Irene Pritchard came by the café today. Did you suggest she talk to me about a job?"

"I said you needed help in the café. She's the one person in town you can hire quickly so you can work on my cookbook."

"Did you forget she badmouthed both of us? She practically accused you of poisoning your dinner guest."

He shrugged. "She wasn't always so cranky. Losing her tea shop a year ago turned her sour. I know how she felt—the same way I did when my last business folded. Too old to do anything useful."

Now that Granddad had achieved status as a newspaper columnist and a budding detective, he was less crotchety than he'd been when Val first moved in with him. Perhaps Irene would undergo a similar transformation and not drive away café customers. "We added to her woes. I got the café contract she expected and you edged her out as the recipe columnist." Was Granddad finally feeling a touch of guilt for winning that job unfairly?

"She'd treat us better if you'd help her out."

Or she might seize her chance to take revenge. Val would have to stay alert for signs of Irene's intentions.

As Granddad turned onto their street, she said, "You take medicine for your high blood pressure, don't you?"

"A beta blocker. I've taken it for ten years. Why are you asking?"

"From what the chief told me, the man who collapsed in the mall parking lot on Saturday might have taken drugs that lowered his blood pressure too much. How common is high blood pressure?"

"My doctor said half the men in their late fifties have it and two-thirds of people over sixty-five. Your grandmother did."

And Grandma had died of a stroke, possibly tied to her blood pressure. With the prevalence of blood pressure problems, a lot of people would have medicine to treat it in their homes. Someone who wanted to collect enough of that medicine for an overdose wouldn't necessarily need a prescription for it, just access to other people's meds. Drop in on older family members or neighbors, check their medicine cabinets, and collect a few pills.

When they went inside, Val asked Granddad to join her in the kitchen for dessert and was surprised when he turned her down.

"Ned and I had dessert pizza," he said. "They put apple pie filling on top of a thin crust. It tasted pretty good, especially with vanilla ice cream on it." He went straight from the door to his bedroom at the end of the hall.

Val headed for the kitchen, put the kettle on,

and reached into the cookie jar. Good. Granddad hadn't eaten all the leftover chocolate chunk cookies. She carried the cookies and a cup of peppermint tea to the front of the house. As she crossed the sitting room to the study, she heard him talking on the hall phone.

"How about nine thirty?" he said.

When he saw her, his eyes widened. He cupped his hand around his mouth, muffled his voice, and turned his back to her.

What was he saying that he didn't want her to hear? It sounded as if he was making an appointment. If he expected something to do something at nine thirty tonight, she'd find out soon enough what it was.

She sat at her computer in the study, the former courting parlor in the Victorian house, and searched for information about Emmett Flint. His Web site listed all the roles he'd played and his contact information. A section of the site was dedicated to his one-man Poe show, the places where he'd performed it, and quotes from favorable reviews. No recent performances were listed, so he'd either not given the show in the last year or not updated his Web site.

She heard the stairs from the hall to the second floor creak. Granddad must be going upstairs, but why? He rarely ventured up there.

She shrugged, turned her attention back to the computer, and googled Rick Usher. Her search resulted in thousands of hits. She narrowed the time frame for the search, requesting Web pages that had been updated in the last month. She skimmed the results. A few reviews of Usher's latest book came up, but no sites mentioned recent personal appearances by the author. Too bad. She'd hoped to find a book signing or other event scheduled for him last Saturday, somewhere Emmett Flint might have gone to impersonate the author.

She heard the stairs creaking again, rushed to the hall to intercept her grandfather, and peered at the waffle cloth garment he was carrying. "Long johns, Granddad? Why do you need them?"

He checked his descent and then continued slowly down the staircase, not saying anything until he reached the landing. "We're expecting a cold snap, maybe even snow late tomorrow. I figured I'd get ready."

Cold temperatures late tomorrow didn't explain why he needed long johns now. What's more, he'd weathered previous cold snaps this season without that extra layer.

He hurried past her toward his bedroom, moving faster than she expected of him this late in the day. He usually fell asleep in front of the television by now. Tonight, he had something to do that required warm clothing. She couldn't stop him from leaving, but she could tail him and intervene if necessary.

She went up to her bedroom for warmer clothes. Too bad she didn't have a thermal underlayer like Granddad's. She donned a sweatshirt on top of her wool sweater. Then she shed her slacks in favor of tights, fleece pants over them, and wool socks. She hurriedly laced her athletic shoes.

Had Granddad slipped away yet? From the window seat on the second floor, she saw his big Buick parked on the street. A compact car pulled up behind it. The night was so dark she could barely make out the silhouettes of the two cars. Then a figure moved along the path from the house to the street. Granddad.

She raced down the staircase, grabbed her parka, and without stopping to put it on, rushed out of the house. He'd just shut the compact's passenger door behind him when she reached the car. Her bare hand froze on the door handle, and not just because it was ice cold. The car was Bethany's.

Val flung open the door. "What's going on?"

A backseat passenger with big teeth barked a reply.

Chapter 10

Val climbed into the backseat of the Hyundai next to Styx, who reluctantly made room for her. Even before she buckled her seat belt, she figured out what was going on. Combine one cadaver dog plus one grandfather who believed a man's death was being covered up, and what do you get? A hunt for a buried corpse. Granddad must have hatched the scheme after picking her up at Bethany's house and learning about Styx's training. Then he'd talked Bethany into it on the phone call he hadn't wanted Val to overhear.

Val leaned toward the front seat as Bethany started the car. "Please tell me you're not going to the Usher place."

"We don't need you to come along, Val," Granddad said.

"Yes, you do." The drive there would give her time to talk him or Bethany into turning around. "You don't have to do this, Bethany, just because my grandfather—"

"I'm okay with it. I don't want Styx's skills to get rusty while he's staying with me. And your grandfather knows exactly where to search."

Granddad nodded. "I saw a mound of dirt near the Usher house yesterday. It looked like someone had dug there recently. I want Styx to sniff and give us a sign if someone's buried there."

"What kind of sign?" Val said. "Barking?"

Bethany glanced back at her. "Styx doesn't bark when he sniffs a cadaver. He's trained to sit as still as a tombstone and he stays put until he gets his treat."

"Suppose someone in the house looks out the window and sees you?"

"They won't," Granddad said. "We'll park off the property and walk along the gravel road to the circular driveway. The windows are mostly on the back of the house, facing the water. If anyone's in a front room, they won't be able to see us in the dark. The moon doesn't come up tonight until almost eleven. We'll be finished before then."

Val foresaw another problem. "They might have motion-detecting flood lights outside, Granddad."

"If bright lights go on, we'll just bolt and forget the whole thing."

Bethany flipped on her high beams as she drove out of Bayport. "Are you absolutely sure they don't have a dog, Mr. Myer? Styx will bark if another dog barks or comes after us."

"They used to have a dog, but he died. They haven't replaced him yet."

Val leaned toward the front seat. "What if they

have a shotgun instead of a dog? Even if they can't see you in the dark, you can get hit with stray pellets."

Bethany accelerated. "You're overly cautious, Val, and really negative. Where's your sense of adventure?"

Val gnashed her teeth. "Your eye for adventure is bigger than your stomach for it, Bethany. Last fall you roped me into going to the haunted corn maze with you. Once we went inside, you were scared silly."

"You're exaggerating, and this is entirely different. We won't meet any zombies on the Usher property like we did in the maze." Bethany glanced sideways at Granddad. "We'll be doing a public service, won't we, Mr. Myer? If the people who make money off Rick Usher's books are covering up his death, they shouldn't get away with it. His fans are being duped."

Granddad obviously hadn't told Bethany he'd also duped Usher fans. Styx changed positions and rested his head on Val's lap.

"I'm glad we're friends now, Styx." She petted him. "You won't meet zombies, Bethany. But you might meet the police, if someone in the house takes you for a prowler and calls 911. You remember what happened last summer when you trespassed, Granddad?"

"Sure. I nailed a murderer."

But not until Val had stormed in to rescue him. "I hope you have a cover story that's less lame than the one you used then."

"Trespassing comes in different flavors. A walk in the woods isn't the same as sneaking into someone's house. Our story is we stopped the car because Styx had a call of nature."

"What's your explanation for driving on the remote road where the Usher house is located?"

Dead silence.

Bethany waved her hand like a pupil who suddenly thought of an answer. "I can say I'm a Rick Usher fan. When your grandfather told me that the Ushers lived nearby, I wanted to know where, so we took a ride. It's all true too."

True, but unconvincing. If Val couldn't stop this folly, maybe she could convince Granddad to stay out of the way and leave the snooping to her, Bethany, and the dog.

Val petted Styx. "There's no guarantee they're all home tonight. Someone might have left for the evening." Assuming Madison was Maddie the actress, she would have gone to a play rehearsal. The rehearsals ended at ten, putting her back here around ten thirty, three quarters of an hour from now. The sooner this foray onto the Usher property was over, the better. "We've got to guard against someone coming back while we're on the property. You should stay in the car as a lookout, Granddad, while Bethany and I go with Styx."

"I hate to miss all the action," he grumbled.

"What action? Styx will sniff and sit down or he'll walk by the mound of dirt. End of story." Or so Val hoped.

"You're right. It might be more exciting to act as the lookout," he said. "I'll call you if a car turns into the driveway. I juiced up my phone before we left."

Val dug her phone from the pocket of her sweat pants and switched it from ring to vibrate. "Can you describe exactly where you saw this mound?"

"On the left as you face the house, where the circular driveway meets the gravel road, there are three cone-shape evergreens. The mound is between them and the strip of lawn."

And how was Val supposed to see the evergreens in the dark? If they couldn't find the mound, they'd have an excuse to give up. But suppose Styx was successful? "I'm calling the chief if the dog sniffs out human remains." Fair warning to Granddad not to take his own sleuthing any further.

As they approached the Ushers' gravel road, he told Bethany to drive past it and make a U-turn. The car would then be facing the right direction for a quick getaway. She parked off the road in a clearing between large bushes, making the car hard for another driver to see.

When Bethany killed the engine, Styx lifted his nose, on the alert.

Granddad passed Val a flashlight. "Don't use this unless you have to, especially when you're walking toward the house."

By daylight the trek along the gravel road to the house would have taken five minutes. Val insisted they walk slowly because the uneven ground could be treacherous in the dark. A twisted ankle would turn this farce into a melodrama.

When her face started turning numb from the cold, she covered her nose and mouth with her gloved hand.

They couldn't see the house for the trees until

they came to the clearing where the road ended and the circular driveway started. Though the front windows were dark, the light from exterior fixtures gave the building a soft glow. The fixtures on the left wing, which jutted toward them, dimly illuminated the conical evergreens and the mound Granddad had mentioned. Too much light for Val's comfort.

She stepped away from the driveway. "Hug the shrubbery, Bethany, so we're not as visible from the house. Will Styx sniff around the mound even if you're not next to him?"

"I think so." Bethany tugged Styx toward the shrubs.

Val stopped at the conical evergreens. "Tell Styx to get to work."

Bethany wrapped the leash around her hand and looked the dog in the eye. "Search." She let up on the leash.

Styx sniffed by the bushes where they stood and then headed toward the woods behind them.

Bethany moved closer to the dirt mound and tightened up on the leash. "No, Styx. Over here." She pointed to the dirt mound.

Styx followed her, his nose to the ground. She stepped back toward the shrubbery as he reached the mound. He sniffed, walked over it, and kept going toward the lawn edging the driveway. Bethany tugged him back.

"I guess there's no one buried there," Val said with relief.

A small animal darted along the driveway. Styx barked and growled. He strained against the leash.

Val's heart raced. What would they do if the dog broke free?

Bethany pulled back on the leash. Styx barked again.

"That's it, Bethany. We've got to leave." Val kept her eye on the house. "Someone might come out to investigate the barking."

"You don't rush out of the house when a dog barks. We should give Styx another chance. Look. He's sniffing near the mound again."

"Dogs sniff all the time. You said he sits if he smells a cadaver. He hasn't done that, so let's get out of—" Val broke off as light flooded from an open door in the wing. She saw someone standing there in a hooded black robe.

"We're being watched," Val hissed. She grabbed the leather leash, wrapped it around her hands, and pulled on it, adding her strength to Bethany's.

The figure in the robe raised his arms and shook them. "Buried alive!" he roared.

Bethany gave a mighty tug on the leash. "Go, Val. I've got Styx."

Val pulled the flashlight from her pocket and lit the way. No reason for stealth now. She ran to the gravel road. Behind her she heard Bethany's feet hitting the gravel.

"Buried alive!" a deep voice bellowed. "Buried alive! My poor—"

Val sped up, her head pounding from fear and exertion. The beam from her flashlight bounced as she ran. She heard panting behind her. Styx? Bethany? Or someone else?

Val didn't dare look back.

Chapter 11

Val's heart raced until they joined the road where the car was parked.

She opened the rear door, and Styx rocketed into the car. She piled in after him. Granddad gaped at them. Bethany wrenched the driver's door open, fired up the car, and zoomed off with a lurch.

"What happened?" Granddad said. "You two are panting as loud as the dog."

Val twisted in the backseat to look out the rear window. No cars were following them or, at least, none with their headlights on. "Slow down, Bethany. You nearly gave me whiplash on your takeoff."

Granddad looked back at her. "Did Styx find a cadaver?"

"He tried, but no one's buried under that mound of dirt." Val petted Styx in case he felt bad about not getting a treat. "Rick Usher's alive."

Bethany let up on the accelerator. "So the man who shouted at us was Usher? He sounded like a character from one of his horror books. Tormented. Crazed."

"Would you two just give me the facts? *Where* was this man? *What* did he say?"

Val relaxed in the backseat, her heart rate finally normal. "Here are the bare bones. Styx sniffed the mound, wandered away, and then barked because an animal ran by him. The door opened in the house wing near us. A man stepped outside, raised his fists, and shouted 'buried alive' twice. We took off. I didn't hear what else he said because I was running away as fast as I could."

Bethany signaled as she approached a turn. "He howled 'my poor sis' as we ran away."

"*Sis* meaning *sister*?" Granddad scratched the knit cap that covered his head. "Usher doesn't have a sister. He's an only child. It must have been some other man."

Sister. Val tensed and startled Styx, who was leaning against her leg. "It makes sense. Sort of. Rick Usher doesn't have a sister, but his namesake, Roderick Usher, had one. In Poe's story 'The Fall of the House of Usher,' Roderick Usher is convinced he buried his sister alive."

Bethany slowed down. "I like it, Val. It's poetic justice. I mean, *Poe*-etic justice. A writer inspired by Poe is trapped inside a story his hero created. It sounds like a plot Rick Usher would come up with."

"He believes he's a character in a story?" Granddad said. "Nah."

"It's not as crazy as it sounds, Granddad. You are what you read. Rick Usher has spent a lifetime steeped in Poe's stories about death, guilt, and madness."

Bethany nodded. "He's possessed. I mean *Poe*-sessed. How do you exorcise a dead writer who's taken over your mind and soul?"

Granddad chuckled. "You usc a *Poe*-tion."

Val groaned. "Enough with the puns. A shaky mental state would explain why Rick Usher doesn't go out in public anymore." And why he needed a stand-in to bolster the fiction that he was still fully functional. "If a man sees two people and a dog in his yard at night, you expect him to yell, *What are you doing here?* or *Get off my property.* You don't expect him to roar, 'Buried alive' twice."

Bethany switched from high beams to low for an oncoming car. "Here's another idea. He could have been talking about himself. He feels buried alive, imprisoned in his own house, by people who want to keep his mental state a secret. Like the woman locked in the attic in *Jane Eyre.*"

"The man you saw wasn't locked in," Granddad said. "And the dirt was recently turned up. That's proof he wasn't talking about himself being buried alive."

Though the meaning of *buried alive* was open to interpretation, Val had all the proof she needed that Rick Usher was very much alive.

Back home at the kitchen table, Granddad sipped the hot toddy he'd asked Val to make for him. "I didn't want to say this in front of Bethany, but she might have messed up the signal she gave Styx."

Val blew on her peppermint tea to cool it. "What

Styx did or didn't do makes no difference. You wanted to know if Usher was buried there. We know he's alive because he came out of the house and shouted at us."

"You don't know for sure that the man you heard was Usher."

"Who else? Not Clancy. He sounds like a radio announcer on a classical music station, smooth and subdued. He doesn't have the pipes to make the rumbling tones we heard tonight." She sipped her tea. "What kind of voice does Usher have?"

"The man I met there had a deep voice, probably the same man you heard tonight." Granddad gulped some toddy. "He shouted that someone was buried there. I'll take a closer look at that dirt tomorrow."

Val's fingers tensed on the handle of her mug. "You have no reason to go there. You said you wouldn't impersonate Usher again."

"But the folks at the Usher house expect me there. I have to pretend I'm going to pose as Usher until they pay me for the hours I already spent on this. And I want to remind Clancy to get in touch with the agent about my cookbook."

"Clancy's quite the go-between. He's arranging for me to cook dinners for the Ushers."

Granddad's eyes popped out. "What?"

She told him about her visit to the Usher house today and her meeting with Rosana. "Clancy called this evening to say the catering contract would be ready tomorrow. He's bringing it to the café in the morning."

"There are funny things going on at the Usher place. You're better off staying away from it."

"I said something like that to you last night, and you brushed it off. Let's make a pact. I'll stay away from the place if you do."

"Hmph." He finished his toddy. "Go ahead and cook there for a couple of days, but don't sign any long-term contract. And ask for double your usual prices. The Ushers have plenty of money."

Val had already quoted prices higher than for her other customers, but not double. "I'm going to have to tell them that you and I are related."

Granddad flicked his wrist. "You might as well. It wouldn't be hard for them to find out on their own."

"The same is true for Simone. She's probably already researched you thoroughly and discovered you're related to the book club's caterer. If she hasn't, I'll tell her because I want to know more about the other Usher stand-in she mentioned." If Simone could identify that man as Emmett Flint, Val could make a stronger case to the chief that Emmett's death and his work for the Ushers might be related.

Granddad yawned. "I'm turning in now. Got a long day tomorrow. What time is Clancy gonna be at the café?"

"Ten thirty." Why did Granddad want to know that? "Are you planning to join us?"

"Nope." He stood up. "Sleep well."

Val climbed the stairs that went from the kitchen to her bedroom above it. She got ready for bed, snuggled under her quilt, and opened *Poe Revisited* to "The Purloined Letter." In Poe's story the French police tried to foil a blackmail attempt by retrieving a stolen letter from the blackmailer's rooms. They failed to find the letter in their painstaking search of possible hiding places. Auguste Dupin, Poe's brilliant detective, located it in plain sight among other letters and stole it back from the blackmailer.

The Rick Usher counterpart to this story, "The Purloined Litter," dealt with the mysterious disappearance of trash from a street in the Latin Quarter. Val fell asleep halfway through the story.

Val was delivering smoothies to two young women when Clancy appeared at the entrance to the café. Though dressed casually, in jeans and a bomber jacket, he carried a leather briefcase appropriate for someone in a three-piece suit.

Val extended her hand. "You found me. Welcome to the Cool Down Café."

He shook hands with her. "This place isn't at all what I expected. I pictured you in a homey eatery with embroidered tablecloths and ruffled curtains, not this sleek, shiny place. I'm happy to say the coffee aroma lives up to my expectations." He sniffed appreciatively.

"The café fits the surroundings. The club is all about hard surfaces and hard bodies toned by exercise. If Poe came back to life among the fitness machines, he'd think he stumbled into a torture chamber."

"Self-inflicted torture. A club for masochists,

except here in the café, of course." He eyed the muffins, biscotti, and breakfast bars under the glass display on the eating bar. "Did you bake those biscotti?"

"Uh-huh." She went behind the counter. "Would you like to try one?"

"Yes, please. The biscotti you buy in cellophane can't compare to homemade ones."

"How about some coffee? On the house."

"Yes to coffee, but not on the house." He put down a ten-dollar bill. "I'm paying and I don't want change."

"Thank you." She poured the coffee. "Let's sit at the table closest to the café entrance so I can spring into action if a customer comes in."

Once he was seated Clancy appeared in no hurry to talk business. He dipped his biscotti in his coffee and ate it with a satisfied smile.

Val broke the silence. "I'm curious how you ended up as Rick Usher's coauthor."

"Ten years ago I was writing software manuals for a company in Baltimore. I went to a lecture Rick gave on how Poe's writing inspired him. Afterward, I introduced myself to him and said we'd both graduated from the same college."

"Where was that?"

"Mount St. Mary's in Emmitsburg, Maryland. We went for a glass of wine. I told him I was writing a horror novel. He offered to read the first fifty pages. He sent them back to me with ideas on how to improve the manuscript and gave me contact information for his agent."

The story surprised Val. Famous authors probably

met wannabe novelists often and had a standard brush-off line. Clancy's writing must have impressed Usher. "That was generous of him. Did his agent take you on?"

Clancy nodded. "And he found a publisher. My book didn't sell as well as I'd hoped. I saw Rick a few years later at a book signing. He remembered me and asked me to work with him on his next paranormal novel."

"Is that when you started staying at his house here?"

"No, he was still living in Baltimore then. He moved here permanently about a year later. I drove here to meet him on weekends and cut down on my hours as a tech writer." Clancy dunked his last piece of biscotti. "About three years ago, he asked me to help write the Gaston Vulpin books as well as the paranormal ones. The writing schedule was so intense that I had to be available all the time. The Ushers had plenty of room in their house and offered me room and board. I quit my job, gave up my apartment, and moved in."

"Do you have time to write under your own name?"

His mouth turned down. "Not now, but I'm learning a lot from Rick. When he's no longer publishing books, I'll write my own. Until then, I'll stick with him."

Val saw no sign of either enthusiasm for working with Rick Usher or resentment of the cloistered living arrangements. "Do you just stay at the house and work, or do you get out for fun sometimes?"

His grinned and raised his eyebrows. "I'm

open to ideas, especially if you'd like to have fun with me."

"I wasn't suggesting—" Val broke off as four middle-aged women came in, carrying athletic bags with tennis rackets stuck in them. "Excuse me, I have to serve these customers."

The women came to the café every Tuesday after their doubles game in the club's tennis bubble and ordered the same thing. Two coffees, two teas, and the muffin special of the day for each of them.

After Val delivered their drinks and muffins, she brought Clancy another biscotti.

"Thank you. You read my mind." He beamed at her. "You were asking what I do in my free time. Helping Rick with two books a year keeps me pretty busy. Still, I make sure I find time to bike outdoors in decent weather and indoors on an exercise bike. Most weekends I visit family in Baltimore." He searched her face. "It's hard to know what you're thinking. Family doesn't include a wife or kids, in case you're wondering."

Val wasn't, but didn't want to discourage him from talking. "You visit your parents on weekends?"

"My father's gone. I spend time with my mother and twin brother. He served in Iraq and lost a leg." Clancy clutched his throat as if he had trouble swallowing. "He also has PTSD."

"I'm sorry to hear that." Val remembered what Granddad had said about Clancy—*he looks into the distance like something out there is haunting him.* His brother's plight must weigh on him. "Is your brother able to manage on his own?"

"The Veteran's Administration took care of most

of his physical needs, including an artificial leg, but his emotional state is still precarious. He can't work. He's depressed and has nightmares. My mother had to give up her job to deal with his problems and drive him to therapy sessions. It takes a toll on her. I try to relieve her on the weekend."

Clancy's job and his family responsibilities didn't give him much time for himself, much less for a wife and children. "Your brother's fortunate to have you as part of his support team."

"It's the least I can do. He served his country. I stayed home. He's broken. I'm whole." Clancy broke off a piece of biscotti. "Sometimes people who lose a limb feel pain where that limb should be. My brother used to wake up shocked to see his left leg was gone. Amazingly, my left leg aches too. I dream it's missing like my brother's leg and, when I wake up, I'm surprised to see it's still attached to me."

Val's eyes burned with nascent tears. Poor Clancy. He had something akin to survivor's guilt and probably wasn't as *whole* as he imagined. "You're doing what you can for him."

"I'm not doing enough." He shook his head as if to clear it. "I apologize. I didn't come here to talk about myself. Rosana liked all of your suggested menus. She drew up a contract for you to sign." He pulled a paper from his briefcase.

"Just to clarify, I'll be making dinner for four people at the house. You, Rick Usher, Rosana Usher, and Madison. What's her last name again? I didn't catch it yesterday."

Clancy grinned. "You had nothing to catch. Madison typically introduces herself by her first name only. Her last name reminds her of a past best forgotten."

Intrigued, Val waited for Clancy to elaborate. Instead, he pushed the contract toward her, leaving her no choice but to prompt him. "Does Madison have a criminal past?"

Clancy laughed. "No, she has a past as a spoiled rich girl and a double-barreled surname to go along with it."

Val knew the kind of name he meant, but frowned to suggest confusion. "Double-barreled?"

"Two names with a hyphen between them. Madison Fox-Norton. A name that belongs at a debutante ball."

But apparently not on the stage, where she was Maddie Norton. The job of cooking for the Ushers came with an unexpected perk—access to the woman who disputed Gunnar's version of his fight with Flint. Val might figure out what motivated Madison's lie by approaching her not as Gunnar's girlfriend, but as a caterer. For now, she'd mine whatever information Clancy had about the woman. "Madison went to a debutante ball? Where do they still have those?"

"Don't take me literally. I meant her pedigree fits the mold. Madison led a pampered life, growing up on the east side of Manhattan, attending private schools. Then her father lost big on risky investments, lost his clients' money too, and sullied the Fox-Norton name. She had to work her way through a state university instead of going to an Ivy on her dad's dollar." Clancy fiddled with his coffee spoon. "Aren't you going to look at the contract?"

"Of course." Clancy would wonder about her motives if she showed too much curiosity about Madison. Val skimmed the single-spaced document. It allowed either party to opt out of a dinner with a day's notice or end the contract with two days' notice. Val couldn't have asked for more flexible terms. But before signing, she'd lay her cards on the table and see if Clancy followed suit. "This looks fine. Just one more question. When did you start hiring Rick Usher impersonators?"

Chapter 12

Clancy went rigid in response to Val's question about impersonators. His ruddy complexion turned the color of vanilla pudding. "What? How do you—I mean, I didn't realize you knew Rick Usher."

"I don't, but I know the man who posed as him on Sunday night. Don Myer is my grandfather. We were amazed to see each other at the book club gathering." Val would like nothing better than for the Ushers to fire Granddad, but not for cause. He deserved to be paid for his work. "He kept his impersonation of Usher a secret, even from me. He fulfilled the terms of his contract, but he couldn't deny what I'd seen with my own eyes."

Clancy's lower lip protruded. "You never said a word about your grandfather when you came to the house yesterday." He looked like a fibbing child peeved by another kid's fib.

"A minor deceit compared to yours. At least I wouldn't enter a business agreement without being completely honest. I doubt you'd have told me about the Usher pretenders if I hadn't raised the subject."

Clancy reddened. "Why would I? I had no reason to tell you anything unrelated to your catering."

Val noticed he hadn't changed her plural *pretenders* to singular. "I won't take the job under false pretenses. You'll have to tell the Ushers I'm aware of their deception, even if it means they withdraw this offer." She pointed to the contract.

"They won't. It doesn't do any good to rescind the offer. We're better off if you're on board with us, since you already know what's going on."

"I wouldn't say I'm on board with it. My grandfather makes his own decisions. I'm not happy with this one, but I won't betray him."

"I couldn't betray the people who pay me." Clancy put his index finger on his lip like a bashful boy. "I was just doing my job."

Doing his job. The same reason Gunnar had given for hiding his true purpose in coming on to her when they first met. She'd forgiven him, but not right away. She might forgive Clancy too as long as he was truthful from now on. "What was the reason for the impersonation hoax?"

"Rick wasn't feeling well last week. Rosana wanted someone to stand in for him so she wouldn't disappoint the book club. She'd seen your grandfather's picture in the newspaper and approached him. He agreed to help her out." Clancy gave her a weak smile. "No harm done."

Val pretended to swallow the story. "Oh, so it was just a onetime hoax?"

Clancy tilted his head left and right, as if weighing

his answer. "We may need your grandfather this coming weekend if Rick isn't feeling well again."

And how many times in the past had Rick not felt well and needed a stand-in? She'd gain nothing by asking Clancy that question. She couldn't count on him for the truth. "I have one more clause to add to the contract."

Clancy smiled, but with a clenched jaw. "You drive a hard bargain."

"I won't do any catering for the Ushers until my grandfather is paid for the work he already did."

Clancy's jaw relaxed. "I'll do what I can to move that along. If Rosana pays him today, will you make dinner for us tomorrow?"

"I can do that." Val added the contingency to the contract, signed it, and gave it back to Clancy.

"Thank you." He tucked it into his briefcase. "By the way, your grandfather's a pistol. I really like him. He reminds me of my grandpa."

"Did your grandpa impersonate Usher too?" She grinned as his eyes widened in surprise. "Just kidding, Clancy. I'm looking forward to meeting the real Rick Usher."

"Alas, I can't promise you that. He often eats in his study, not in the dining room with the rest of us."

Yesterday morning Val might have taken those words as support for Granddad's theory that Rick Usher was dead. Now she knew better. The anguished shouts of *buried alive* must have come from the author inspired by Poe.

She noticed Irene at the entrance to the café and

acknowledged her with a wave. "I'll be right with you, Irene."

Clancy's head swiveled toward the entrance.

Irene's face lit up with a broad smile. "Clancy!"

His smile matched hers. He stood up and greeted her with a hug.

How did they know each other? "Are you two old friends?" Val asked.

"Clancy was my tea shop's writer-in-residence. He sat typing in the corner for hours."

"I missed the tea shop once it closed." His lips pressed together and downward, making an upside-down smiley mouth. "You took good care of your customers."

Val listened in surprise to Clancy's praise and hoped Irene's people skills hadn't dried up in the ten months since her business went under.

"All good things must come to an end." Irene patted him on the shoulder. "How is your brother?"

"About the same. Thank you." Clancy pushed up the sleeve of his sweater, revealing a digital watch with a nylon band. "Time to return to my keyboard. Wonderful to see you both."

Irene waved as he left the café. "Does he come here often?"

"This was his first visit."

Val greeted three men in their sixties who came into the café every Tuesday and Thursday morning. They seated themselves at the rectangular table in the far corner.

Irene sat at the eating bar. "I'll wait until you aren't busy with customers."

After Val served the three men, she sat on the

stool next to Irene's and got down to business. "Clancy gave you a great endorsement. I hope we can reach an agreement for both you and Jeremy to work here. Lunch deliveries will work best if we have regular customers and get a commitment up front for a certain number of lunches. I'll have flyers for Jeremy to distribute by tomorrow. I hope he'll have time to do that."

Smile lines appeared around Irene's eyes, cracks in her usually icy demeanor. "He'll make time."

"I'll also work on getting some press coverage in the *Treadwell Gazette* for the delivery service. Do you have any suggestions about the lunch deliveries?"

"I've been studying your sandwich menu. You have lots of different breads, meats, cheeses, and spreads. A simplified menu with set combinations might work better for delivery orders."

She had a point. The limited menu Val had offered at the town festival last fall had streamlined ordering and prep. "Great idea. I'll work on a shorter menu for lunch deliveries. I'll also create a survey to find out what kinds of food the club members would like us to have in the evening."

Irene drummed her fingers on the eating bar. "We still haven't discussed money."

The tricky part. "I'll pay you the same hourly rate as my other assistant, Bethany O'Shay. In addition, because you're managing the café in the evening, you'll get a percent of the sales and, of course, all the tips."

Irene's eyebrows rose. "That sounds fair."

Apparently, she hadn't expected fair wages, but she probably expected to work more hours at that pay than Val wanted. "I'll pay that for the hours from four to seven, but not for the midafternoon time. I don't anticipate selling much food between two and four."

Irene pursed her lips. "Do you plan to close the café during those hours?"

Val shook her head. Time to sweeten the deal. "I'd like to hire someone I could pay less than you because there won't be any cooking involved. I was thinking Jeremy might be interested. Do you think you can train him to sell snacks and make coffee and smoothies?"

Irene's eyebrows reached new heights. "I'm sure I can. He used to help me in the tea shop."

"I'll pay him minimum wage for working behind the counter and for the time he spends delivering lunches. He should make good tips."

Irene focused on the bar and ran her fingers along its edge. "We don't always see eye to eye, but I haven't forgotten that you helped Jeremy out last summer." She raised her head. "I'm grateful that you're willing to trust him now. You won't be sorry."

Her response gave Val hope that they could co-operate in the future, whatever their differences in the past. "I'm sure Jeremy will do a good job." She liked the shy young man. His mother wanted him to succeed so much that she would spend the time working with him. "I'll draw up contracts for each of you and have them ready later in the week. Let's plan on switching to the extended café hours next week. That'll give us time to get the word out."

Val would have felt more confident about putting the café plans into action if she didn't also have to cater at the Usher house, keep Granddad from further exploration of the burial mound there, and try to prove Gunner innocent of murder. *The Codger's Cookbook* would have to go on the back burner for a while.

After Irene left, Val tuned the TV on the wall to the local station, hoping to hear the latest about Emmett Flint's death. The subject came up toward the end of the noon news.

A spokesperson for the county sheriff made a brief announcement. "We are awaiting the final autopsy report and conducting a preliminary investigation, a standard practice when questions are raised about the cause of death. We have nothing further to report at this time."

The newscaster announced that a reporter had interviewed the victim's sister. The video cut to the interview outside Emmett Flint's Bayport home.

A statuesque woman in her fifties, Amy Flint complained on camera about the lack of progress in the police investigation.

"For the last three days, the only things I've heard about my brother's death are theories that have no basis in fact. I don't see how he could have died from an overdose of blood pressure meds. He wouldn't have committed suicide or taken too many pills by accident. It's past time for the police to get to the bottom of this."

As the reporter signed off, Val decided to cram one more task into her busy schedule. She whipped out her phone and searched for Emmett Flint's address. On her way home, she would stop at the house in hopes that his sister hadn't yet left town.

So far Val had heard about the victim from only one person—Gunnar, who hadn't gotten along with him. Amy Flint would have a different view, possibly biased in the other direction, but any information was better than none. Val's previous attempts to identify suspects in a murder had convinced her that understanding the victim's character was essential to solving the crime. Though she hated to intrude on someone in mourning, she also didn't want to pass up a chance to find out more about the man Gunnar might be accused of murdering.

At the café's closing time, she stacked a paper plate with brownies and pecan mini-muffins. But what if Flint's sister didn't have a sweet tooth? Val added cheddar cheese cookies to the plate. She served them with vegetable soup at the café, but they made a good snack too.

Fifteen minutes after leaving the club, Val drove down the street where Emmett Flint had lived. His house, a square two-story cube clad in white vinyl siding, looked neither historic nor modern, just ugly. The few windows on the house, positioned asymmetrically, had black shutters, the single decorative touch on the house's façade. A white picket fence surrounded a small yard without a single shrub or tree on it. The street's other houses with their foundation plants blended better into the landscape.

A tan compact car sat at the curb in front of the house. Val parked across the street. She rang the doorbell with her plate of treats in hand.

A woman cracked the front door open. "Yes?"

Val saw enough of her to recognize the woman interviewed on TV. "Hello. I'm Val Deniston. I'm looking for Emmett Flint's sister. I wanted to express my condolences."

The woman glanced at the plate of cookies Val carried and opened the door wider. "I'm Amy Flint, his sister. Please come in."

"I hope I'm not intruding."

"Not at all. I'm taking a break from sorting through Emmett's books and papers." She led Val into the living room decorated in black and white. The spines of books on the floor-to-ceiling shelves created the only colorful touch in the room. On the floor near the shelves were paper grocery bags, a few filled with books, but most of them empty. Amy would have a big job emptying those shelves.

Val held out the plate. "I brought you some sweets and savories."

"Thank you. You're my first visitor." Amy set the plate on the coffee table next to an open bottle of wine and a stemmed glass with an inch of red wine left in it. She gestured toward a black leather sofa. "Please sit down. Would you like something to drink? Emmett had expensive wine tastes. I just opened one of his reds, and I prefer not to drink alone. Or else I could make you tea. I used the last of his coffee this morning." Her clear resonant voice broke.

"Don't go to any trouble. A splash of wine sounds good. The cheddar cookies I brought would go well with it."

"Wine and cheese," Amy said in her low, vibrant voice. "Perfect. I'll get you a glass."

While she was in the kitchen, Val scanned the bookshelves. One section held books about the theater and acting editions of plays. The top shelves in another section were devoted to Poe. Below them were plays by and books about Tennessee Williams. The next shelf down held Rick Usher books. Black marble composition books were interspersed among the volumes on many of the shelves. Val remembered a teacher who'd mandated that type of stitched notebook because it would last longer than spiral or loose-leaf notebooks, as if anyone would consult their school notes years later.

Amy returned and sat on a white leather chair at right angles to the sofa. She poured Val more than a splash of wine and refilled her own glass. She leaned back in the chair. "Did you know Emmett well?"

"I saw him in a local theater production a few months ago, and I was at the mall when he collapsed on Saturday. I gave him CPR."

Amy's eyes glistened with tears. "Thank you for trying to save him . . . and for coming here. I appreciate the company."

Val gazed into her wineglass, feeling guilty about visiting with an ulterior motive. Then she reminded herself that her goal matched Amy's. They both wanted to know the truth about Emmett's death. And Amy, who'd had no visitors offering condolences, probably needed to talk about her brother. "I was looking at Emmett's book collection. He must have been quite a fan of Edgar Allan Poe."

"He played Poe and some of Poe's characters in a one-man show." Amy held up her glass as if toasting. "Here's to Edgar and Emmett."

Val raised her glass a few inches. She'd drink to Edgar but not to Emmett. "A one-man show must be a huge challenge for any actor. You're on the stage the whole time."

Amy took a cheddar cheese cookie from the plate. "That type of role suited him."

Because other actors irritated him? Because he wanted to be center stage the whole time? Because as writer, director, and actor, he could control everything? Was Emmett a loner, a narcissist, a control freak, or all of the above? Val sipped her wine. "Was his one-man show a hit?"

"He was booked solid in 2009, Poe's two hundredth birthday, and has gotten some mileage out of the show since then, despite fierce competition. You wouldn't believe how many Poe performers are out there. There's a Poe museum, house, or memorial in every big city from Boston to Richmond, and Emmett performed his show in all those cities." Amy brushed crumbs from her lap. "These cheese things are delicious."

"Thank you." Val couldn't keep her eyes from straying toward the shelf with Rick Usher's books. Should she ask about them? Not yet. Better to talk about another writer first so her interest in Usher would be less obvious. "Your brother collected a lot of books on Tennessee Williams. Plays, stories, and memoirs. Not as extensive as the set of Poe books, but close."

"Emmett had parts in Tennessee Williams's plays

over the years and was rehearsing a play that parodied three of them. It's scheduled to open next week." She sighed and drank some wine. "He steeped himself in any role he was playing and in the author who created the character. See all the composition books on the shelves? Emmett took extensive notes to prepare for each role."

Val counted four such notebooks on the Poe shelf, two near the Williams plays, and one near the Usher novels. Rick Usher books on a side table or a nightstand would suggest pleasure reading. Emmett had shelved them amid volumes related to his work as an actor, perhaps because he'd played the role of Usher, but not on a stage. "Did your brother have another one-man show in the offing?"

"He was working on a two-person show and wanted me to play all the female parts. I've never done anything like that, so it would have been a challenge. I studied drama and did some acting when I was younger, off-Broadway and on TV. Voice-overs and audiobooks are my bread and butter now."

"I can understand that. You have a wonderful voice." And she was using it to raise questions about her brother's death out of loyalty to him, not because she craved camera time, as the chief had implied. Val sipped her wine. "Do you live in New York?"

"In Washington. Emmett was on his way to my house when he died. He was going to perform the first scene of the two-person play for me. He was convinced that once I saw it, I'd agree to be in it."

The drive from here to Washington would have

taken Emmett right by the outlet mall. He must have pulled off the road when he started feeling bad. "What was the subject of his new play?"

"He was going to tell me all about it on Saturday over dinner." Amy added wine to her nearly empty glass. "The police said he had theatrical makeup on when he died. I assume he planned to give me the full effect of the scene he'd written by appearing as he would on stage."

Was Emmett going to play a character based on Rick Usher? That would explain why he'd had Usher's signature tinted glasses and hat with him on Saturday. Maybe Emmett mentioned Rick Usher to his sister. Val put her glass down, walked toward the bookshelves, and pulled a copy of *The Murders in the Rue Cler* from the shelf. "Your brother must have liked Rick Usher's novels. Here's the latest one."

"I'm not familiar with him." Amy joined Val at the bookcase and peered at the shelf with Usher's books on it. "Have you read any of his books?"

"I'm reading one now. I'd like to read more."

"I don't have room for Emmett's books in my apartment. You're welcome to take everything on that shelf."

"That's very generous."

"Fair trade for the cookies. Fill a bag or two with books." Amy returned to the coffee table and downed the rest of her wine.

Val loaded the Usher books into one paper bag. She hesitated before putting the composition book in the bag, but only for a moment. Amy had told her to take everything on that shelf.

She walked Val to the door. "I'm glad you stopped by."

"It was good to meet you, Amy. Once again, I'm sorry for your loss. And thank you for the books."

Val crossed the street to her Saturn. She stowed the bag of books in the backseat, closed the rear door, and was about to climb into the car when a sheriff's department patrol car drove slowly down the street in her direction. It veered slightly left, blocking the middle of the narrow street, and stopped abruptly. The driver's window rolled down to reveal the doughy face and narrowed eyes of Deputy Holtzman.

Val's stomach churned. She was never glad to see the obnoxious deputy, but better now than thirty seconds ago. If he'd caught her carrying a bag from Emmett Flint's house, he would have confiscated it and probably even accused her of tampering with evidence. Having made that wild accusation in the past, he wouldn't hesitate to do it again.

Chapter 13

Deputy Holtzman leaned out the window of his patrol car. "I can't say I'm surprised to see you here, Ms. Deniston. You've gotten involved in every suspicious death in this area since you moved here. What are you doing parked near the deceased's house?"

It's a free country and I can go where I like. Val bit back the sassy reply. She should try to make nice with him, even though he wouldn't appreciate it. "I came to offer my condolences to the victim's sister."

"Personal friend of yours? Did you suggest she complain to the media about the pace of the investigation?"

Val raised her hand as if taking an oath. "Not guilty. I talked to her for the first time half an hour ago." The media campaign apparently bothered Holtzman. If he tried to bully Amy into giving it up, he wouldn't succeed. She cared about her brother and wanted justice for him.

The deputy fixed Val with his bulging eyes. "I'm

aware you have a personal reason for interfering in the investigation."

A personal reason named Gunnar. "I'm not interfering with your investigation." *I'm just carrying on a parallel one.* Her previous *interference* had saved Holtzman from arresting the wrong person. She was still waiting for him to thank her for that.

"If you have something to report, bring it to me, not Chief Yardley."

Then Holtzman could once again sneer at her for playing Nancy Drew. The chief at least took what Val said seriously enough to argue against it. "Nothing to report now, but I'll keep that in mind." She opened her car door, climbed in, and turned her key in the ignition.

He took his time before driving on, showing her who was boss. She pulled out as soon as he stopped blocking her and watched in the rearview mirror as he made a U-turn and parked in the space she'd vacated. He climbed out and crossed the street to Emmett Flint's house.

She imagined Deputy Holtzman warning Amy not to share information with Val, and Amy admitting she'd given Val her brother's notes. The deputy might then demand the notebook from Val. She'd better make copies of its pages fast, but not at home because Holtzman knew where she lived. He'd gone there last summer to intimidate Granddad.

She drove to the small print shop on a side street in Bayport and used the high-speed copier to duplicate the twenty-odd pages in Emmett's notebook that had writing on them. While there, she told the printer she would e-mail the text for her café flyers and surveys. He promised a fast turnaround on them.

Back at home, she hid the copy of Emmett's notes in a folder of recipes. Then she flipped through the notebook itself. It contained a list of sources about Rick Usher, including online videos featuring him. Based on those, Emmett described Usher's physical traits, typical gestures, and manner of speaking. A year-by-year record of Usher's professional life included where he'd lived, studied, and taught, along with the books he'd published and the speeches he'd given.

Nothing in Emmett's notes suggested he'd met Rick Usher or posed as him. Yet Val wasn't ready to admit she'd reached the wrong conclusion. Simone remained the best hope of connecting the dead actor to the impersonation hoax. She might be able to identify Emmett as the imposter if Val showed her a photo of him in the role of an older man.

Val searched online for images of Emmett Flint and found only flattering pictures that made him look twenty years younger than he really was. Either the photos were taken years ago, or Emmett had hired a photographer who knew his way around Photoshop. She needed a photographer who could add, rather than subtract, wrinkles to make Emmett look as old as Rick Usher. She sat up straighter. Her cousin could do it, but was Monique back from Florida yet?

Val speed-dialed Monique and was thrilled when she reached something other than voice mail. "You're back!"

"Just walked in the door. We're exhausted. The kids loved the theme parks and wore us out." Monique talked over the voices of her two preschoolers clamoring for a treat.

Val raised her voice. "I want to hear more about your trip when you're less busy, but now I have a favor to ask. If I e-mail you a headshot of a man, can you make him look twenty years older?"

"I have software that does that. All it takes is a click to age a photo. Hold on, Val. The kids won't quiet down without a snack."

While waiting for her cousin to come back on the line, Val came up with a better way to find out if Simone could identify the man she'd seen posing as Usher. If it was easy to age a photo, Val might as well show Simone headshots of more than one man and ask if any of them resembled the impersonator. It would be like a police lineup, less biased than presenting a picture of just one man.

"I'm back," Monique said. "Send me the photo you want aged."

"You said it just took only a click to age someone. So may I send you photos of three men?" Val didn't wait for a response. "Besides aging them, could you put tinted glasses and a gray beard on them?"

"That will take longer. To speed up the process, send me a picture of a man with the type of glasses and beard you want me to superimpose on the other photos. Try to find photos of the other men in similar poses. The kids are squabbling." Monique told her children to stop fighting and came back on the line. "The last time you asked me to do something like this, you were trying to identify a murderer."

"That's not the purpose this time."

"I'll work on the photos in the morning and bring them to the café. Then you can tell me what's going on."

"I really appreciate this. See you tomorrow."

Val brought up Rick Usher's Web site on her computer. The site's media page included two pictures of him, the headshot that was usually on the cover of his book and a photo of him standing next to Poe's grave. She copied the close-up. Then she found half a dozen headshots on Emmett Flint's Web site and copied the one most similar to Usher's. Now for the two more headshots.

Val searched through photos on her computer and found one of her ex-fiancé, Tony, in a formal pose, a picture taken shortly after he joined his law firm. Too bad she didn't have a suitable picture of Gunnar. His acting career hadn't progressed far enough for him to bother with publicity shots, but she could take a picture of him in the right pose.

She phoned him. He said he'd be home for the next hour and then leave for a rehearsal. She promised to be there within half an hour. Before she did anything else, she had to create the flyer announcing the café's lunch delivery and e-mail it to the printer. Otherwise, it wouldn't be ready for Jeremy to distribute tomorrow.

Half an hour later, with that job done, she jumped into the car and drove to Gunnar's house.

As she turned onto Maple Street, she spotted a

sheriff's department car parked in front of Gunnar's place. Uh-oh. Deputy Holtzman again? Probably.

She drove past Gunnar's Miata, the deputy's car in front of it, and the SUV belonging to Gunnar's neighbor before she parked her Saturn. She pulled out the ignition key and sat in the car, unsure what to do. Her presence might not help Gunnar. She brought out the worst in Holtzman. She and the deputy had rubbed each other the wrong way the first time they met. After she'd complained about his unprofessional behavior to his boss, the tension between them had never let up. If she hadn't gone over his head, he might have been less hostile to her in their later encounters.

Nah. Hostility coursed through his veins. He'd badgered her and Granddad. Before Gunnar left his government job, he'd worked undercover with Federal investigators. That experience would probably make him less susceptible to badgering. Still, he might want her beside him for moral support. She'd leave it up to him.

She got out of the car, marched to the tiny, one-story brick house he rented, and tapped the knocker on the front door lightly. Normally, she would follow that up by letting herself in and calling out to him. Today she waited.

Gunnar opened the storm door, anxiety apparent in his rigid jaw. "Come in."

"Are you sure?" she whispered.

He nodded and held the door open for her. "Don't react to him," he said in her ear as she went past him.

Gunnar had set up the living room as an office, with his desk, a file cabinet, and a table that doubled as a small conference table. The only other furniture in the room was a loveseat and a chair near the window. She exchanged nods with Holtzman and sat across the table from him next to Gunnar. The deputy showed no surprise at seeing her. Gunnar must have told him he was expecting her.

Holtzman tapped a ballpoint pen on his spiral notebook. "I'd like to get some background information, Mr. Swensen. You were living in Washington until you quit your government job six months ago and moved here to start an accounting business." At Gunnar's nod, Holtzman continued, "At that time you'd just come into some money. Who gave that to you?"

Val had expected Deputy Holtzman to ask about more recent events. The deputy didn't make small talk. Apparently, he thought Gunnar's background had a bearing on the Emmett Flint case.

"I inherited money from my great-aunt," Gunnar said with no inflection or emotion, like an actor trying hard not to get a part.

"When did she die?" Holtzman said.

"Last April."

"When was the last time you saw her alive?"

"The day before she died. I was visiting my mother in Indiana. We took my aunt some soup."

"Huh. You visited your aunt shortly before she died." The deputy leaned forward at the edge of his chair, like an audience member at the climax of a play. "What did your aunt die of?"

Val cringed inwardly, convinced that the deputy already knew the cause of death and had planned this chain of questions. She couldn't tell anything from Gunnar's poker face, but his hands gave him away.

His knuckles whitened as he gripped the seat of his folding chair. "Heart failure. She had a history of heart ailments."

"Was she treated for high blood pressure?"

Gunnar shrugged. "Possibly. It runs in that side of the family."

"Who cleared out the place where she lived after she died?"

"I helped my mother do it."

A shudder passed through Val. Emmett's assault complaint and threat to sue gave Gunnar a motive for murder. He'd also had access to Emmett's burrito and, apparently in Holtzman's eyes, to the meds the actor had OD'd on.

The deputy stood up. "That will be all for now. I'll let myself out."

He was finished *for now.* Would he return to ask more questions or did he already have sufficient reason to charge Gunnar with Emmett's murder?

When the door closed behind Holtzman, Gunnar shot out of his chair and paced the room. "He's not going after me only for Emmett's murder. He insinuated I murdered my aunt for her money."

"It's just a ploy to rattle you. That's how he works." Val tried to sound calmer than she felt. She walked to the window, peered between the slats of the blinds, and watched the deputy drive away. "He can't possibly think you killed your aunt."

"Before you arrived, he asked to use the bathroom. I'll bet he wanted to look in the medicine cabinet." Gunnar ran his hand through his hair. "Not giving me much credit. If I'd murdered someone with pills, I wouldn't keep the rest of them around."

"He was looking for the kind of pills that killed Emmett." Val was sure the deputy hadn't found anything incriminating in the medicine cabinet, unless Gunnar had medical problems he hadn't mentioned to her. "You don't have high blood pressure, do you?"

Gunnar winced. "No, but I have my aunt's meds."

Chapter 14

Val tugged Gunnar toward the loveseat under the window. He'd better have a good explanation for holding on to his aunt's medicine, and she better not have died from an overdose of them. "Why do you have your aunt's meds?"

"I took them to dispose of them safely. I never got around to it when I was clearing out my apartment in Washington. I threw the pills in a footlocker with a bunch of other things I didn't have time to sort through."

"Where's the footlocker now?"

"In the storage unit with all the stuff I won't need until I move to an unfurnished place."

The rent was so reasonable on this fully equipped house that he could afford to store his own furniture until his lease was up. Val knew the deputy would find out before long where Gunnar had stored things. "You could get your aunt's medicines from the unit and dispose of them."

"If I'm caught, I'll look more guilty than I do now."

True. "We need to figure out who killed Emmett before Holtzman gets a search warrant for your storage unit. Did you find out if any cast members saw Emmett after Saturday's rehearsal?"

He nodded. "One of them noticed him leaving around twelve with his hair and beard grayed."

"Three hours later he collapsed in the mall parking lot. He stopped there on his way to visit his sister." Val told Gunnar what she'd read in Emmett's notebook and heard from his sister. "I think he was creating a show based on Rick Usher's books and dressed as him to perform a scene for his sister."

"So he was writing a play and not impersonating Rick Usher?"

"He might have done both. I'm going to visit the woman who said she saw an Usher impersonator. I'll show her a photo lineup of men resembling him and see if she picks out Emmett as the impersonator." Val fished her phone from her shoulder bag. "May I take your picture?"

"Is it for a mug shot?"

Val could tell from Gunnar's lopsided smile that he wasn't serious. Even when he was worried, he could make a joke, a trait she found endearing.

She kissed him and explained her plan for Monique to age Emmett's photo. "She'll age your photo, Emmett's, and one other man's for the lineup."

"Don't show me my picture after Monique ages me. I'd rather not know how I'll look when I'm paroled after forty years."

Val framed his face in the camera display. He looked grim. "Aim for the Mona Lisa look. Attractive and enigmatic." That got a laugh out of him. She waited until he looked more serious and then snapped half a dozen photos. She tucked her phone away. "Do you happen to have a picture of Maddie?"

"I might. When I was watching the early rehearsals, I took photos of Emmett's scenes, in case I had to take over for him as Big Daddy. She should be in a few of them." Gunnar scrolled through the pictures on his phone. "Here's one where she's facing the camera."

The photo confirmed Val's assumption. "Her full name is Madison Fox-Norton. She works for the Ushers and lives in their house."

"So she's another thread between the Ushers and Emmett. Don't pull too hard on that thread. Just tell Chief Yardley about it." He squeezed her hand. "Now I'm kicking you out. I need time alone to get into Big Daddy's head for the rehearsal."

As Val went into the house, Granddad was talking on the hall phone. She waved to him on her way to the study. He went through the same motions as he had the night before when he didn't want her to know about his cadaver-dog scheme. He turned away and covered his mouth. What was he up to now?

She threw her jacket on the sofa in the study, sat at her computer, and jiggled the mouse.

Granddad poked his head into the room. "I've got to go out for a bit. I'll be back before six."

"Okay." No point in asking where he was going. He wouldn't tell her, but at least she could find out who had been on the other end of his phone call. Once he drove away, she went into the hall and pressed the phone's redial button.

A man picked up. "Good afternoon. Althea Johnson Law Office. May I help you?"

It took Val a moment to get over her surprise. Her friend and tennis teammate, Althea, had a legal practice in Bayport with a focus on family law. Did Granddad need legal advice? "Good afternoon. This is Val Deniston. May I talk to Althea, please?"

"Please hold on. I'll see if she's busy."

Althea wouldn't break a client's confidentiality and say whether Granddad was consulting her, but Val had other reasons to talk to her friend.

"Hi, Val. I can't talk long because I have an appointment in a few minutes."

An appointment with Granddad? "Just a quick question. Can you suggest a good criminal lawyer in Maryland?"

"The same attorneys I recommended to Monique last summer. I'll e-mail you their contact information as soon as I can. You're not in any kind of trouble, are you?"

"I'm not the one who needs the lawyer, if that's what you mean." Val didn't want to tell anyone about Gunnar's trouble without his permission, not even a good friend like Althea.

After they hung up, Val attached photos of Emmett Flint, her former fiancé, Gunnar, and Rick Usher to an e-mail message, identifying them only by number. She asked Monique to age the men in the first, second, and third photos, and then to superimpose the hat, glasses, and beard from the last photo onto the other three.

With that out of the way, Val pored over Emmett's notes tracking Rick Usher's life from birth to the present. The author was born eighty-two years ago as Richard Ugla—not far off from his Poe-related pen name. Rather than spend time reading about his early life, Val flipped to the last pages in the Usher bio and worked backward.

For the years since 2010, when the Ushers moved to the house where they now lived, Emmett had noted only titles and release dates of books. October 2009 was the date of Rick Usher's last public appearance that Emmett recorded. He'd written a marginal note about it: *Usher fled.*

What did that mean?

Val turned to her computer and typed *Rick Usher October 2009* in the Google search box. She clicked on a link titled "Writer Channels Poe" and read the first paragraph: *Celebrating a birthday by holding a funeral makes sense if the ghost of honor is Edgar Allan Poe. In one of many events marking Poe's two-hundredth birthday, hundreds gathered to attend a belated funeral service for him in Baltimore, where he died and was buried in 1849. Rick Usher, best-selling author of Poe-inspired novels, gave a lecture after the mock funeral.*

According to the online article, the audience for the lecture included several men and one woman dressed to resemble Poe. They wore black jackets, some with a white shirt and dark cravat, others with a white scarf around their neck. The woman wore a fake mustache.

Rick Usher gave a eulogy punctuated with dramatic readings from Poe's works. Then he began talking as if he were Poe, which he'd done at other presentations. The audience loved it, even the part in which Usher exhibited the paranoia that Poe had shown in the last year of his life.

The article then described an incident from the summer of 1849. Poe jumped off a train in Philadelphia because he'd overheard two passengers plotting to kill him. He ended up in a city jail, hallucinating and suspected of temporary insanity. After being identified as "that Raven guy," he was released, whereupon he took refuge with a friend and described his lucky escape from death. He insisted on having his mustache shaved off, apparently to prevent his would-be killers from recognizing him. A few months later, Poe died in Baltimore under mysterious circumstances. *To this day*, the article said, *no one knows what killed Poe but murder is a possible explanation.*

The article went on to say that Rick Usher exhibited paranoia similar to Poe's. At the end of his 2009 lecture, he pointed toward the audience, accused someone of stalking him, and shouted, *I'm not ready to die. You can't take me yet.* He then ran to the exit at the back of the room, pursued by a boyish Poe look-alike seated in the front row. No one else in the audience left, apparently expecting the two men to reappear for applause, but neither returned.

The last paragraph in the online article read:

Those who've attended other Rick Usher lectures know that he concludes them by speaking as if he were Poe and by basking in the applause of the audience. This time he didn't return to the room for his ovation. Why not? It's a mystery.

A mystery Val would like to solve. What motivated Usher's dramatic departure—the performance, his own paranoia, or real peril? Fleeing the room as Poe had fled the train made an apt climax to a program in which Poe's fear of being murdered played a role. Usher's retreat from the public eye after that evening suggested he might have had similar fears. Val couldn't rule out that he'd had a reason for those fears. Not long after that lecture, the Ushers moved away from Baltimore and eventually hired an impersonator, possibly because Rick Usher still feared for his life.

Val's stomach knotted. She'd better make sure Granddad never posed as the author again. Though he'd told her he wouldn't do another impersonation, he might change his mind. He couldn't do it, though, if she took his costume away.

Where had he put the tinted glasses? She dashed from the study to his bedroom. Not on the dresser or his night table. Not in his bathroom either. She checked the table in the hall and the one next to his chair in the living room. No glasses. She would have seen them in the kitchen if he'd left them there. Where else could they be?

He'd worn them Sunday night at the book club meeting, but when Val saw him later at home, he was wearing his bifocals. He might have left the tinted glasses in the car or the pocket of his new overcoat. She opened the hall closet, checked his coat pockets, and found them. She also confiscated the tweed driver's cap from the shelf in the closet. Now for the black shirt. She found it in the hamper of his bathroom. She took the three items up to her room and put them among her own clothes in a suitcase under her bed.

Back downstairs, she read the article about Rick Usher's lecture again. Could what happened that night explain Emmett's murder? He might have been killed by someone who'd stalked and intended to kill Usher. Yes, she was leaping to a conclusion, but a tentative one. Solving a murder was like creating a new dish. You introduced ingredients one at a time, corrected the seasoning, and tasted it. If it didn't work, you could add more to the pot or start from scratch. Arriving at the recipe that worked best could take several tries.

Her phone rang.

"I'm at the supermarket," Granddad said. "Do you want me to pick up anything?"

"We'll eat the leftover beef from the book club dinner. We're running low on salad greens, so please get some lettuce." He could save her time by buying the food for tomorrow's dinner too. If the Ushers had paid him today, she'd have to make dinner, not just for the two of them, but also for the four at the Usher house. "Did Rosana Usher pay you today?"

"Sure did. I deposited the money as soon as I got back in town. I didn't want to carry around that much cash."

A cash transaction meant no paper trail for the shady business of impersonation. Though Granddad had a contract, it might contain vague wording about his duties. Val had signed a contract that wasn't at all vague. Now that Granddad had been paid, she had to cook. "I'm making dinner at the Usher house starting tomorrow."

"I know. They invited me to stay for it."

Val had already decided what to make for the first dinner there. "Would you please buy four Cornish hens?" She'd split them in half, leaving two extra portions in case anyone had a massive appetite or a guest showed up at the last minute. She gave Granddad the rest of her grocery list.

After hanging up, she continued searching for online sources that mentioned Rick Usher's last stand in front of the public. None of them had any more information than the article she'd already read, but she found some photos people had posted on Facebook after the event. The pictures showed the author at the podium from various angles. In two of them he pointed to the audience, his face contorted with fear.

She also found photos of the audience taken from the front and sides. One showed a young dark-haired man with a mustache. His deep-set eyes, white scarf, and high-collared black jacket guaranteed he'd beat every other contestant in a Poe look-alike contest. No one else in the front row fit the description of the man who followed Usher out of the room.

Val picked up Emmett's composition book and turned to his notes on Rick Usher as a young man, his graduation from high school and his military service in Korea after the armistice agreement. He had that in common with Granddad, who'd also been stationed in Korea in the 1950s. When Rick Usher came back from overseas, he went to college on the G.I. bill and taught in a high school while going to graduate school. He then won a teaching fellowship and a faculty appointment at the University of Virginia. In 1974 he married Rosana and left UVA. Emmett had written notes next to that section of the bio: *Rosana UVA grad 1974.*

Hmm. Maybe Rosana had been one of Rick Usher's students.

Val saw Granddad's Buick stop at the curb. She opened the front door for him and took the grocery bags to the kitchen while he hung up his jacket.

He joined her there and went to the refrigerator for a beer. "Busy day at the Usher place. I found out what's under that mound of dirt."

Val's jaw dropped. She had a vision of him digging in the yard. "Did you take a shovel with you today?"

He popped open his beer. "I had one in the car, but I didn't need it. Rick told me what was buried there."

Rick? "You're calling the man you thought was dead by his first name?"

"I was wrong about that." Granddad sat at the small kitchen table. "But you were wrong about what he meant when he shouted *buried alive*. He wasn't talking about something from a Poe story."

Did that mean someone had been buried alive there?

Chapter 15

Val joined Granddad at the small table in the kitchen. "Please explain how you got to talk to Rick Usher and what he meant by *buried alive.*"

"I went to his house early. I knew that Clancy wouldn't be there because he was going to the café to talk to you and that Rosana and Madison work together every morning."

"You were hoping to catch Rick Usher alone."

He nodded. "Even if I didn't, I wanted to take another look at the dirt mound. When I got there, he was by himself, standing by the mound. I walked up to him. He remembered meeting me last week, but forgot my name. *You're the man who's going to represent me at book signings,* he said."

Represent. If Granddad's contract described him as a representative, the Ushers could deny they'd hired an impersonator. "What was he doing there by the mound?"

"Looking like a man at a cemetery. His dog is buried there." Granddad leaned toward her as if he had a secret to reveal. "His dog Cicero."

If Val had been in a cartoon, a light bulb would have appeared over her head. "He started to say *My poor Cicero* last night, not *My poor sister.* Okay, he's not crazy enough to think he's a Poe character, but he has the same obsession with live burial as Poe. Why would he think his dog was buried alive?"

"He dozed off in his study last night and woke up when he heard barking. He went outside and saw two people and a dog near the mound. He thought prowlers had dug up his dog alive."

Val jerked to attention. "Rick Usher has a good memory for faces. He knew who you were from a brief meeting a week ago. He might recognize me as one of the people he saw last night."

Granddad gave her a smug smile. "That occurred to me too. I asked him to describe the prowlers. He couldn't. They were too far away and he was focused on the dog. He assumed you and Bethany were teenage boys."

"Whew." She mimicked wiping sweat from her forehead. "I feel bad about the way we upset the poor man. I hope he didn't stay out in the cold for long."

"When you all ran away, he went inside and talked to Rosana. She told him he'd had a dream. He wasn't convinced, so this morning he went out to check on Cicero's resting place. He even asked me if I could see any sign of digging there. I said the mound looked the same today as two days ago." Granddad stood up. "Speaking of dreams, I had one last night that reminded me of something I should do." He left the kitchen.

"I'll start dinner." She took the leftover beef daube

from the fridge. While it heated in a pot, she peeled potatoes, cubed them, and added them to the beef, turning the heat down to a simmer. She was scraping carrots when Granddad came back.

He marched up to the counter. "You hid my new hat and glasses. Why?"

Just her luck. For the first time in years, he remembered where he put a pair of glasses. "Why do you need them? You said you weren't going to impersonate Usher anymore and—"

"And you didn't believe me." He pointed his index finger at her. "You've got to stop treating me like a child. How would you like it if I hid your stuff?"

Of course she wouldn't like it. He had every right to be angry. "I'm sorry. I shouldn't have done that."

He went on as if she hadn't apologized. "Last night I dreamed that a thief got in the house and stole my Usher getup. The dream about a thief came true." He glared at her.

Now he was really rubbing it in. "I said I was sorry, and I meant it."

He waggled his finger at her. "Bring me those things right now, young lady."

Feeling like a naughty six-year-old, she went upstairs and got them. He grabbed them from her, turned, and left her alone in the kitchen.

Alone with her regret. A year ago, when she quit her job in New York, broke off her engagement, and moved in with him, her mother had assigned her a role—to save Granddad from himself. Val was supposed to put him on a healthier diet, encourage him to do something besides watch old movies, and prod him to sell the big house. He ate better now that she was cooking for him. He'd taken up writing a recipe column for the newspaper and started a half-baked business as a sleuth. He no longer spent all day in his lounge chair watching the TV screen. But he wouldn't budge on the house sale. She respected that decision. Even her mother was happy with two out of three and absolved her of further responsibility for him. Occasionally, though, Val slipped back into her role of grandfather protector. Last summer her protectiveness had saved his life, though he didn't give her credit for that. This time, though, her intervention had backfired. He might even retaliate against her by clamming up, refusing to tell her anything more about his visit to the Usher house today.

The aroma of beef simmering in wine and garlic brought him back to the kitchen sooner than she expected. He set the table in silence. She poured two glasses of red wine, hoping it would make them both more mellow.

She took the food to the table and sat across from him. "I want to explain why I hid your glasses and hat. I thought, if they were within easy reach, you might wear them because you look good in them." A little flattery went a long way with him. "Today I found out that someone might have stalked and tried to kill Rick Usher before he moved here. I was afraid you'd be in danger if you resembled him."

Granddad put his salad aside and took a generous helping of beef. "How do you figure that?"

She told him what she'd read about the author's

behavior at his last public appearance. "He moved here a few months later and went into seclusion, possibly because he feared for his life. Recently he hired a stand-in. Why? Maybe to test whether he's still in danger."

Granddad pointed his fork at her. "You're wrong about why he's holed up in that house. And you're wrong about him. He's not the kind of man who'd put someone else in danger to save his own skin." He went back to eating.

She'd rather smooth over their differences tonight than challenge Granddad's conclusions about a man he'd just met. She speared some salad. "I don't understand why a famous author would want another man to pretend to be him."

"Who says he wanted that? He told me that he always talked like Poe at lectures and he didn't mind if I talked *like* Rick Usher. He never saw me in the clothes and glasses that made me look like him." Granddad reached for his wineglass. "Either Rosana didn't tell him what I was doing or he forgot."

"Rosana might want to know if a killer is still after her husband. But is she ruthless enough to put someone else in jeopardy to find out?"

Granddad rolled his eyes. "Why do you keep saying someone wants to kill him? He acted paranoid when he gave that speech because he was showing how Poe acted."

"And then he moved here and never went out in public again."

"He was in his seventies. He retired. What's the

big deal? Anyway, he had other reasons to move here."

Val waited for Granddad to say more, but he took a mouthful of beef instead. So this was her punishment for hiding his hat and the tinted glasses. He was tantalizing her with bits of information and leaving her hanging. "You're right. People his age retire. A lot of retirees move to this area. But no one's hired to masquerade as them. Three days ago, an actor who made himself look like Rick Usher died under suspicious circumstances. He may be dead because his killer mistook him for a famous author."

"You have no proof someone wanted to kill the famous author." Granddad sipped his wine. "Look for evidence that someone wanted to kill the actor."

"The police have been doing that." And reached the wrong conclusion. "They've found evidence against Gunnar."

Granddad's eyes widened. "How's Gunner involved?"

"He, Emmett, and Madison have roles in the Treadwell Players' upcoming show. Gunnar intervened when Emmett harassed Madison. Emmett tried to punch him. He forced Gunnar to defend himself and then filed an assault complaint and a lawsuit against him."

Granddad stared at the wall behind Val. "Huh. Now that's weird."

"What's weird?"

"Something Rick said."

"Over Cicero's grave?"

"No. Later." Granddad mounded beef onto his fork. "What else makes Gunnar look guilty?"

Val drank some wine and suppressed her annoyance with his evasions. Then she told him about Gunnar's access to Emmett's burrito, his lack of an alibi, and his possible possession of the medicine Emmett had OD'd on. Granddad's frown deepened as she talked. Though his attitude toward Gunnar had improved in the last few months, she sensed it could turn negative quickly.

"So Gunnar has motive, opportunity, and means." Granddad put down his fork. "I warned you against him when he first showed up here. I knew he wasn't being straight with you. Giving up a solid job at his age to take up acting didn't sit well with me either. But I never figured him for a murderer, especially not by giving a man pills. That's like poisoning. It's a woman's weapon. I can't see Gunnar using it."

Val rarely let Granddad get away with a generalization about women, but she let this one go. It worked in her favor. "You want to blame a woman? I've got one who makes an excellent suspect. Madison." Val summarized the case against Rosana's assistant. Emmett tried to blackmail her. She lied about it to the police. She had as much chance to tamper with his burrito as Gunnar did.

"Emmett sounds like a nasty piece of work. What else do you know about him?"

Val ran through what she'd learned about Emmett. When she mentioned his one-man show, Granddad interrupted her. "Aha! Would you call him a Poe expert?"

What did that *Aha* mean? "Emmett researched

Poe for the play he wrote for himself. Why do you ask?"

"Rick mentioned him today, though not by name. He didn't much like the guy."

Another thread connecting Emmett to the Ushers! Val kept her excitement in check. If Rick Usher hadn't mentioned Emmett by name, Granddad's conclusion might be wrong. "How did Usher go from mourning his dead dog to dissing a Poe performer?"

When Granddad's face lit up, she saw she'd hit on the right way to extract information from him. He stubbornly avoided answering simple questions, but he couldn't pass up the chance to spin a yarn.

He went to the sink and brought a large glass of water back to the table, like a lecturer afraid his mouth would run dry before he finished. "While we were at Cicero's grave, we traded dog stories. Rick said he never imagined Cicero would die before he did. He started crying. Not just tears rolling down his cheeks. I mean bawling his eyes out. It was embarrassing to be there, but I didn't want to leave him either. All of a sudden he stopped and apologized. I told him I understood. I grieved a lot when my dog died."

"I guess you didn't tell him Chessie died ten years ago."

"Not important. It made him feel better to think somebody understood what he was going through. The Ushers bought the house here as a summer place about the same time as Cicero joined the family. That's how Usher put it. The dog loved running free here. He hated Baltimore, the noise, the crowds, and, probably most of all, the leash. So the Ushers decided to move here permanently and sold their place in the city."

"The dog made them do it?" Val didn't believe it. "I'm sure Cicero preferred living in the country to living in the city, but he didn't demand that Rick Usher give up contact with his fans."

Granddad shrugged. "Folks slow down when they get older. He asked how long I'd lived on the Eastern Shore. When I told him all my life, except for my stint in Korea in the fifties, he got excited. He was stationed there too, four years before I was. We reminisced about the place. Then he invited me to go inside with him. We went in by the door in the wing that leads directly to his study."

Val mimicked tipping her hat to Granddad. "Bravo. You penetrated Rick Usher's wall of isolation."

He smiled for the first time since she'd taken his glasses and hat. "You should see his study. Books on all four walls, floor to ceiling. Everything from ancient history to Stephen King. We sat in armchairs in front of the fireplace and talked about growing up in the forties. He's a few years older than me. I married earlier, straight out of high school. He didn't get hitched 'til he was almost forty."

"He married a younger woman."

"Yep. Rosana's a baby boomer, only a few years older than your mother. Usher and I hit it off because we're from the same generation. We speak the same language. Men who go for younger wives miss out on that kind of bond."

Val suppressed a smile. "I guess they have other compensations."

"Those don't last forever." Granddad sipped his wine. "Usher's a lonely man. The next time Ned and I go to dinner and poker night at the retirement village, I'll ask him to join us. I think he'd enjoy meeting some people his own age."

"He appreciated your company. Whether he likes poker is another question."

"Only one way to find out." Granddad stopped talking long enough to take another bite of his dinner. "This beef tastes great."

"Thanks. It's one of the few dishes that's good when you make it, better the following day, and best two or three days later."

"I'm glad a few things improve with age." He reached for his wineglass. "Rick's different from most people I know. He asked me a question no one else ever did—*What's your philosophy of old age?* What would you say to that?"

Easy question for Val. "Old age is better than the alternative."

"That's a young person's answer. Not all old folks would agree." Granddad sipped his wine. "My approach to being old is to try new things to replace what I can't have or can't do anymore. That's what I told him."

Unless Val redirected the conversation, she'd have to listen to Rick Usher's philosophy of old age when she wanted to hear about his reaction to Emmett Flint. "What else did you talk about?"

"Our families. We both raised one daughter and no other children." Granddad poured another half glass of wine. "Now for the sad part. His daughter died when she was fifteen. The mother of her friend was driving the two girls home after a party. A drunk driver hit them."

Val's last bite of beef stuck in her throat. "That's terrible. How do you get over something like that?"

"I don't know. Rick sank into depression and couldn't write anything for a couple of years. When he went back to it, he did it with a vengeance. Two books a year instead of one. *My books are my children,* he told me. *I want them taken care of when I'm gone.* He said the man who managed Poe's literary legacy destroyed his reputation. Rick's afraid the same thing will happen to him. He's looking for the right person to take care of his legacy."

"His wife's not the right person?"

"He said the house and their savings would go to Rosana, but he needed someone else to manage what he's written. She handles the finances, which never interested him, but he doesn't want to burden her with making decisions about his works."

"Or he doesn't trust her to make them," Val said.

"He talked to one man, a Poe expert who asked to interview him. Rick wanted to get to know him before saying anything about his literary legacy."

Granddad's *Aha* now made sense to Val. "You think he talked to Emmett Flint?"

He nodded. "The guy gave him advice on how to profit from his fame. Instead of paying a writer like Clancy to work with him, Rick should find writers willing to pay him to put his name on their books. Then he could make money without doing any work."

"Exploiting other people. That sounds like Emmett."

"Rick said this Poe expert was like Mr. Proffit in Poe's story 'The Business Man.' Mr. Proffit puts up eyesores that people pay him to remove. He starts fights with people on the streets and then sues them for attacking him." Granddad turned his hand palm up as if offering her a plate. "That's what I said was weird. Emmett doing what Mr. Proffit did."

"Clearly he wasn't the right person to enhance Usher's reputation." Val added a splash of wine to her glass. "Rick Usher rejected him and Rosana as literary executors. Why not appoint Clancy? He knows more than anybody about the Usher books."

"I asked Rick the same question. He told me how the two of them work together. Rick dreams up the plots and gives them to Clancy to write a first draft. The draft always comes back with unnecessary characters and complications. He said if Fancy Clancy wrote Peter Pan, Captain Hook wouldn't just have a crocodile chasing him. He'd also have a school of sharks and a great white whale. And Tinker Bell would have two mean stepsisters."

Val laughed. "Clancy won't be writing drafts of books after Usher dies, so his fancy touches don't matter." How important could Rick Usher's literary legacy be? His books sold well, but he wouldn't make anyone's list of the top hundred American writers. "What does Rick Usher expect his literary executor to do?"

"I asked him that. The executor would make decisions. Who should get access to his papers?

Who should write an official biography? Should another writer continue his series with the French detective? When should those books come out?"

Val saw opportunities for Clancy to profit as the literary executor. "Clancy would want to choose himself as the biographer and the writer of follow-on books. But I'll bet Rick Usher can specify in his will that the executor, whoever it is, can't give himself those plum jobs." Val caught Granddad's twitch when she mentioned a will. Before dinner he'd phoned Althea, a lawyer who could draw up a will. "Is Usher going to change his will?"

Motionless for a second, Granddad then shrugged. "How would I know?" He stood up. "Mighty good dinner. I'll eat dessert later. I gotta think through some things."

He didn't usually put off eating dessert. His reaction made her suspect Rick Usher had asked him to arrange a lawyer for him, possibly to handle a change in a will. But why would the author ask a virtual stranger to do that? Maybe because he didn't want interference from anyone close to him. Reading and watching murder mysteries had taught Val a lesson about wills: Don't alert your heirs of impending changes, or you might not live long enough to make them.

Chapter 16

When Val finished cleaning up after dinner, she went into the sitting room and found Granddad in his lounge chair. He usually watched television, read the newspaper, or napped in that chair. Tonight, it had apparently turned into his thinking chair. He stared at the TV, which wasn't even on.

"Can I get you anything, Granddad?"

"Nope." He massaged his forehead.

She went into the study and left the door open so she could see him. She checked her e-mail. Althea had sent her the names of two criminal lawyers in Annapolis. She forwarded the message to Gunnar.

Then Val opened Emmett's composition book to the 1974 page. Beneath the statement that Rick Usher married Rosana in that year, Emmett had jotted other notes: *What made Usher leave UVA? Didn't get tenure? Library job? Affair with student? Lazy and married money?*

Except for *library job,* whatever that meant, Emmett had chalked up Usher's departure to failures or weaknesses. Val had a more positive take on why the author might have left the university. He was in his late thirties, wanted to write novels, and decided to focus on that—similar to what Gunnar had done in leaving a secure government job to pursue his ambition of acting. Gunnar had received an inheritance. Perhaps Rosana's money served the same function for Rick.

Val reread Emmett's jottings. She found it hard to believe that an affair with a student would cause anyone's removal from the faculty. But at a conservative school like UVA in the 1970s, it might have jeopardized Rick Usher's chances for tenure.

Emmett's notebook contained no information about the author for the five years after he left the University of Virginia. Usher might have spent those years writing fiction. His first historical mystery about Gaston Vulpin hit the best-seller list in 1979. Another Vulpin book came out two years later and then every year after that including 1988, when Usher returned to academia as a visiting professor at Boston University.

Didn't Simone study there? Val turned to her computer. She went to the Web site for Chesapeake College, where Simone taught, and brought up the faculty list. Sure enough. Simone had earned a Master's degree from Boston University in 1988 and a Ph.D. there five years later. No way to know if she'd taken a course from Rick Usher, but with her research focused on Poe, surely she would have known him. By then he was in his fifties. She must have been in her twenties in the late 1980s. Had he become romantically involved with Simone in Boston as he had with Rosana at UVA? A liaison between the Ph.D. candidate and the visiting professor would explain her intense interest in him.

Thinking about Simone reminded Val to arrange a meeting with her. Monique would have the photos of the digitally aged men ready in the morning. Val called the number she'd found online for S. Wingard in Treadwell. The woman who answered sounded like Simone.

"Hi. This is Val Deniston, the caterer who made dinner at the book club meeting Sunday night."

"The caterer." Simone sounded bemused. "Oh, yes. You sent Judith your onion soup recipe, and she forwarded it. Thank you for that, but I don't need a caterer."

"That's not why I'm calling. I have some news for you about Rick Usher and something to show you related to him. I'd like to make an appointment to meet you, tomorrow afternoon if possible."

The silence on the line ended after three seconds. "You want to *show* me something about Rick? What is it?"

"I'll explain tomorrow afternoon if we can get together then. I can meet you at your house or office or at my house in Bayport, whatever's most convenient."

"I'll be home by three tomorrow." Simone rattled off her address in Treadwell.

"See you then."

Val hung up and glanced at Granddad in the sitting room. He hadn't moved out of his lounge chair. She went back to Emmett's notebook. For 1989, the year after Usher taught at Boston University, Emmett noted one major event—the death of

Usher's daughter. Emmett's notes for the next few years, or rather the lack of them, confirmed what Granddad had said. No Usher books came out until four years after the girl died, when Usher's first horror book was published. From then on, one or two Usher books came out every year.

Val looked up as Granddad came into the study. Would he tell her what he'd spent the last half hour pondering? She swiveled in the desk chair to face him.

He sat on the sofa. "I want your opinion on something Rick told me. When he asked me my philosophy of old age, I talked about finding new interests. He told me I was making the most of the present, but he cared more about the past and the future. He needed to put a few things right. Then he could *die in peace.*"

Val could tell from Granddad's emphasis that Rick Usher's reference to dying bothered him. She struggled to interpret the comment in a matter-of-fact way. "Don't make too much of it. We'd all like to die in peace, but we don't expect it to happen right away."

"He said he made up his mind a long time ago where and how he wants to die." Granddad hugged himself as if chilled. "I'm afraid he's going to kill himself."

An understandable worry. Val had read about the high suicide rates among men in their eighties. She abandoned the desk chair and sat next to her grandfather on the sofa. "He didn't decide recently how to leave this world. He came up with a plan in the past and he's been living with it for a while.

There's no reason to think he's going to act on it now."

The worry lines in Granddad's forehead showed no signs of smoothing out. "He must be very depressed. That's why he's talking about dying."

She feared the author's depression might spread to her grandfather. "Talking about dying doesn't mean he's going to commit suicide. Maybe the doctor gave him bad news. Knowing he doesn't have long to live means he has to take care of unfinished business."

Granddad took off his bifocals and wiped them on his shirt. "You may be right, but if I don't do anything and Usher takes his own life, I'd blame myself for not speaking up. But if I go behind his back and tell Rosana what he said, he won't trust me anymore. I'd like to help him if I can. Getting him out of the house to meet more people might cure what ails him. I can coax him to do that, but not if he's mad at me."

Val finally grasped the dilemma. "You don't know whether you'd be making the situation better or worse by telling Rosana." He'd come to her for advice. She wouldn't tell him what to do, but maybe she could convince him that he didn't have to do anything immediately. She reached for his hand. "I think you can put off a decision until you know more about his state of mind. Whether or not he's contemplating suicide, he said he's not ready to die until he sets something right."

"I was hoping you'd say that." Granddad squeezed her hand and released it. "He asked me to help him do a few things."

Val hadn't cared for the way Granddad had helped Rick Usher previously. At least this time he was alerting her in advance. "He's living with three people whose sole purpose is to help him. He needs you too?"

"He doesn't want them to know what's bothering him. Besides, I might do a better job than they would. He'd like to locate something he misplaced and someone he lost touch with."

Val groaned inwardly, guessing how Granddad had responded. "You told him you learned how to track down people in your private investigator course and you've had great success in finding missing items." Like the strayed cats and misplaced keys he'd recovered for the residents of the retirement village.

"I sure did." Granddad leaned toward her as if telling her a secret. "He pointed to the highest shelves in the room and said I wasn't tall enough to find what he was looking for. When he was going up a ladder to search there last weekend, Rosana stopped him. She told him he was too old to climb it and took the ladder away. So now he needs a man tall enough to reach the top shelf by standing on a chair."

Or someone who brings a ladder with him, but Val didn't say that because Granddad might decide to do exactly that. She was no happier about him balancing on a ladder than Rosana was about Usher doing it. "He must have shelved something up there. It's got to be a book or a small item he tucked behind the books. You could phone a few handymen and ask them how tall they are."

"I can't just call anybody to do this job. He wants someone who wouldn't steal what's there or blab about it." Granddad leaned forward. "Do you think Gunnar would do it?"

Val stifled a smile. Gunnar was neither thief nor blabbermouth, a strong testimonial from Granddad, who'd been deeply suspicious of him six months ago. She now understood why he'd confided in her. He wanted Gunnar's help. "I'm sure Gunnar wouldn't mind, as long as he doesn't have to do it right away. He's getting ready for the biggest role he ever had on stage."

"This won't take long. Find out if he can spare some time tomorrow morning around nine thirty. That's when Rick's expecting me back. He said the other three in the house would be busy then. He'll let me in the side door to the study. I'll take Gunnar in with me."

She would text Gunnar to phone her when his rehearsal ended tonight. "If he's willing to do it, I'll tell him to meet you here at nine. He may ask me a lot of questions. I'll have to explain how you know Rick Usher."

"Okay, but he's not allowed to tell anyone else." Granddad yawned and glanced with longing at his comfortable chair in the sitting room.

Val was on a roll getting answers from him and didn't want him falling asleep yet. "Let's go to the kitchen and eat some brownies." An offer he couldn't refuse.

She waited until they were seated at the kitchen table with the tea and brownies in front of them before tossing more questions at him. "You came up with a way to help Usher find something he lost. Who's the person he lost and wants you to locate?"

"His son." Granddad bit into a brownie.

She was surprised Granddad had answered her question. Did he want her help with locating the son? "Wait a minute. I thought you said he had one child, a daughter who died."

"She was his only child with Rosana. The son was from another relationship." Granddad sipped his tea. "I told Rick I could get on his computer and look up his son on the Internet. I just needed a name and a birth date. He said his computer wasn't connected to the Internet. He uses it only for writing. He also wasn't sure of the son's last name or birthday."

Val nearly choked on her brownie. She swallowed some tea to wash it down. "Did he explain why he didn't know his son's name or birthday?"

"He had no chance. Rosana interrupted us."

"Maybe the boy was put up for adoption." If so, it wouldn't be easy to locate him. "How did Rosana react when she saw you with Usher?"

"Surprised, but she treated me like an honored guest. Rick said that he'd waylaid me and that we'd had a great time talking about the fifties and sixties. The next thing I know, we're all sitting around eating canned soup and crackers for lunch. No wonder they hired you to make meals." Granddad yawned again. "After lunch she handed me off to Clancy."

"What did you and Clancy do?"

"He gave me some stuff to read about Poe. Then he set me up with earphones so I could listen to a talk Rick gave. I'm supposed to try to sound like him. That's in case he backs out of his event this weekend. He's done it before, so I have to prepare to take his place."

"When are you going to tell Clancy *you're* backing out?"

"Not yet. I'm hoping to convince Rick to go. Then I'll get paid for my work this week. I can't ask for my pay if I refuse to go." Granddad ate the last of his brownie.

"I wonder why he's trying to find his son after so many years."

"Like I said, he's fixin' to die."

"But not by his own hand. He wouldn't locate his son and then commit suicide. Only a monster would inflict that kind of pain on a young man. Rick Usher doesn't sound like a monster. He wants to *set things right.* He feels guilty, possibly because he didn't reach out sooner to his son. Now he hopes to make up for that somehow."

Granddad finished his tea. "He might want to change his will and provide for his son. He asked me to find a lawyer who'd take care of business for him over the phone, so he doesn't have to go to a law office. He didn't tell me why he wanted a lawyer. I talked to your lawyer friend, Althea. She'd need a face-to-face meeting and a picture ID for anything related to a legal document."

"I'll bet every other lawyer would say the same thing."

"She makes house and hospital calls for clients who can't make it to her office. That won't work for

Rick since he doesn't want his wife to know what he's doing. Maybe I can spring him loose."

Bad idea. "Don't get in the middle of anything to do with his will, Granddad. That man is worth a lot of money. If he designates a new heir, someone's getting a smaller piece of the pie and won't be happy about it."

Granddad shrugged. "He can do what he wants with his money."

Val foresaw trouble. "Suppose his current heirs get wind of the plan? They can't try to stop him without making him angry. They wouldn't want to do that to the man who's leaving them money." She pointed her teaspoon at Granddad. "Instead, they'll prevent you from springing him loose, whatever it takes."

Granddad glowered at her. "Again, you're trying to protect me from a threat that's all in your head. You're always jumping to conclusions, and you've been wrong before." He stood up. "I'm going to turn in. It's been a long day."

She couldn't reason with him when he was tired and grouchy. Even if he were rested, she would face an uphill battle. Now that he had a personal relationship with Rick Usher, she'd have a hard time convincing him to stay away from the author and his house.

Chapter 17

Val returned to the study and drafted the survey about the café's evening menu. It was nine thirty by the time she e-mailed it to the printer. He'd promised a quick turnaround for a job request that came by early morning. When he arrived at work tomorrow, he would have both the survey and the flyer she'd sent earlier.

She texted Gunnar to call her when his rehearsal ended. Then she skimmed Emmett's notes about Rick Usher's speaking engagements. The author had given lectures on Poe, conducted workshops on creative writing, and delivered keynote addresses at conferences over several decades, but none after he moved to the Eastern Shore. In case Emmett hadn't gotten around to recording the author's more recent appearances, she checked online references to Rick Usher for the last seven years. She found announcements of forthcoming books, fanfare about their publication, and reviews, but nothing about speaking engagements.

Speculations about Usher's health popped up

occasionally over those years. They became more frequent and went viral last summer. In quick succession, various fan sites reported not only that Usher was gravely ill but also that someone else was writing the books under his name. Though denied by an unnamed spokesperson for the Usher family, those speculations continued. They petered out in November when announcements appeared about Usher's upcoming book signings.

Quelling those rumors might have been the reason the Ushers scheduled events and hired a stand-in for the author. Why had the rumors gained more traction six months ago than they previously had? A concerted campaign could have revived old speculations about Usher. Val combed through the online reports of his poor health but couldn't trace them to any one source.

Her phone rang. Gunnar greeted her when she answered.

"Hi, Gunnar. How did your rehearsal go?"

"Not as well as I'd like."

Val heard the dejection in his voice. Here was his first chance to show what he could do with a big part, and the threat of arrest dragged him down. "You'll do better tomorrow." Unless Holtzman harassed him again.

"Did you ask me to call so you could cheer me up?"

"Of course, and for other reasons. A few months ago, you mentioned a computer forensics expert you got to know when you were tracing laundered money. I'd like to find the source of information that was repeated on various Web sites. Maybe your friend can help." She explained her suspicion that the widespread rumors about Usher's health might have come from a single source.

"E-mail me the search terms you used to locate the sites where the rumors appeared. My friend can take it from there."

"Thank you. Granddad has a request too."

"I can't pass up a chance to improve my standing with your grandfather."

"He doesn't love you as much as I do yet, but you're his first choice as a sidekick for this secret mission."

She explained what he needed to do and, as she expected, he peppered her with questions. She ended up telling him about Granddad's impersonation and his new friendship with Rick Usher.

"So that's why you thought Emmett had impersonated Usher—because your grandfather did it too. I hope you warned him to avoid looking like Rick Usher from now on."

"Yes, and I may have even convinced him. Can you meet him here at nine tomorrow morning? This shouldn't take more than an hour, including the trip to and from the Usher house."

"Okay. I'll call you tomorrow and let you know what we find."

"Thanks, Gunnar."

Val went upstairs, got ready for bed, and opened *Poe Revisited* to "The Cask of Amontillado." Poe's story, delving into the mind of a murderer executing an elaborate revenge, riveted her. She was too tired to tackle the companion story by Rick Usher, "The Case of Amontillado."

* * *

When she arrived in the café Wednesday morning, Val tuned the TV mounted on the wall to the local news, anxious to hear the latest about Emmett Flint's murder. If there was any news, she missed it while making and serving breakfast to customers.

Monique phoned to say she'd finished aging the photos of the three men and would drop them off at the café later in the morning. Val asked her to stop at the printer's shop to pick up the flyers and surveys.

Gunnar called at ten fifteen. "Hey, Val. I'm back from the Usher place. I thought you'd want to know I didn't find what Usher was looking for."

"What was it?"

"An old book of poetry. *Tamerlane and Other Poems* by a writer identified as *A Bostonian.*"

The title and nameless author tickled a memory from Val's trivia nights at a pub. "That was the first book Poe ever published."

"Usher wanted me to keep searching. He was upset that I didn't find it. I ended up taking photos of the books on each shelf so he could see for himself that it wasn't there."

"It must be a rare book or one that has sentimental value." Val saw that a couple who'd come in five minutes earlier looked ready to order. "I have to get back to work, Gunnar. One quick question. Did Granddad stay behind at the Usher house?"

"No. Usher told us when we arrived that we'd have to finish by ten. He had a meeting scheduled with the guy who works with him on his books. Good luck with your dinner tonight."

"Thanks." Val tucked her phone away and helped her customers.

She'd just delivered their order when Monique arrived. She gave Val the digitally aged photos.

Val was surprised by Emmett's picture. He resembled Rick Usher and looked like a healthier version of the man Val had tried to revive with CPR. She studied the photos of her former fiancé and of Gunnar side by side. In the originals she'd sent Monique, Tony was far more handsome. Forty years from now, though, no one would say one man looked any more attractive than the other. "Wrinkles level the playing field."

Monique nodded. "Up to a point. You'd never mistake Gunnar for either of the others."

Val looked again at the photos. With gray hair, a beard, and dark glasses, Tony could have passed for Usher as easily as Emmett had. Gunnar, though, had a squarer face and a larger mouth. "You're right."

"I want to know what you're going to do with those pictures, but first tell me about these." Monique pointed to the print jobs she'd picked up for Val. "You're delivering lunches now and surveying the club members about their dinner preferences? What's going on?"

Val explained her plan to increase the café revenue and hire Irene Pritchard to help. "If I don't, or possibly even if I do, the manager will put a sportswear boutique here in place of the café."

"That guy's clueless. No one's going to buy clothes

here. It's not like anybody at this club is a fashion plate."

"Except a few tennis players. Remember Chatty." Their former tennis teammate had comforted herself after losing a match by buying a new outfit for the courts, though her closet already contained one in every hue and style.

"Even *she* didn't buy clothes every day. I'm going to start a petition to save the café from clothes horses." Monique flounced out, bent on a mission.

She'd be even more incensed if Val told her about the manager's flirtation with the clothes horse who wanted to run the boutique. By the time Monique poked her head into the café again, the tables were full and Val was too busy to talk to her cousin.

Irene came into the café after the crowd thinned and gave Val two handwritten pages. "Here are my proposals for afternoon tea and evening menus."

"Thank you." Val hadn't planned to offer a teatime menu or to cede control of the evening menu to Irene. "I want to get the survey results before finalizing the evening menu."

Irene's face turned stony. "I thought you wanted to move fast. Waiting for survey results will just delay you, but that's your choice." She glanced at a menu. "Where does your bread come from?"

"The baker in Treadwell. It's delivered fresh each morning. I usually have three types—sourdough, rye or pumpernickel, and whole grain. If the baker has a special bread on sale, I'll order that too."

"I make sandwiches with white bread. Then you

can taste what's on the sandwich, not the bread itself."

Val had more misgivings than ever about hiring Irene. "The bread and the filling work together. They don't cancel each other out."

She'd kept one eye on the TV all morning. Now, as Irene explained why spongy bread was better than grainy bread, a picture of Emmett Flint flashed on the screen. "Excuse me, Irene." Val turned up the sound on the TV.

The sheriff's department and the Bayport police had issued a statement that they were making progress in the investigation of the actor's death. Val marveled at the ability of TV anchors to make much of no news.

Irene pointed to the screen. "I've seen that man at my tea shop."

Now that was a piece of news worth having. Val didn't even try to hide her surprise. She lowered the volume on the TV. "I always picture women in tea shops. Now I hear that Clancy and that man"—Val pointed at the TV though Emmett's picture wasn't on it anymore—"both went to your tea shop. Did they know each other?"

Irene looked up as if she had a memory stored on the ceiling. "I only saw them together once, about a month before the shop closed. The other tables were all taken. Clancy had his usual spot to himself, typing into his computer. The other man went over to him, sat at the table, and started talking. I could see Clancy didn't like being interrupted. He packed up and left when he finished his tea."

A chance encounter wasn't what Val had hoped for. Collusion between the two men would have added a new wrinkle to the intrigue surrounding Rick Usher.

As another wave of customers arrived, Val cut off further discussion with Irene. "Thank you for the menu ideas and the pricing." She gave Irene the flyers. "These are for Jeremy to distribute to businesses in Treadwell and Bayport. Remind him to keep track of the hours he spends so I can pay him for his time."

While Val served her last customers of the day, she planned the rest of her afternoon. Before leaving for the Usher house to make dinner, she would talk to Simone and, if time allowed, visit Chief Yardley. She took snacks to give each of them.

Simone lived in a town house development on the outer edges of Treadwell. The straggly trees in the green strip along the curb suggested the houses had gone up in the last ten years on converted farmland. Val drove slowly along the street lined by two-story houses clad with vinyl siding, searching for Simone's address. From inside the car on this dreary day, she could barely make out the brass house numbers.

She parked her Saturn in front of a house with a FOR SALE sign on it, tucked the snack container into her shoulder tote, and walked half a block before finding Simone's house. The Suzuki motorcycle parked in front of the house surprised Val. She had trouble imagining the fiftyish Professor Simone, elegant in high-heeled boots and a narrow skirt, commuting to work on a motorcycle in the dead of winter. The Suzuki must belong to a neighbor. Val rang the bell. No one opened the door. Not surprising, since she was fifteen minutes early.

Back on the sidewalk, she surveyed the small house. No room upstairs for more than two bedrooms or possibly three tiny ones. A curtain covering the upstairs window parted slightly. Val couldn't see who had moved the curtain aside. Maybe Simone hadn't heard the bell. Val went back and banged the knocker hard against the front door. Again, no response. Had Simone changed her mind about the meeting? Or did another person live in the house too, someone unable or unwilling to open the door?

A neighbor might know. The SUV parked outside the house two doors away suggested Val might find someone home there. According to the mailbox, the Smiths lived in the house.

She knocked on the door. A twenty-something woman with a toddler on her hip answered the knock. She had dark circles under curious eyes.

Val hoped the woman would welcome adult conversation. "Hi! I saw the FOR SALE sign on the house down the street. The house is a perfect size for me, but I'm not familiar with the neighborhood. Can you tell me anything about it?"

The young mother smiled. "I'd be happy to. We've been here about six years. We like it a lot, but we're going to put our house on the market in the spring because our family's growing." She jiggled the baby. "Please, come in. I don't want this little guy to get chilled."

"Thank you." Val closed the door behind her.

"What did you want to know about the neighborhood?"

Val came up with a question a would-be buyer her age might ask. "Do any singles and young adults live on this street, or are there mostly families?"

"It's a mix of couples, families, and singles, in different age groups. The neighbors are all friendly without being nosy."

Val smiled. "I was more concerned about noisy than nosy after seeing the motorcycle parked two doors down."

"That belongs to Raven. He lives there with his mother. We hear the motorcycle only when he starts it up to go to work. It's not like he's in and out all the time, so I wouldn't call it noisy here."

Val hoped the woman could tell her more about Simone's son. "Does he work a night shift? Is that why the motorcycle's there now?"

"He works at the supermarket pharmacy. I think they're open from nine to nine. He might have the late shift today." Mrs. Smith put the toddler down. "Raven keeps to himself. He's nearly thirty. If he ever had wild parties, he's past that stage. No one his age even comes to visit."

Hardly surprising if Raven never opened the door to any visitors. "Good to hear. That answers all my questions for now. Thank you for your help."

"If you're not in a hurry to buy a house, this one will be up for sale soon." She grabbed the toddler by the hand as he took tentative steps toward the living room. "Wave bye-bye to the nice lady."

The little boy smiled and waved. Val did the same.

As the door closed behind her, a postal truck crept away from the mailbox in front of Simone's house. A lean man with longish dark hair and a mustache dashed out of the house. He collected the mail and shuffled through it. Val saw his face clearly for a second, and her heart skipped a beat. He looked like the guy in the front row at Rick Usher's last public appearance. Was he the young Poe look-alike who'd followed Usher out of the room?

She huddled near a holly in the Smiths' front yard, hoping he didn't notice her staring at him. Just because he had the same build, haircut, and mustache as the man at Usher's talk didn't mean he was the same person. If she'd glimpsed him anywhere else, she would have walked right by him without noting the resemblance. But she couldn't avoid the obvious conclusion once she'd seen him emerge from Simone's house—he was her son, Raven, named for Poe's most famous poem. Her interest in Poe and Rick Usher might have rubbed off on him, explaining his presence at the Usher talk. Or did an even closer connection exist between the young man and Rick Usher? Could Raven be the son he was looking for?

Raven took the mail into the house and emerged seconds later, wearing a helmet. He climbed on the motorcycle, revved up the engine, and drove off with a roar.

She checked her watch. Ten minutes to go until her appointment with his mother. Val went back to her car to stay warm while waiting. Based on what Mrs. Smith had said about Raven's age, he could have born around the time or shortly after Simone had studied and Usher taught at Boston University. Val kept herself from leaping to the conclusion that Raven was Usher's son. Instead, she'd call it a working hypothesis. Nothing she knew so far contradicted it. One person could confirm it—the woman she was about to meet. But Val wouldn't ask her anything so personal.

A red Toyota passed by Val's parked car and pulled into the space where the motorcycle had been. A dark-haired woman climbed out. Simone. She wore boots, as she had to the book club, but with lower heels, and skinny pants instead of the narrow skirt she'd worn Sunday night. She slung a bulging tote bag, large enough for a laptop computer, over her shoulder and went inside the house.

Val waited five minutes and then retraced her steps to Simone's front door.

Chapter 18

Simone opened the door and peered at Val over reading glasses. "I vaguely remember seeing you at the book club. Come in."

The aroma of freshly brewed coffee pervaded the house. Val inhaled deeply. "The coffee smells wonderful."

"I combine coffee beans from different regions to make it." Simone pointed to a clothes tree in the foyer. "Hang your jacket there."

She led Val to a dining el off the living room and slid aside a pile of books on the table. "Sit here. I'll be right back."

Val obeyed, feeling like a student on the first day of class.

She glanced at the living room with its spare and square Swedish furniture—black and white and red all over. Crimson throw pillows on the black sofa matched the drapes that hung from the ceiling to the white-carpeted floor. Along the wall opposite the sofa, a tall white bookcase held an assortment of red vases, bowls, and pitchers, and a couple of photos of a dark-haired young man, probably Raven. The bookcase was sandwiched between two red shelving units full of books. Simone matched the décor in her white sweater, black pants, and red scarf.

She came back from the kitchen with a tray holding two mugs of coffee, a sugar bowl, and a creamer, all red. She set them on the table and sat down across from Val.

"Thank you." Val took the snack container from her shoulder bag, unsnapped the lid, and put it in the center of the table. "Spiced pecans, oatmeal cookies, and dark chocolate turtles to go with the coffee."

Simone glanced at the sweets and looked away. "You came to show me something about Rick Usher. How do you know him?"

"I never met him." Spotting him while looking for a cadaver in his yard didn't count. "I know him only by association. Don Myer is my grandfather. He's—"

"The imposter at the book club! So you were in on that hoax." Simone pointed an accusing finger at Val.

"No. I was shocked to see my grandfather. He was equally surprised to see me there." Val sipped her coffee, a rich dark roast that tasted as strong as it smelled. "I have something to show you related to the other man you saw pretending to be Rick Usher. Do you happen to know his real name?"

Simone shook her head. "He was at a book signing in Salisbury the weekend before last. I was going to follow him when he left the Barnes & Noble, but he lost me."

If she didn't know the impersonator's name, she had no reason to connect him to a murdered actor who was twenty years younger. Good. Val would just as soon not bring up Emmett's murder if she could avoid it.

She reached into her bag for the photos her cousin had touched up. "Could any of these be the man you saw at the bookstore?" She handed the pictures to Simone.

Simone looked at each picture for about three seconds, her face as unchanged as a mask. "The three of them are trying to look like Rick Usher. Did they all pretend to be him?"

Val shook her head. "Two of them didn't. One of them might have."

"So this is why you came? To give me a multiple-choice test. A. B. C." She put one photo on the table as she spoke each letter, lining them up in a column. "Or D—none of the above. Why do you care who impersonated Rick Usher?"

Professor Simone wouldn't respond to the multiple-choice question until Val passed an oral exam. She'd flunk if her answer wasn't convincing. She'd better stick close to the truth. "One of those men filed a false report to the police about somebody I love. I want to convince them not to trust what he told them."

Simone held up her hand like a traffic cop. "What makes you think that same man posed as Rick?"

Val chose her words carefully. "The last time I saw

that man, he resembled Rick Usher in his publicity photo." Val cradled her coffee mug. "If he posed as Usher, it's proof of dishonesty that I can take to the police."

"Your grandfather was similarly dishonest."

"Once. He won't do it again." Val sipped her coffee. Maybe she needed to sweeten the pot with more than the snacks she'd brought to coax Simone into picking out the impersonator. *Give information to get information.* "My grandfather took you seriously when you said Rick Usher might be dead. He dropped in at the Usher house early in the morning and managed to speak with Rick in private for two hours. They exchanged stories about Korea in the 1950s. Hard to believe that another eighty-year-old with the same looks and background as Rick Usher has taken up permanent residence in that house."

Simone raised one eyebrow until it went halfway to her hairline. "If he's fine, why isn't he at book signings? I'll believe he's alive and well when *I* see him in person." She selected a chocolate turtle from the snack collection.

Val remembered what Simone had said about not being welcome at the Usher house. Had she tried to see the author or just assumed Rosana would turn her away at the door? "You may be able to see him in person. Usher invited my grandfather to come back again when Rosana isn't around. You could go with him."

Simone took another candy turtle. "Rosana's not the only obstacle. Rick may not want to see me either. He's never tried, though that's my fault more than his." She bit off the head of the chocolate turtle.

"How do you know him?"

"He was a visiting professor at Boston University when I was in grad school there. Our fields overlapped. He'd specialized in nineteenth century American history. I was focusing on American lit from that period. We shared a scholarly interest in Poe." Simone stood up and walked to the sliding door leading to the deck. "The storm clouds are rolling in already. Freezing rain will drive away the last of the diehards hoping to see the Poe toaster tonight."

Val interpreted Simone's abrupt change of subject as reluctance to talk about Rick Usher. "The Poe toaster?"

"The annual visitor to Poe's grave. Beginning a hundred years after Poe's death, or possibly somewhat earlier, a mysterious figure went to Poe's grave between midnight and daybreak on January nineteenth, Poe's birthday. He drank a toast to Poe and left a partial bottle of cognac and three roses at the grave. Crowds used to gather outside the cemetery in the dead of night, in the January cold, to catch a glimpse of him. His last visit was in 2009, the two hundredth anniversary of Poe's birth. A few people come back every year, still hoping to catch sight of the visitor whose identity no one has ever discovered."

Thank you for the lecture, Professor. Now it was Val's turn to change the subject. She pointed to the photos on the white bookcase. "I arrived here a little early, just in time to see that young man leave the house. He rode off on a motorcycle."

"My son, Raven." Simone returned to the table.

"I was startled by how much he looked like Edgar Allan Poe."

"Fascination with Poe runs in the family." Simone flashed a wry half smile and then lifted her mug to her lips. She drank some coffee and set the mug down again. "Raven would like to follow in Poe's footsteps as a writer. But looking like a writer doesn't make you a writer. Which brings me back to your photos—three men who look like a famous writer but aren't him. Will the real imposter please stand up?" She lifted Emmett's photo from the table and faced it toward Val.

At last! "Thank you." Val collected the photos and put them in her bag.

"I take it that's the answer you wanted."

Val nodded. Now that she had one answer, she was greedy for more. "Something good came from my grandfather's attempt to find out if Rick Usher was dead or alive. The two of them hit it off. They had a lot in common, including similar experiences in the army. After they'd talked a while, Rick said he needed to do a few things and then he could die in peace."

Simone's hand flew to her mouth. "Die in peace? That sounds as if he doesn't expect to live long. He must be very sick." She blinked rapidly. "Did he say what he needs to do?"

"Find his son." No three words Val had ever said produced such a dramatic effect.

Simone squeezed her eyes shut and pressed her

lips together as if trying to bottle up an erupting volcano. She trembled with the effort.

Then she gave up. She covered her eyes with her hand. Tears dripped down her face. "What do I do now?"

Val was asking herself the same question. Should she give Simone privacy or comfort? How do you comfort a distraught woman you barely know? Val decided to encourage her to talk and give her a sympathetic ear.

She took a tissue from her bag and offered it to Simone. "Raven is Rick Usher's son?"

Simone took the tissue and nodded. "I gave Rick an ultimatum when I became pregnant. Rosana or me. If he chose her, he would never see me again and never meet his child."

"He decided not to leave her?"

Simone blew her nose. "He couldn't even bring himself to tell her about us. I used the only leverage I had to ensure my child's future. In return for my not telling Rosana about the baby, I demanded Rick set up a trust fund to be administered by my lawyer. I instructed the lawyer not to tell Rick how to contact us."

No wonder she'd said it was her fault he'd never tried to see her. "He agreed to it?"

"Yes. I gave him a chance to change his mind. The money was supposed to go into the trust a month after the child was born. I sent him an *It's-a-boy* announcement and a baby picture. I left the baby's name and date of birth blank in case Rosana saw it. A few days after I mailed it, I found out Rick and Rosana's daughter had just died."

Val gasped. She sympathized with all of them—the man, his wife, his lover, the dead daughter, and the newborn son. Her eyes stung with tears. "He couldn't leave Rosana at a time like that."

"I'd have thought less of him if he had." Simone blotted her eyes. "Rick had always struggled with guilt over his success as a writer. He didn't feel he deserved the acclaim. After his daughter died, he had something else to feel guilty about. I imagine he viewed her death as cosmic punishment for our brief moments of joy . . . and our separation as a way to atone for it."

Val sipped her coffee. "It couldn't have been easy for you as a single mom."

"Easier than a lot of women have it. My parents helped me take care of the baby so I could finish my doctorate. Raven had a grandfather who took the place of a father. A couple of years later, I married Wingard, and he adopted Raven. The marriage lasted until Raven was in high school."

How odd that Simone called her ex by his surname. "You kept your husband's last name after the divorce."

"By then I'd gotten a Ph.D. and published under that name. I saw no reason to go through the rigmarole of changing it."

"Does Raven know who his biological father is?"

"My ex's parting shot when our marriage broke up was to tell him that his real father, the famous Rick Usher, had abandoned him. Wingard wanted to make the point that he wasn't such a bad guy, compared to Raven's other father." Simone drank up the rest of her coffee. "Within the space of a year, the kid lost his grandfather to cancer and his stepfather to a bitter divorce. Then he found out his biological father had written him off. I couldn't tell him the truth, that it was my fault his father had nothing to do with him."

"You were the only person Raven had." Val used to believe that the truth trumped everything. Now she wasn't so sure. "Sometimes the truth does more harm than good."

"But if you hide it, it comes back to haunt you. What do I do now? Should I help Rick fulfill what sounds like his dying wish to see his son? How would that affect Raven? What would it mean to my relationship with my son?" Simone jerked as if she'd just come out of a trance. "You're leaving me with a lot to think about."

Val took the hint that it was time for her to go. She fished a café business card from her wallet and jotted her cell phone number on the back. "I appreciate your taking the time to see me. Call me if you want to talk again."

A blast of frigid air hit her as she walked back to her car. Thick gray clouds totally obscured the sun. In the short time she'd been at Simone's house, the temperature must have dropped almost ten degrees.

Back in the car, Val read a text message from Gunnar. His computer-savvy friend had combed social media for references to Rick Usher in the last year. Comments about Usher's ill health and inability to write, in blogs apparently by different people, tracked back to accounts Emmett Flint created. He'd also posted on Facebook and tweeted from a fake account. Other people with legitimate accounts linked to, shared, and retweeted what he'd written.

Val tucked her phone away. Had Emmett waged the campaign against Rick Usher out of spite or in hopes of profiting from it? Whatever the motive, the campaign and Emmett's impersonation of the author ought to convince Chief Yardley of the connection between him and the Ushers. More than that, her information would present the chief with alternatives to Gunnar as a murder suspect.

Chapter 19

Half an hour after leaving Simone's house, Val sat in the metal visitor chair in Chief Yardley's office.

The chief reached across his desk to take one of the oatmeal raisin cookies she'd brought him. "You only bring me sweets when you want to poke your nose into an investigation."

"I made a New Year's resolution to bring you them more often so you won't be on your guard when I visit." She grinned at him. "The TV newscast showed Emmett Flint's photo this morning with a request that anyone who saw him Saturday afternoon contact the police. Since that request has been out there for days, I assume few witnesses came forward. I can explain why."

The chief munched his cookie and didn't dispute her assumption about the tepid response to the police request for information.

She took three photos from her tote bag and put Emmett's publicity shot on the chief's desk. "The media is using this picture. That's not how he looked when he died."

"We generally don't give the media photos of dead people."

"Understood. But Emmett walked around looking like an older man for three hours before he dropped dead. After the Treadwell Players' rehearsal Saturday morning, he made himself look two decades older with theatrical makeup. A member of the theater group saw him drive away, looking something like this." Val handed the chief a photo of the digitally aged actor.

He glanced at it. "Where did this come from?"

"My cousin took Emmett's publicity shot and used software to make him look older. She also added glasses and a hat like the ones he wore when I saw him walking in the mall parking lot." Val presented the chief with photo exhibit three, Rick Usher's publicity photo. "Here's a picture of another man dressed similarly."

The chief put the two pictures side by side. "I see the resemblance. Who is this man?"

"The author Rick Usher." With the caffeine coursing through her system from Simone's high-test coffee, Val could no longer sit still.

She stood up like a lawyer making a closing argument in court. The chief munched an oatmeal cookie as she wove together the connections between Emmett Flint and the people who lived at the Usher house. Rick Usher had a meeting with Emmett Flint last summer. Shortly after that meeting, the news circulated online that Usher was dying and someone else had taken over writing his books. A computer expert tracked the rumors back to Emmett. The gossip about Usher died down as the news broke that he would appear in public after an absence of seven years.

As the chief took another cookie, Val got to the key point. "Ten days ago Emmett impersonated Usher at a bookstore in Salisbury." She anticipated the chief's skepticism and tried to forestall it. "A woman who knew Usher well twenty-some years ago recognized the man who pretended to be him as an imposter. She identified the imposter as Emmett from that touched-up photo I showed her, the one I gave you."

"Why would Emmett impersonate Rick Usher?"

"The Usher family probably paid him to do it."

"Probably? You're only guessing." The chief brushed away cookie crumbs along with her argument.

His skepticism convinced Val that she'd have to break down and tell him about Granddad. "I'm not just guessing. After Emmett died, the Ushers paid someone else to act as a stand-in for the author."

The chief said nothing for a moment. "I'm waiting for you to tell me who this someone else is."

Val took a break from pacing the room and perched on the edge of the metal chair. "Granddad."

Chief Yardley's mouth dropped. "Nobody can keep that man down. How did that come about?"

"Rick Usher's wife, Rosana, recruited him. Usher's coauthor, Clancy Curren, trained him and accompanied him when he appeared as Usher last weekend. Granddad promised me he wouldn't do it again." Val noticed the chief's stern look soften. "From what I've heard about Emmett, he'd have tried to squeeze more money from the Ushers.

Maybe he threatened to tell the world that they hired him to impersonate the author."

"That's not a reason to murder him. The Ushers can say he tricked them. Their word would carry more weight than his."

She couldn't argue against the chief's reasoning. The Ushers wouldn't have put it in writing that he was supposed to impersonate Rick. Val had yet to see Granddad's contract with them, but it probably said he could represent Usher, which could mean anything. Clancy knew about the impersonations, but he also knew who buttered his bread. He'd side with the Ushers in any dispute about the meaning of the agreement.

"Okay, Chief. I concede that Rosana and Rick Usher don't have a strong motive for murder." Val wouldn't go so far as to say they had no reason to kill Emmett. She just needed to find a more compelling motive for them.

"Tell me what you know about Clancy." The chief put a half-eaten cookie on his desk and picked up his pen. He took notes while she talked. Then he looked up. "How is he paid for his work? Does he get a percent of the sales or is he on salary?"

"No idea." Val made a mental note to ask Clancy that question. "Clancy needs money to take care of his brother's medical bills. If sales of Usher's books declined because of rumors about his health and Clancy's compensation is tied to those sales, he'd want to make sure the rumors didn't resurface. Maybe he found out Emmett was behind them."

The chief flicked his wrist. "*Ifs* and *maybes*."

Val moved toward more solid ground. "The person

at the Usher house with the most obvious reason to get rid of Emmett is Madison Fox-Norton, known as Maddie Norton in the theater group. Gunnar overheard Emmett blackmailing her. She had the opportunity to add meds to Emmett's burrito during the rehearsal. Did she and the other people at the Usher house have access to blood pressure meds?"

"We have no probable cause to search the Usher house for meds, if that's what you're hoping. To get a court order for a search, we need compelling evidence tying someone to a crime."

Val was disappointed, but not surprised. "Granddad and I will be at the house this evening. Maybe we can find out something that will give you a reason to conduct a search."

The chief threw up his hands in an I-give-up gesture. "You just tried to convince me that someone in that house is a murderer. If you're right, it could be dangerous for both of you. Stay away from there."

She wasn't going there only to snoop. "I have a contract to cook dinner for the Ushers. They're expecting me there tonight."

"The forecast is calling for freezing rain tonight. Tell them you can't make it."

"The bad weather's arriving late. We'll be home before it starts." She hurried to change the subject. "Given that Emmett looked and dressed like Rick Usher on Saturday afternoon and impersonated Usher the week before, he may have been murdered by someone who mistook him for Rick Usher."

Chief Yardley squinted at her. "Who'd want to murder Rick Usher?"

Val described how Rick Usher behaved at his final public appearance, fleeing the room after declaring that he wasn't ready to die. "After that night, he went into seclusion and moved away from Baltimore, possibly because he feared being killed."

"And seven years later, someone kills a man who resembles him? That's your most far-fetched theory yet."

The chief would call her theory that Raven Wingard killed his father even more far-fetched. Without any evidence to support it, she didn't dare bring it up.

The motion-sensing outdoor lights turned on as Val drove along the circular driveway to the Usher house. Maybe because of the chief's warning, the house that had looked gloomy on her last visit now struck her as menacing. She parked behind Granddad's Buick. As she climbed out of the car, he rushed out the front door of the house, shoving his arms into his parka.

His unusual speed alarmed her. "What's wrong?"

"I gotta tell you something."

"Out here?" She opened the trunk and took out the recyclable grocery bags with tonight's food. "You could have waited until I was inside."

"Can't talk inside. The walls have ears."

The Ushers' front door opened again, and Clancy stuck his head out. "You need some help?"

"No!" Granddad shouted. "We've got it covered." He watched Clancy shut the door. "I found a bug in Rick's study. Other rooms could have bugs too.

Don't stand there gaping at me. Act like you're reorganizing the stuff in the trunk in case somebody's watching us."

Val tried to think of reasons for planting a listening device in the study. "Maybe Rosana wants to make sure he's okay."

"It's not like a baby monitor. It's a voice-activated recorder. Whoever put it there can download the recorded conversations wirelessly. I was going to remove the thing, but I didn't want to tip them off that I found it."

"Where is it?"

"On a shelf where Usher's writing awards are displayed. It was sitting near the trophies. Weird trophies—two shaped like haunted houses, and three like Edgar Allan Poe heads."

"Good hiding spot. Nobody moves trophies once they're in place." Val shifted the grocery bags in her trunk again. "Are you sure it's a bug?"

"Positive. We studied listening devices in my investigation course. You told me I was wasting my money on that online course, but I learned a lot. I'm gonna put one lesson to use right now. If we stay out here talking in the freezing cold, that would look suspicious. So we gotta do something to make it look natural." Granddad took a grocery bag from the trunk, peeked in it, and then spilled the contents, accidentally on purpose. "I've got more to tell you. Take your time picking up that stuff."

"Gee, thanks." Val crouched to pick up the vegetables and salad ingredients strewn on the ground. Fortunately, they were all in plastic bags. "What else did you discover besides a bug?"

"Rick has a prescription for beta blockers, the same blood pressure pills I take. He doesn't like how they make him feel. He checks his pressure and only takes them when it goes up. Rosana delivers the pills to his study every morning. He treats them like a squirrel with acorns. Puts them in a desk drawer, behind the drapes, or on shelves higher than Rosana can see."

"Madison is taller and so is Clancy. They could see the pills on the high shelves."

"Rosana controls the supply. All of them had access to that medicine."

Val finished refilling the grocery bag. "Were you in Rick Usher's study, talking about the meds?" When Granddad nodded, she continued, "How did the subject come up?"

"I told him I took medicine to lower my blood pressure and asked him if he did."

A frightening thought hit her. "Every conversation you had with him was recorded. Suppose the person who put the bug in Usher's study is also Emmett's murderer? Your question about blood pressure meds sounds like you're fishing for information about the murder weapon."

"It sounds like an ordinary question to me."

She looked up at him. "Not to a paranoid killer. Usher asked you yesterday to find him a lawyer. Whoever hears that on the recorder would probably assume what we did—that he wants to change his will. Somebody in the house might not like that and try to keep you from finding a lawyer."

"I already found a lawyer. They're too late to stop me."

"They don't know that." She stood up, her stomach in knots. "Why don't you plead a headache and go home? I'll feel better if no one in this place can get to you."

"Are you going home now?"

"I agreed to make dinner. I have to do it."

He took the last grocery bag from the trunk. "If you're staying, I'm staying. You're not any safer here than I am. The person who bugged the study would assume I told you what Usher said. So we're a whole lot better off staying together."

She knew better than to waste her breath trying to change his mind. "Don't eat or drink anything in the Usher house unless I give it to you."

Chapter 20

The door of the Usher house swung open as if by an invisible hand as Val and Granddad approached it. The walls had not only ears, as he'd said, but apparently eyes too.

A raspy voice came from behind the door. "Welcome to the house of Usher. Make yourself at home . . . if you dare."

Val smiled at Clancy's mock eerie tones. The watchful eyes belonged to him, but the listening ears might not. Though she couldn't rule him out as the bug planter, Rosana made a more likely spy. Vendors of hidden cameras and recorders probably sold most of their wares to spouses who suspected infidelity, and Rick Usher had cheated on her in the past.

Clancy emerged from behind the door, his nose in the air and his mouth pursed. "I am the butler. May I take your coats?" He maintained a stiff posture as he helped them off with their jackets and hung them up.

Val glanced at the bouquet of lilies perfuming

the hall air. Did Rosana fear a May-December romance had blossomed under her nose? Her husband and Madison might not have a physical relationship, but emotional infidelity could damage a marriage too. Even a platonic relationship might lead an older man to remember a younger woman in his will. If that's what Rosana feared, hearing that Usher wanted to talk to a lawyer without her being there would chill her.

Clancy dropped his butler-in-a-haunted-house act once they were in the kitchen, emptying the grocery bags. "What's for dinner, Val?"

"Orange-glazed Cornish hen, roasted root vegetables, and a salad of baby spinach with dried cranberries and feta cheese." And maybe a random leaf from one of the hanging plants. Val glanced at the green canopy over the kitchen island. Was it her imagination or had the plants grown and multiplied over the last two days? Val liked kitchens with hanging pots, the sort that could be used for cooking, not the kind from which poisonous plants like ivy and philodendron cascaded.

"Cornish hen." Granddad flicked his wrist as if shooing birds away. "A lot of work. Not much payoff."

Clancy flashed him a toothy grin. "The menu's a welcome change from what we've been eating here lately. Before leaving, the personal chef made batches of one-dish meals for us and froze them, but we're down to only four choices. And we have the same dessert every night—ice cream." He covered his mouth with his hand. "Oops. I should have asked what you were serving for dessert, Val, before I heaped scorn on ice cream."

"I'm making warm chocolate tart." She was happy to see two pairs of eyes light up in anticipation.

Granddad moseyed around the kitchen. He inspected the plants on the shelves and the windowsill. "How long since the chef went away?"

"Ten days." Clancy unloaded sweet potatoes, parsnips, and beets from a grocery bag. "We've set up a routine for dinner. Madison dishes up and serves, and I clear the table and clean up the kitchen. She doesn't like touching dirty dishes."

Val took the salad fixings to the counter near the sink. "When I cater a dinner, I normally cook, serve, and clean up. But tonight, I'd appreciate it if you could handle the cleanup. Because of the weather forecast, I'd like to leave for home as soon as I serve the dessert."

"Glad to help out," Clancy said cheerily, "when you're cooking."

Granddad snatched the beets and parsnips from the counter where Clancy had put them and took them to the refrigerator. Val was about to tell him to leave them out when she saw what he was doing. As he stuffed the vegetables into the crisper, he ran his hand along the top of the fridge, no doubt checking for bugs.

"Who's been cooking your food for the last ten days?" Val hoped her question would draw Clancy's attention away from Granddad.

"If you can call it cooking," Clancy said in a low voice, "Rosana nukes a frozen casserole and dumps the salad from a cellophane bag into a bowl."

Granddad closed the fridge door, went to the far end of the counter, and peered behind the coffee-maker and the toaster on the counter, continuing his search for a bug.

Val pulled the freezer drawer open to see what kind of casseroles the chef had made. Stacked there were microwavable containers with labels: creamed chicken with chipped beef, quiche, chicken pot pie, and mac and cheese. "I promise not to make any pasta or main-dish pies. You've all had your fill of those."

Clancy nodded. "Amen to that."

Rosana glided into the room on rubber-soled flats, carrying a copper watering can with a long thin spout. "How nice to see you again, Val. So glad you made it here tonight. I was afraid the weather report would keep you from coming."

This effusive welcome struck Val as more appropriate for a garden party guest than for the hired help. "To be honest, the forecast worries me. Though it didn't keep me from coming here to cook tonight, I'd like to serve dinner earlier than you usually eat so I can beat the storm home."

Rosana pursed her lips. "You can cook the meal earlier if you want. We'll just keep the food warm until seven thirty."

Behind her back, Clancy rolled his eyes. He doubtless wanted to eat the food when it was hot as much as Val wanted to serve it then, but she wouldn't risk a road accident because of the hostess's inflexibility. "Whatever you like. Dinner will be ready at six thirty."

Rosana turned to Granddad. "You'll stay and eat with us, won't you, Don?"

He shook his head. "I'm gonna leave when Val does."

"Oh, dear. Rick said he'd join us because you'd be there. He's been eating alone too often lately." Rosana's brow furrowed. "Let's have dinner an hour early then. Don, will you please let Rick know that dinner will be at six thirty? Please stay and talk to him in his study until then."

"I'll stay if he wants me to." Granddad crossed the foyer toward the Ushers' private wing.

Rosana watered the plants on the windowsill. "Your grandfather's a breath of fresh air in our *ménage.* He's not a reporter or a fan, like the other people who come here hoping to talk to Rick. I'm happy Rick's found someone whose company he enjoys."

Did that mean he no longer enjoyed his wife's company? Val turned on the oven to preheat. "They seem to get along well."

"Rick needs someone at the moment. He's depressed because our dog died."

Val mixed the glaze for the Cornish hens. "It took a while for my grandfather to get over his dog's death. When did your dog die?"

"On Saturday."

The same day Emmett died! Could there be a connection between the human's death and the canine's? Val heated the glaze in the microwave. "Was the dog sick long?"

"He seemed listless and weak for a few days," Clancy said.

Rosana turned away from the windowsill. "Really? I didn't notice. Would you water the hanging plants, Clancy? I don't want to bother getting the stepladder."

"Sure." Clancy filled the watering can and made quick work of giving the plants a drink.

"You're welcome to join us at the table for dinner, Val. Madison has a play rehearsal tonight and won't be here. So that makes five of us including Rick." Rosana took a bottle of white wine from the refrigerator and removed two stemmed glasses hanging upside-down from a wine rack. "Can I pour you some wine, Val?"

"No, thank you." Wine paired well with cooking, but not with hunting for murder suspects or driving through a winter storm.

"I'll take some," Clancy said.

Rosana raised her brows at him. "Oh, you're finished with today's chapter?"

"Not yet. I'll have it done before dinner. Excuse me." He left the kitchen.

Val saw no sign that it bothered him to be treated like a schoolboy who had to complete his homework before he could eat or drink. Did Rosana think a glass of wine would make him less productive? Maybe he had a tendency to keep drinking once he started.

Rosana opened the wine, poured herself a glass, and sat on a barstool at the island counter. "Your grandfather told me you run a café at an athletic club. I don't know how well that pays, but I imagine you'd make more money as a personal chef."

"Possibly." Val basted the hens with balsamic glaze.

Running the café gave her a chance to chat with customers and friends. By comparison, a personal chef had limited contact with others. The job had never appealed to her. But if she lost the café contract, she might consider it as a stopgap.

"If our chef doesn't return next week, I'd like to have someone ready to take over. Would you be interested in that?"

Understudy to the chef at the house of Usher—that entry would make her résumé unique. "I'll think about it. Thank you for suggesting it."

Val was glad Rosana wanted something from her. She might answer prying questions more readily. Usher's wife obviously favored contingency plans and redundant systems, and not just for cooks. She'd hired a backup for her husband and then a backup for the backup. When she approached Granddad last week, did she have a reason to think Emmett, backup number one, wouldn't be around long?

Val took out the hens she'd cut in half at home and arranged them on a roasting rack. "What made you get in touch with my grandfather?"

"I saw an article in the local newspaper about him. He described himself as a problem solver, and I had a problem." Rosana sipped her wine. "Rick and I have been very isolated since we moved here. That didn't bother him for years, but lately he's been depressed. Before we moved here, he loved talking to his fans. I hoped to chase his doldrums away by arranging for him to interact with some fans. He agreed to go to the book club on Sunday and then, at the last minute, he changed his mind."

"So you hired a stand-in for him in case that happened. Did he back out of a signing or other event ever before?" Like when Emmett Flint stood in for him at the bookstore?

"Rick did that a few times when we lived in Baltimore. He had a reason then. He was convinced someone was following him, stalking him, probably a crazed fan. Rick was so worried he didn't want to leave the house. He couldn't concentrate on his writing either. That's why we moved here."

Val basted the hens with half the glaze and put the roasting pan in the oven. "Did you report the stalking to the police?"

"No. Rick believed someone was following him, but *I* wasn't convinced of it." Rosana smiled ruefully. "He said the man was Edgar Allan Poe, wanting revenge because Rick used his plots and characters. Obviously, Rick's nerves were acting up."

Or maybe he was being stalked by his son, Raven, who looked and dressed like Poe. "Has he gotten over that?"

"Living along the water is very calming. He isn't afraid of a stalker anymore, but something else has been bothering him lately. He won't talk about it." She gulped her wine and muttered into her glass, "I've dedicated my life to that man. After all these years, he's shutting me out."

Val guessed why Rosana had been so forthcoming about her private life. Like her husband, she was isolated and needed someone to talk to, especially now that he had withdrawn from her.

"When did you two meet?" Val hadn't forgotten Emmett's notes about Rick and Rosana at the University of Virginia. No harm in verifying them with the source.

Rosana smiled, maybe because she had happy memories. "He was teaching at the University of Virginia. I was in his class."

Emmett's speculations had been correct on that. Val remembered his note about a job at the library. "I thought he worked at the library. Granddad must have said something that gave me that idea."

"Rick didn't work there, but he haunted it. The university has a large collection of nineteenth-century American artifacts, manuscripts, and letters. That was Rick's field."

"Did you work at the library?"

Rosana laughed quietly. "No, but I knew that's where I'd find Rick. He was the right man for me. I couldn't let him get away. I hung around the library, so I could bump into him. I figured if he saw me there often enough, he'd notice me. And he did." She finished her wine and stood up. "I'll go set the table and then freshen up for dinner. Don't worry about the wine. I'll bring it to the table."

Val would have offered to set the table except that she was already on a tight schedule to make dinner early.

At six twenty all the food was ready to serve except the warm chocolate tart. Val would remove it from the oven before sitting down to dinner. She tossed the salad and distributed it among five plates, leaving some in the large salad bowl for seconds. When she put the salads on the table, she noticed raindrops trickling down the dining room window. At least they weren't ice drops . . . yet.

Rosana hurried into the room and took five dishes from the sideboard. "Please don't forget to warm the plates before you put the food on them." She followed Val to the kitchen. "You can do that either in the oven on low or in the dishwasher."

"Thank you for the reminder." And the explicit instructions on how to accomplish a simple task. Val loaded the plates in the dishwasher and set it on the dry cycle. She'd previously suspected Rosana of being a micromanager. Now she was sure of it.

Rosana put the white wine she'd opened earlier in a wine chiller and filled a pitcher with water. "I'll put these on the table. There's another bottle of wine like this one in the refrigerator in case we run low. If you're ready to serve, I'll let Rick and your grandfather know."

"I'm ready."

A brief cough came from behind Val. She and Rosana turned toward the cougher.

Madison stood in the doorway to the dining room, balancing on stylish, high-heeled shoes. "Excuse me. May I speak to you, Rosana?"

Rosana crossed the kitchen toward her. "I thought you went to a rehearsal tonight."

"The director called it off because he didn't want us driving home in the snow and sleet."

They moved into the dining room. Val heard

only murmurs. She went over to the shelves near the doorway to the dining room and pretended to study the plants. Rosana's voice drifted toward her.

"One evening a year, Madison. That's all we've asked of you. Rick will be so disappointed if you go back on your word."

"I planned to go with you tomorrow. It's not my fault that tonight's rehearsal was called off." Madison's voice verged on a whine. "I don't think I can do a good job without another rehearsal. The play's opening next week."

"Surely you can arrange for someone in the drama group to rehearse with you before the opening. I'll give you free time to do that next week. Tomorrow night you have an essential role with us," Rosana cajoled in a voice as smooth as honey, synthetic honey. "We can't do it any other night, and no one can stand in for you."

"All right. I'll be there." Madison paused between each syllable as if she had to force it out of herself.

"Thank you. Would you please set another place at the table for yourself? Val's in the kitchen. You'll need to tell her that you'll be joining us."

Val scooted back across the room. What was happening that required Madison's presence tomorrow night?

Madison came into the kitchen, carrying a plate. "Hello, Val. I assume you'll be dishing up and serving the food tonight."

"Of course. It's part of my job." Even if it weren't, Val didn't want anyone in the Usher house near her food or Granddad's.

"Kitchen duty isn't part of my job description, but I get to do it anyway." Madison added her plate to the others warming in the dishwasher and then left.

A few minutes later, as Val put the food on the plates, she heard Granddad's voice. He was talking with another man in the foyer.

"I'd like to meet your granddaughter," the man with the deep, rumbling voice said.

She looked forward to meeting, at long last, the real Rick Usher.

Chapter 21

When Rick Usher and Granddad came into the kitchen, Val was struck more by the differences between them than by their similarity. Though they were close in size and age and had similar beards, the author's shoulders were more rounded. Granddad wore gold-rimmed bifocals with clear lenses and Usher the frameless tinted glasses. Had he always looked at the world through gray-colored lenses?

Even behind those lenses, Usher's dark eyes, one of them larger than the other, mesmerized Val with their intensity.

He clasped her outstretched hand in both his hands. "Welcome to my house. I've heard wonderful things about you from your grandfather."

Really? Nice to know that Granddad said good things about her behind her back, even if not to her face. "Happy to meet you. I'm enjoying the stories in your *Poe Revisited* book." The Poe stories more than the Usher ones.

"Thank you for the kind words. I'm looking

forward to your dinner." Usher progressed at a stately pace toward the dining room.

Val could usually read Granddad's mood by his gait. He either walked on springs or trudged in a swamp. This evening his lively step made him look like Rick Usher's happy-go-lucky younger brother.

Clancy poured wine while Val delivered the plates. The golden brown hens garnished with fresh orange slices, the tricolor mix of roasted vegetables, and the bright green spinach studded with cranberries and feta made dinner look appetizing. After delivering everyone's food, Val took the empty chair next to the host, who sat at the head of the table. Madison sat across from her.

"*Bon appétit*, everyone." Rosana picked up her fork. "Rick, we're so glad you joined us for dinner tonight."

His glasses glinted in the light from the chandelier. "From now on, I'll be joining you anytime a visitor is here."

At the other end of the table, Rosana beamed, either missing or ignoring her husband's grim tone. "Wonderful. I'll arrange to have company more often." She cut into her Cornish hen.

Her husband did the same. "I don't crave company, but it's bad luck for me to eat alone when we have a guest. The last time I did that, my dog died."

Val's heart skipped a beat and she stopped chewing. Could Emmett have been that guest?

"It's a coincidence, Rick, not bad luck," Rosana said. "The food is delicious. Did you teach your granddaughter to cook, Don?"

"I taught her a few things in the kitchen," Granddad said, "but she makes fancier dishes than I do."

Name one thing you taught me in the kitchen. Val forked a large piece of the hen into her mouth to keep from challenging her grandfather.

Rosana took control of the table talk by quizzing Val on her background—where she'd grown up, gone to college, and worked. Then the hostess switched her attention to Madison and asked her about the play she was rehearsing.

Madison, who'd been systematically slicing meat from the hen, put down her knife and fork. "*The Glass Mendacity* is a comedy with characters from three different plays by Tennessee Williams. Big Daddy is dying and can't decide who should inherit the family estate. He's trying to find the person who can manage it and is worthy of it."

"A familiar plot." Rick leaned toward her. "What role do you play?"

"Big Daddy's daughter, Laura, the shy, disabled girl from *The Glass Menagerie.*" She didn't look at all shy as she returned his steady gaze. "Unlike his other two children, Laura loves Big Daddy for himself, not for what she'll inherit from him."

Granddad broke the silence that followed Madison's statement. "Why is the play called *The Glass Mendacity*?"

"Because all the characters lie." Madison looked from left to right at her tablemates. "Big Daddy accuses the others of mendacity and deceit, but he lies to himself. He believes what he wants to believe, not the truth."

Val wondered if Madison justified lying to the police by convincing herself that everyone lies.

"Poe was guilty of mendacity too," Rick said in his sonorous, professorial voice. "He told tall tales about his past and his family connections to impress people. Why do the characters in the play lie?"

"My character lies out of shame and feels guilty about it." Madison resumed cutting meat from the hen. "Big Daddy's other children lie to get more of his inheritance and cut each other out. His wife lies too. She sugarcoats reality and insists Big Daddy is perfectly healthy."

Granddad grimaced. "That play sure doesn't sound like a comedy."

Madison heaped the meat she'd cut into a pile. "I didn't want to tell you the funny parts because that would spoil the show for you. Trust me, it's hilarious. If you go to the play and don't laugh, I'll reimburse you for the ticket."

"That settles it. You can count on laughing." Clancy swallowed the last of the wine in his glass. "Madison wouldn't make that offer unless she knew it wouldn't cost her a cent." He poured himself more wine.

Val had trouble reading Clancy's comment. Was it hostile or teasing? The relationship between the two "children" at the table tonight might be like the one between Val and her brother. As teenagers, they'd added large helpings of rivalry and mockery to Deniston family dinners.

Madison cut the last of the meat from the hen's leg, laying bare its bones. "Here's an example of the play's humor. Big Daddy has a son named Brick, the alcoholic from *Cat on a Hot Tin Roof.*" She trained a laser look on Clancy. "Brick is a milquetoast who'll never amount to anything. In the play we're rehearsing, he isn't even played by an actor. He's a life-size mannequin. It's very funny when the other characters cart him around the stage and pretend he has ideas of his own."

Whoa. Val had no trouble picking up on the hostility in that comment.

Rosana gave Madison an icy look and turned to Clancy. "I hope your brother is doing better."

Clancy described his brother's slow improvement and his continuing challenges. While he talked, sleet pelted the window.

Rick interrupted him. "How long will this bad weather last?"

"The forecast says it will clear up tomorrow morning," his wife said. "Don't worry about it, Rick."

He stared at the window as if a menacing presence stood there watching them. "Forecasters aren't always right."

For a man who rarely left the house, he was certainly obsessing about tomorrow's weather. Val eyed the window uneasily too, worrying more about tonight's weather than tomorrow's.

She rested her knife and fork on her nearly empty plate. "Excuse me. I'd like to dish up the dessert so I can get on the road before it gets icy."

"I'll clear the table." Clancy started to stand up.

Rosana laid a restraining hand on his arm. "Not

yet. Madison is still eating. Val, you go ahead and get the dessert ready to serve."

She sounded like a strict parent, excusing one child from the table and not excusing the other.

Val went to the kitchen, cut the chocolate tart, and put slices on four cake plates.

Clancy brought in a stack of plates, apparently having been excused at last. "Just four pieces? Who's not eating pie?"

"Granddad and I will skip dessert if the weather's bad. I'm going outside to see what's happening. Then I'll decide if we should stay any longer."

She went into the foyer and opened the front door. The gravel looked wet, but not icy. Without bothering to go back for her jacket, she crossed the covered entry deck for a closer look at the driveway and went down the two steps to the concrete walk. When her foot hit the concrete, she slid on glazed ice. In an instant, she was lying on her back, being hit by freezing rain. She sat up. Nothing hurt except her tailbone. With her hands on the cold ground, she tried to stand up but her foot skidded as soon as she put weight on it. She fell back again.

"Val! Are you hurt?" Clancy called from the door.

"No, but it's too icy for me to get any footing. I could use some help." She held out her hand. "Stay on the steps and pull me toward you."

He tugged her toward the stairs and then lifted her under her arms until she was sitting on a step. "Thank you."

"You're welcome. If the walkway is covered with ice, so are the roads. You'd better not try to drive." He held out his hand to help her up off the step.

"Ready for a dark and stormy night at the house of Usher?"

Val took his hand and scrambled to her feet. "Bring it on, if dry clothes and central heat are included in the price."

She went into the dining room and explained why she was soaking wet. "Before I went outside, I should have put on my coat, but I didn't expect to be out there long. I slipped on the icy walk and had trouble getting up."

Granddad looked alarmed. "Are you hurt?"

"No broken bones or even bumps." She couldn't rule out bruises.

"You must take off those wet clothes," Rosana said. "Madison, can you lend her something to wear?"

Madison stood up. "Come with me."

She pointed out Rosana's office as she took Val past it and into a small hallway. A door at the end of the hall led to a staircase.

Madison's large room above the three-car garage had a sitting area and a sleeping zone. Though the sloped side roof and dormer windows made the space look cozy, it was cooler than the main part of the house. Val shivered in her wet clothes.

Madison opened a cedar closet. She took out gray knit pants, a matching zip-up jacket, and a red sleeveless sweater. "The pants are roomy and a little short on me so they should fit you just fine."

"Thanks." Val could have done without the reminder that Madison was taller and thinner than she was. Who'd want to have a stick figure anyway?

"Put your wet clothes on a towel rack in there for

now." Madison pointed to the bathroom. "Later you can hang them up in the laundry room downstairs."

Later? Val had planned to go back to the first floor immediately, but Madison seemed to have other plans for her. In the bathroom Val hurriedly removed her top and slacks. Fortunately, the rain hadn't penetrated through to her underwear.

She took Madison's clothes off the hanger, amazed at how soft they were. Cashmere, all three pieces. A Bergdorf Goodman label was sewn below the designer label in the pants and jacket. To afford these clothes, she must have overcome the financial problems she'd faced after her father's investments tanked.

When Val came out of the bathroom, Madison was removing the cork from a bottle of wine. "Care for some Pinot Noir?"

An invitation Val hadn't expected. Until now, Madison had treated her more like a servant than a guest. Why the sudden hospitality? "Yes, I'd like a little."

Okay, Val had failed to follow the advice she'd given Granddad, but surely it was safe to drink wine poured from a just-opened bottle. As an added precaution, Val wouldn't take a sip of the Pinot Noir until her hostess had drunk some.

"Have a seat." Madison gestured toward a pair of barrel swivel chairs that flanked a small table under the dormer window.

Val took the chair that gave her a view of the wet bar and the staircase. "I noticed you didn't drink the wine at dinner. Is that because you don't care for white wine?"

Madison twisted the corkscrew like an expert. "I never drink the wine at dinner because Rosana doesn't serve it at the right temperature. The white wine goes straight from the fridge to the table, so it's ten degrees too cold. The red wine is at least ten degrees warmer than it should be. Room temperature in a house where the thermostat's set at seventy-five isn't the same as room temperature in a wine cellar." The cork came out with a pop. "I don't say anything to Rosana about the wine at the table. I just don't drink it."

Val sat in the chair and glanced at the small wine fridge near the wet bar. Madison had her own wine stock here, no doubt kept at the right temperature. Did she usually drink alone here or did she invite Clancy? Bad idea if Clancy had alcohol problems as she seemed to imply tonight at dinner. Not wanting to drink alone might be the reason she invited Val to join her.

Whatever the reason, Val couldn't pass up a chance to talk to Madison in private.

Or was it private? This room, like Rick Usher's study, might be bugged.

Chapter 22

Val scanned the room for a place where a bug might hide, though she couldn't imagine why anyone would bug Madison's room. Because of the sloped roof, there weren't any tall bookcases where such a device could go unnoticed, as it did in Rick Usher's study. With Madison focused on pouring the wine, Val reached under the small table next to her chair and felt around for a bug. Nothing there.

Madison handed her a glass. "Cheers." She clinked her glass with Val's, took a healthy swig, and then fiddled with the CD player on a low bookcase in the sitting area. Classical music filled the room.

As long as they stayed in this spot, the music would drown out their conversation. Relieved, Val put her glass on the side table between the two chairs. "I appreciate your lending me these warm clothes. They're really comfortable and, like everything you wear, beautiful."

Madison smiled. "With my sensitive skin, I have to wear good clothing. The labels on most clothes scratch me and sometimes the fabrics do too.

I can't stand to wear anything synthetic. Even cheap cashmere is uncomfortable."

Nothing less than three-ply cashmere would do. Fortunately for Val's budget, she'd never gotten used to such luxury. "I'll get these clothes cleaned and return them to you in a few days."

"Please don't do that. Dry cleaning makes cashmere itchy. I hand-wash all my cashmere things to keep them fluffy. But I don't want you to wash the clothes. I have special laundry soap for cashmere only."

Val figured Madison would pass the princess-and-the-pea test with flying colors. "I enjoyed hearing about the play you're rehearsing. I'm not familiar with it, but I've seen *The Glass Menagerie.* You strike me as perfect for the part of Laura."

Madison looked as startled as if Val had discovered a deep dark secret. "Why do say that? I'm not shy like her. I don't have a disability."

"You have the right body type for the role. You can project an air of fragility. I'll bet you have other things in common with the character." *Like that you're both liars.*

The actress gazed into her wineglass. "You're right. Playing Laura has made me realize something about myself. I've withdrawn from the world like she has. I don't polish glass animals, but I endlessly polish an author's reputation."

"You get paid to do it, and you must like the job or you'd leave it."

"I might earn as much at another job, but with this one I don't have to fork out anything for food or a roof over my head. I'm saving money now so I can live the way I want in the future."

She couldn't save much if she bought designer clothes, but maybe her wardrobe consisted of leftovers from her life as a rich girl. "Are you saving for anything in particular?"

"A house. My fiancé teaches in a charter school in Washington, D.C. He loves the job, but it doesn't pay enough for us to live in a nice place. I don't want to live in a bad neighborhood or a tiny apartment. That's all we can afford when we combine our salaries. He's not happy about us living so far apart." She looked around the room. "I don't know how much longer I can stand it here. I feel like I'm entombed in this house."

As tombs go, it was spacious. Val sipped her wine. "Can you live elsewhere and work remotely?"

"I suggested that. Rosana wouldn't hear of it. I'm not allowed to post anything online about Rick until she approves it. She looks over my shoulder when I'm at the computer. I could e-mail her my drafts to approve, but she refuses to put her fingers on a keyboard or a touch screen. She says she doesn't *trust the computer.*" Madison made air quotes around the last three words.

"She doesn't trust herself to use it." Or Madison to do her job.

"Rosana hovers over me because she needs something to do. Her whole life has been about her husband. He worships at the shrine of Poe. She worships at the shrine of Rick Usher. So do Clancy and I." Madison swigged her wine. "We all need to get out of this house more."

"You're free to do what you want every evening, aren't you?" *Except for tomorrow evening.*

"There's not much to do around here unless I'm rehearsing a play. Most weekends I visit my fiancé."

Val's hope that Madison would blurt out what she was doing tomorrow evening was dashed, but at least she'd mentioned the theater group, another subject Val wanted to explore. "The rehearsals get you out of this house and give you a chance to socialize with other people. It must have been a shock for all of you when one of the cast members died suddenly."

Madison jumped as if someone had poked her with a skewer. "Yes, it was." She topped off the wine in her glass and held up the bottle. "More for you?"

Val shook her head. She would bring up Emmett again, once Madison had drunk more wine and relaxed. "What got you interested in acting?"

"The theater has always fascinated me, even when I was a child. I grew up in Manhattan and loved going to the plays. It was like magic to sit in the dark when the curtain rose and a different world opened up. I saw everything from Broadway to Off-Off-Broadway." She returned to her chair and sighed. "But after my family moved away from the city, I didn't have many chances to go to the theater. I read a lot of plays, though, and I would stage them in my head."

"Did you ever consider the theater as a career?"

"Considered and rejected it. I couldn't face living hand-to-mouth like most actors when they're starting out. Very few people make it big on the stage."

"Do you expect to make it big in your current job?" *Maybe by inheriting money from Rick Usher?*

"No, but it's a steady income, which actors don't usually have." Madison glanced at her watch. "This is about the time I call my fiancé."

Val ignored the hint to leave. With the clock running down on this game, she might as well go for broke. "You've obviously seen and read a lot of plays. Maybe you can tell me what play a snippet of dialogue comes from." She paused to remember the threat that Gunnar had overheard Emmett make Thursday night and that Madison had claimed was a line from a play. "*I'm calling the shots now. Do what I say unless you want your secret to get out.*"

The actress blanched and froze for an instant. Then she put her wineglass on the table with a shaky hand. "I don't recognize that dialogue." She pulled her long braid to the front and grabbed it like a lifeline.

Liar. "Funny. You heard it less than a week ago. And you weren't the only one who heard it."

"Not the only—? Ah, I get it. You've talked to Gunnar." Madison let go of her braid and stood up. "I think it's time you left."

Val didn't budge. "It's time you told the truth. Gunnar was trying to protect you. In return, you lied about his fight with Emmett. I can understand your lying if Emmett pressured you. Now that he's dead, he can't hurt you, but lying to the police can get you in trouble."

Madison clutched her braid again. "I was so upset by what he said that I didn't pay any attention to what was going on between him and Gunnar."

She'd fiddled with that braid both times when she wasn't telling the truth. What she'd just said contradicted the story she'd given the police.

Val pounced on the discrepancy. "Why would Emmett's words upset you if he was just practicing lines from a play? That's what you claimed they were." Having caught Madison in a lie, Val wanted to push her advantage, but not too far. She wouldn't get anywhere by asking Madison what kind of hold Emmett had over her. Madison would be more willing to reveal his secrets than her own. "What did Emmett want you to do?"

Looking relieved, Madison sat down. "To search for a poetry book in Rick's study."

Val hadn't seen that coming. She'd assumed Emmett wanted to extort money or sexual favors. "What book?" *The same one Rick Usher was trying to find?*

"Something by Poe. I wasn't paying attention because I couldn't search for it even if I wanted to. Rosana's never far away if I'm in Rick's study. Emmett didn't believe me." Madison took a long drink of wine. "By Thursday, when he had the fight with Gunnar, he'd come up with a new idea. He would give me some sleeping pills to crush into the food Rick, Rosana, and Clancy ate for dinner. He wanted me to search Rick's study after they'd all gone to bed. Totally nuts."

Her volley of words surprised Val. She didn't doubt the story. It was too weird for anyone to make it up, and Madison had delivered it fast without touching her braid. But why was she willing to give so many details? Maybe she was using the truth as a smokescreen. This story diverted attention from a subject she hoped wouldn't come up—why Emmett assumed he could make such demands on her.

Val broke a long silence. "Emmett wanted you to steal the book?"

"He knew I wouldn't do that. I was supposed to take a picture of the book on the shelf. He didn't say why. I told him I'd try, just to get him off my back." Madison's glower suggested she wanted Val off her back too.

Val wasn't ready to leave. "You told him that after the rehearsal on Saturday?"

Madison shook her head. "On Thursday, when he had the fight with Gunnar. I didn't see Emmett after Saturday's rehearsal."

Val waited for Madison to reach for her braid, but this time the actress passed the hairy lie-detector test. Not necessarily conclusive. Even sophisticated lie detectors sometimes failed. "You came straight back here for lunch after the rehearsal?"

"No. I don't usually eat here on weekends. I went to Bayport."

"That's where I live. Bayport has some great restaurants. Which one did you go to?"

"I wasn't hungry after snacking in the rehearsal hall. I just . . . uh, window-shopped." Madison fiddled with her braid.

Window-shopped on a cold, blustery day? Right. Maybe she was trying to avoid the man who was pressuring her. "Did you go to Bayport because you knew Emmett was coming here for lunch?"

"I didn't know it ahead of time. I came back here

around two. I was a quarter of a mile from the house when I saw his car coming toward me."

Madison answered without hesitation or braid clutching. She'd just confirmed Val's guess about Emmett's visit here on Saturday.

The room struck Val as eerily quiet. Too quiet. Sometime, while she was focused on grilling Madison, the music had stopped. From then on, any bug in the room would have picked up their voices. The recording would convey how fixated Val was on Emmett and his visit here. A new worry gnawed at her. Someone in the Usher house, maybe more than one person, would rather the police not know about the man who came to lunch.

She still had more questions, but she'd like to ask them with the music on. "Do you mind if I turn on the CD player?" Without waiting for a response, she punched the play button. It hit her what was odd about Madison's claim that she'd seen Emmett's leaving. "I don't usually look closely at who's driving a car coming toward me. What made you notice Emmett's car?"

"The road doesn't get much traffic because there are only a few houses along it. When he whizzed past me, I was so surprised that I took my eye off the road, swerved, and nearly hit an oncoming—"

The lights went out and the music stopped.

Chapter 23

"The power's gone off," Madison said. "It's happened before during storms."

Val couldn't even see her own hands. "Do you have a flashlight?"

"Yeah, but I can't find it in the dark. Ha. Ha. My phone would give us some light if only I knew where I put it."

Val knew exactly where she'd left her phone—in her bag in the kitchen. "My phone's downstairs. I'm afraid you're stuck with me a little longer."

The lack of power left her without a lie detector. In the dark she couldn't see when Madison stroked her braid. Lies had tripped off the woman's tongue while the lights were on. No reason why they'd stop now. Without music to interfere with the reception of sound, Val would have to watch what she said. A bug small enough to hide would run on a battery without any need of AC power. From now on, she'd avoid the subject of Emmett Flint.

"Don't panic!" Clancy's voice carried up the

staircase. "I'm going to gather flashlights. I'll bring one up to you."

"Who's panicking?" Madison sounded annoyed.

"You and Clancy seem to get on each other's nerves," Val said. "At dinner you two sounded more like rivals than teammates in the Usher enterprise."

"Clancy's the one who started with the digs. He thinks his work is more important than mine, just because he's *the writer.* He can't write anything without a detailed outline and, even so, Rick has to fix Clancy's scenes. Since Rick stopped giving talks and going to book signings, I'm the one who keeps him in the public eye. Clancy wouldn't have a job if it weren't for me."

"What did you do before you worked for the Ushers?"

"My first job was at a public relations firm, doing social media campaigns for clients. Then I handled publicity for mysteries and thrillers put out by Rick's publisher. After I met the man I'm now engaged to, I wanted to move from New York to Washington. When Rick heard I was leaving the publishing company, he offered me a job as his assistant and publicist."

Val wondered if Madison had known then that she'd work under Rosana. "That's when you moved in with the Ushers?"

"No, they still lived in Baltimore. I rented a place halfway between their house and Washington. I gave up my apartment after they moved here and offered me a room."

Val saw a chance to nudge the conversation in a

direction she wanted. "Rosana told me they moved here because Rick feared a stalker."

Madison laughed. "I'm not sure the stalker exists. Rick had an infection that made him paranoid. He even hallucinated. The doctor put him in the hospital, pumped him full of antibiotics, and cured him. A month or so later, the cycle repeated. Infection, weird behavior, antibiotics, recovery. Rosana was afraid he'd act crazy in public and damage his reputation. She canceled all his events and convinced him to move away from Baltimore."

Though Rosana had told Val a different story about the move, she and Madison had agreed on one thing—that no one had stalked Rick. Val shelved her suspicion that Raven Wingard had stalked his father.

A light came from the stairwell, weak but welcome.

"Let there be light." Clancy arrived at the top of the stairs. The beam from his small LED flashlight danced around the room and stopped when it lit up Val and Madison. He pulled a second small flashlight from his pocket and held it out to them.

Madison jumped up and grabbed it. "I'll use this to find my own flashlight. Then you can have it, Val." Madison walked toward the sleeping area, rummaged in a dresser, and pulled out an old-fashioned flashlight in metal housing, sturdy enough to bash someone. She turned it on. "Still operational. The last time the power went out, the furnace didn't work. Any idea how long this outage will last?"

"I called the electric company. They're fixing a

downed power line but can't estimate how long it will take," Clancy said. "We can all huddle around the gas fireplace in the living room if the house gets too cold."

Madison gave Val the small flashlight. "Until then, I'll stay here, under my down comforter, with my Kindle full of books to keep me warm."

Val counted on the cashmere outfit and her parka to fend off the cold for as long as she was stuck here. She also needed something to ward off harm. "I'm going to call the Bayport Chief of Police when I go downstairs. He's a good friend of my grandfather's. I'll tell him where we are and ask him for an update on the roads between here and town. Maybe we won't have to stay here much longer." She turned to Clancy. "Do the Ushers have any sand to put on the walk and the driveway?"

"I can check down there." He pointed to the garage below Madison's room. "I doubt they have enough sand to treat the whole driveway."

"I'll get my wet clothes." Val fetched them from the bathroom. "Thanks again for lending me some dry clothes, Madison."

"No problem. By the way, Clancy, Val mentioned that Emmett Flint ate lunch here on Saturday. Why was he here?"

Val groaned inwardly. She'd planned to work up to that question with Clancy, not hit him in the face with it. Madison apparently wanted to put him on the spot. They seemed to enjoy making each other uncomfortable.

Clancy didn't miss a beat. "He dropped by to talk to Rick. Rosana invited him to lunch."

Based on what Rick Usher had said at the table tonight, he'd passed on eating lunch with a guest, but they might have met before the meal in the privacy of the study. If so, the author would have come face-to-face with his double, a disconcerting experience for anyone.

Clancy had already started down the stairs, lighting the way for her. She followed.

He waited for her at the bottom. "Your grandfather's in the living room with Rick and Rosana. There were phone noises coming from your handbag in the kitchen while I was cleaning up after dinner."

"Thanks, I'll check my messages. First I'll deal with my wet clothing. Can you point me to the laundry room?"

"I'll show you." He waited while she hung up the clothes. "On a night like this, I appreciate Rosana's preparations for an emergency. Using the light from my phone, she found six flashlights she'd stowed in various places around the house." He walked to the kitchen with Val.

She fished her phone from her bag and saw that Gunnar had texted her. She would call him later, from a place where no one could overhear her. "If you'll excuse me, I need to find someone to cover the café in case the weather doesn't improve by morning."

"Okay. I'll go work on my computer. Its battery should last a while."

When he left, she went into the living room and told Granddad and the Ushers that she would call Chief Yardley to get an update on the roads between here and Bayport.

Her phone rang as she returned to the kitchen.

"Hey, Val. It's Bethany. I just called your house to talk to your grandfather. No one answered."

"He's with me." Val lowered her voice. "We're both marooned at the Ushers' house because of the freezing rain, and the power just went out."

"Yipes! That's worse than hunting for a cadaver in the dark. I just watched the news. The roads in town are fine and so are the main roads. It's only that last stretch on the side roads you have to worry about. The meteorologist said we're right on the line between rain and freezing rain."

Val crossed her fingers that the front would shift north before morning. "Why did you want to talk to Granddad?"

"To tell him what I found out about cadaver dogs, but you can tell him. My neighbor returned today and came over to pick up Styx." Bethany giggled. "Good pun. She told me how she works with the dog. Styx was never going to pay any attention to my signal. He only searches for a cadaver when his handler gives the signal."

Val laughed. "Thanks for telling me. Too bad we didn't know two days ago." They might not be spending the night here if they hadn't gone cadaver hunting. Rick Usher's shout of *buried alive* had brought Granddad back for another look at the mound and led to his surprising bond with the author. Then, to make sure Granddad wasn't in danger, she'd taken the catering gig here. Funny how one thing led to another.

After she got off the phone with Bethany, she called Irene Pritchard and explained she might not be able to return to Bayport by morning. "If you can get around in the morning and I can't, would you mind opening the café?"

"That depends on the weather. Jeremy has four-wheel drive. He'll be able to drive me there, unless the roads are iced up."

"If they are, the club won't open. I appreciate your doing this, Irene. I'll call you in the morning and let you know if I'm stuck."

"I usually get up by six thirty," Irene said.

Val thanked her and hung up. Irene had been cooperative, though not friendly. Good enough for now.

Clancy poked his head into the kitchen from the foyer. "I'm happy to lend you my e-reader tonight, but I'm not sure the books I have would match your taste."

"I'm working my way through *Poe Revisited.* If I can borrow a copy, I'll read it by flashlight, or better yet, by candlelight. That will put me in the spirit of Poe."

He laughed. "I have a copy in my room. Go up the spiral staircase and give me a shout when you want it."

Val put on her parka and then went outside to the covered front porch. She called Chief Yardley's cell phone number and left a message on his voice mail, saying she and Granddad were stranded at the Usher house. She ended with a tidbit she hoped would prompt him to investigate the people who lived here. "Emmett Flint had lunch here on

Saturday, a couple of hours before he collapsed. And everyone here has access to beta blockers." She would tell him about the dog's death the next time they talked.

Now to call Gunnar. He had texted earlier to tell her that the rehearsal was canceled and that he hoped to ride out the storm with her.

"Sorry I can't be with you," she said when he answered his phone. "Granddad and I are iced in at the Usher house." She gave him the same information she'd left for the chief, but in more detail.

"Great, Val. You've proven that the gang there had the means and opportunity to murder Emmett. That's the good news. The bad news is that you're stuck overnight in a house with them. Would you please stop snooping?"

"Okay, but I need you to do some research about the book Usher wanted you to find on his shelves. Go online and see if there's an early edition of *Tamerlane* that could be valuable."

"Okay. I'll call you back."

Val walked to the porch railing. With no outdoor lights working, she couldn't see what was falling from the sky, but she could hear rain hit the pavement and the porch roof. Holding on to the stair railing, she went down two steps, took off a glove, and bent to touch the concrete walk. Still icy.

She'd just gone back inside the house when Gunnar called her.

"Your hunch was right," he said. "A first edition of *Tamerlane* is worth a lot of money. In 2009 a copy sold at auction for more than any other book by an American writer—six hundred fifty thousand dollars."

Wow. Worth stealing if you needed money for a house or for your brother's medical bills. Val felt the blood pumping through her veins and warming her. "How many first editions are there?"

"A dozen are known to still exist. One of those was stolen from the University of Virginia library, along with some manuscripts and historical artifacts."

"When did that happen?"

"They were discovered missing in 1973."

When Rick Usher was at the University of Virginia. The significance of Emmett's note about a *library job* hit Val. It didn't refer to where Rick or Rosana had worked, but to the slang meaning of a *job*—a robbery.

Chapter 24

Val clutched her phone. Was the theft of a rare book decades ago somehow related to Emmett's murder? "Hold on, Gunnar, while I grab my coat and go back outside. It's a little warm in here."

"By *warm* you mean someone might be listening to you?"

"Yes." The Ushers sat in the living room, only steps away. Clancy or Madison could be lurking in a dark corner not far from the foyer. Once outside, Val said, "Do you know exactly what else was taken in that theft from the library?"

"Letters written by George Washington and Thomas Jefferson. Papers that belonged to Mark Twain, Aaron Burr, and Robert E. Lee. Those are just a few of the items."

Rick Usher, who specialized in American history, must have had access to those materials for his research. That didn't mean he'd stolen them. He'd asked Gunnar to search for a copy of the *Tamerlane* book, but it could have been a different edition. If Usher had a rare book, wouldn't he have put it in a safe-deposit box or another secure location? Not if he'd drawn a lesson from "The Purloined Letter," Poe's story about concealing something in plain sight. The best place to hide a valuable book was on shelves with other books.

"Those items disappeared from the library when Rick Usher was teaching at the University of Virginia. According to his wife, he spent a lot of time in the library." Val told Gunnar about Emmett's chronology of Usher's life. "Emmett came up with possible reasons why Usher left the university in 1974. Failure to get tenure. An affair with a student. *And the library job.* I think he suspected Usher of stealing that first edition or buying it from the thief."

"He projected his own rottenness onto other people. What evidence could he have that Usher stole anything?"

"Emmett was trying to get the evidence. Madison said he wanted her to look for it on the bookshelves in the study."

Gunnar said nothing for a moment. "Maybe she saw it, stole it, and then killed Emmett because he accused her of theft."

Val doubted it. Gunnar was letting his anger at her lies cloud his judgment. "She wouldn't have told me about the book if she'd stolen it and killed Emmett because of it. But she might have murdered him for another reason. I caught her lying a couple of times."

"Please tell me you didn't confront her about her lies."

Val couldn't say that without lying herself. "I pointed out contradictions."

He groaned. "Rule of thumb, Val—when stuck in a house with murder suspects, talk about the weather. Speaking of that, I'll let you know as soon as the roads are safe."

"Okay. Love you."

"Love you too. Good night and be careful."

Val went inside and hung up her coat. She peeked into the living room.

Rosana motioned for her to join them. "Your grandfather has been telling us about your parents and your brother and his children."

"I'll be back. Clancy said he'd lend me a book. I was just going to pick it up."

She turned around, went up the spiral staircase in the foyer, and called his name.

He met her at the top of the stairs, carrying a hurricane lamp with a candle in it. "Perfect timing. I'm ready to knock off for the night." He showed her into a long narrow room about eight feet wide and twice as long. "This is my work and living area. The door over there leads to my bedroom and bath."

The space had probably been intended as a loft overlooking the living room below, but a solid wall now closed it off from the lower floor. His living area consisted of a love seat, an armchair, a lamp table, and a coffee table.

Clancy put the hurricane lamp on his cluttered computer desk. The shelves in the hutch above his desk held books stacked horizontally. "I know you came for the book, Val, but I hope you'll stay and keep me company. I just poured some cognac. Would you like some?"

She glanced at the coffee table, where a bottle and two brandy snifters rested, one empty and the other half filled. "No cognac for me, thank you, but I'll keep you company for a while." She sat in the armchair and put her flashlight on the lamp table with its beam pointing at the ceiling. "What have you been working on this evening? An Usher book or one of your own?"

Clancy sat on the love seat. "I was doing research for Rick's next Gaston Vulpin book. Rick uses Poe's 'The Mystery of Marie Roget' as a model for his French detective series. Poe started with a real crime that occurred in this country and shifted the setting to Paris. Rick does the same."

"How does he choose his ripped-from-the-headlines crimes?"

"I do the initial research online and identify intriguing cases he might use. After he picks one, I research it in detail and come up with plot variations." Clancy swirled the cognac in his glass. "Rick decides which variation to use. Then I do the first draft."

Madison had implied Clancy did hack work, but he'd just described his role in every stage of a book's creation. At the book club, Simone had noted that the writing style and the emphasis on food in *The Murders in the Rue Cler* suggested Usher's protégé had authored much of the novel. Even so, Rick Usher made all the decisions about the books. Val would hate to cook only the recipes a master chef dictated. *Uh-oh.* She cringed inwardly. She was acting like that chef, asking Irene to stifle her creativity, just as Usher stifled Clancy's creativity. She made up her mind to give Irene leeway to develop an evening menu herself. Well, maybe half of it.

Val remembered the chief's questions about how Clancy was paid. "I didn't realize your work included researching, brainstorming, *and* writing. Do you get a cut of the royalties?"

Clancy snickered. "I get a fixed amount for each book. It's at the low end of the ghostwriter pay scale. But steady employment, and my name on the cover with Rick Usher's are worth more than another ten or twenty thousand per project."

The famous author could afford to pay better. Val would demand a raise if she were Clancy. "You spend all your time working on books Rick Usher wants to publish. If you were writing your own books, would they take off from Poe's stories, like Usher's books?"

"No!" Clancy banged the brandy snifter down on the coffee table, the first time he'd let go of it. "I want to tell my brother's story. What it's like to be in the military fighting in the Middle East. What it's like to come home with physical and psychological wounds."

Channeling his brother might give him more satisfaction than channeling Poe, but it would also take an emotional toll on Clancy. "I look forward to reading your book."

"With a cheerleader like you next to me, I might actually write it." He sat forward on the love seat and perched his head on one side. "Are you seeing anyone?"

A strategic lie might make him more willing to answer questions and share information, but it wouldn't be fair to either him or Gunnar. "Yes, I am."

Clancy's face fell. "Too bad. I hope you'll let me know if your romance fizzles."

"I don't expect that to happen, but no one ever does." Val couldn't resist the chance to bring up Emmett Flint, though Gunnar had advised talking only about the weather. "The man I'm seeing has a role in *The Glass Mendacity* with Madison. He was Emmett Flint's understudy for the part of Big Daddy."

"So your boyfriend's an older guy?" Clancy sounded more cheerful.

"No. Stage makeup can add years to an actor." Would he pick up on her cue and mention Emmett's ability to age himself? Clancy said nothing. Val would have to adopt a more direct approach to get answers out of him. "How did you know Emmett?"

Clancy swallowed some cognac. "He struck up a conversation with me at Irene's tea shop. I told him I was a writer working with Rick Usher. I never expected to see Emmett again. He contacted me a few months later through my Web site."

Val hesitated a moment before deciding to push for more. "About what?"

"He wanted to pitch an idea for a show based on Rick's life and writing. Emmett had a one-man Poe show. He had something similar in mind for an Usher show."

Probably the two-person show Emmett's sister had mentioned. "Did he ever get a chance to pitch his idea to Rick?"

"He asked me to give Rick his résumé. I was surprised when Rick agreed to meet with him. Emmett impressed him with how much he knew about Poe. But Rick didn't want his books reworked into a show."

That must have been the meeting Rick mentioned to Granddad, when he assessed and rejected Emmett as a literary executor. "I'm surprised Rick turned down the idea. A show would help him sell more books."

"Not if a second-rate playwright and actor put it on." Clancy held up the cognac bottle. "This is almost empty. Wouldn't you like to help me finish it off?"

She'd just watched him pour his own drink from that bottle. The cognac probably wouldn't kill her. The more he drank, the more he might tell her, so she might as well stick around. "Just a taste, please."

He poured an inch of cognac in the brandy snifter for her and two inches for himself. Val watched him sip his drink with his eyes closed, as if his sense of sight might interfere with his sense of taste. She tried the cognac. Smooth. Intense. She liked it more than she'd expected. "So Emmett gave up on the idea of a Rick Usher show."

"Not at all. When I ran into him in Bayport a few months later, he said he'd done more research on Rick and was working on a scene to present to him. He was sure his writing and acting ability would convince Rick to change his mind."

"Did he want you to arrange another meeting with Rick?"

"No, he was still working on his audition, and since he'd already met Rick, he didn't need me in the middle . . . for that. He wanted me in the middle of something else. He asked me to check Rick's shelves for an old copy of *Tamerlane and Other Poems.* Emmett said he'd make it worth my while to look for that book." Clancy drank more cognac. "Emmett convinced himself that Rick had a stolen a rare edition of that book, Poe's first publication. Can you believe that?"

Val not only believed it, she'd guessed as much. But it surprised her that Clancy, who'd kept Emmett's impersonation of Rick Usher a secret from her, was now telling her so much about the actor. Maybe Clancy, like Madison, was using the book story to distract Val from asking about other subjects. "Why did Emmett think Rick had stolen the book?"

"A first edition of it disappeared from the archives at the University of Virginia library while Rick was teaching there. Rick was obsessed with Poe and left the university shortly after the theft was discovered. Ergo, he must have stolen it or known the person who did. I pointed out the flaws in this reasoning, but logic didn't enter into Emmett's calculations."

"Was he going to steal the book and sell it?" The perfect theft: stealing from a thief who couldn't report the loss without incriminating himself.

"I suspected that. I researched the book and learned it's worthless. The library copy has unique inscriptions, visible under ultraviolet light. Anyone trying to sell it to a collector would be charged with possession of stolen property. I e-mailed Emmett and told him that."

And yet, as Val had heard from Madison, Emmett still had that book on his mind. The possibility of stealing the book might have tempted Clancy, too, until he found out no reputable collector would buy it.

Val reminded herself to talk about something other than Emmett. "I've never heard of a person or place named Tamerlane. What is that poem about?"

"Tamerlane is a Mongol ruler, nearing the end of his life. He regrets the choices he's made. He lost the love of his life because of his quest for fame and power. Some biographers have said 'Tamerlane' reflects Poe's feelings about a woman he loved and lost."

Did it also reflect Rick Usher's regrets about his lost love Simone? Val heard a faint but insistent jingling sound. "What's that?"

"Rosana's favorite dinner bell. She wants one or both of us downstairs."

"Madison couldn't possibly hear that bell in her apartment over the garage. Is there a gong to tell her when to descend?"

"It's called a cell phone. Rosana summons *me* the old-fashioned way."

Val didn't detect any annoyance in his tone, but how could it not bother him? She stood up. "Do you have the book you were going to lend me?"

The bell from downstairs jingled again as Clancy

took *Poe Revisited* from a bookcase and the hurricane lamp with a chunky candle from his desk. "Bell, book, and candle." He grinned.

Val couldn't help liking him though she didn't trust him. She was sure he wouldn't have told her Emmett had eaten lunch here if Madison hadn't forced him to confirm it.

When they went downstairs, Val noticed that Rick Usher, Granddad, and Rosana were sitting closer to the fire than they had earlier. The large living room was colder than Clancy's cozy space upstairs.

Rosana stood up. "We talked about staying close to the fireplace tonight, but with the big windows and high ceiling, this room is chilly even with the fire. We'd be better off in the bedrooms, in warm clothes, under blankets. I've put extra blankets in the rooms on this floor. If you have what you need, Clancy, I'll show Val and her grandfather to their rooms."

"I'll be warm enough, thank you. Good night, everyone." He retraced his steps to the staircase.

Rosana led them toward the other side of the house from the Usher wing and Clancy's quarters. She trained her flashlight into a room with a sofa and a huge desk. "I hope you don't mind sleeping on the sofa in the office here, Val. Your grandfather will be in the guestroom next to you."

"That's fine." Val would have preferred everyone together in front of the fireplace, instead of her and Granddad isolated in one corner of the big house. "We're going to leave early, assuming the roads aren't icy. If I don't see you in the morning, thank you for your hospitality."

"We enjoyed your dinner. I forgot to tell you that you can skip cooking dinner for us tomorrow night. I'll expect you back on Friday."

"That's fine." Val already knew something out of the ordinary was happening tomorrow night, requiring Madison's presence. The change in dinner plans suggested everyone in the Usher household would be involved.

Five minutes after Rosana left her, Val knocked on the guestroom door. "It's me, Granddad."

He opened the door. "I was about to go get you. I don't want you in that room by yourself." His voice was barely above a whisper.

She trained her flashlight around the guest room until the beam lit up a recliner in the corner. "I'll take the chair. You take the bed."

"Nope. Other way around. I sleep in a chair like that all the time when I'm watching TV. I'm used to it."

She didn't plan to sleep. Staying awake would be easier in the chair than in the bed. "How about if we take shifts? I'll go first in the chair. We'll switch places halfway through the night." But only if he woke up on his own before morning. She wouldn't wake him.

"Okay." He beckoned her toward the guest bathroom and opened the taps in the sink. "In case the guest quarters are bugged, the splashing water will make it hard to record us. When Rosana left the living room to find blankets, Rick told me he wasn't ready to see a lawyer after all."

"Second thoughts about what he planned to do, I guess." The snoop who bugged Rick Usher's study might have overheard him ask Granddad to find him a lawyer. Maybe the bug planter then talked Rick out of seeing a lawyer.

"Did you catch what Rick said at dinner about his dog dying after a guest visited?" When she nodded, Granddad continued. "I know when that happened. Cicero died Saturday afternoon. He took a nap and never woke up."

Emmett had died the same afternoon. Val doubted that was a coincidence. She moved closer to Granddad and spoke into his ear. "According to Clancy, Emmett ate lunch here on Saturday. Cicero might have eaten scraps from Emmett's plate."

"That lets Rick out as a suspect. Even if he somehow managed to put meds in Emmett's food, Rick would have made darn sure the dog didn't eat the same thing. We're left with Madison, Clancy, and Rosana as suspects."

"Madison said she skipped Saturday lunch here. She's in the clear, but only if the dog and Emmett OD'd on the same meds. To prove that, Granddad, we'll have to convince the police to exhume Cicero and do a doggie autopsy." The Ushers might oppose digging up the dog. Then the police would need a strong case against someone to get a court order for digging up Cicero. Val would tackle that problem tomorrow. "First, we have to make it through the night under the same roof as a murderer."

Chapter 25

Val huddled beneath two blankets in the recliner and opened *Poe Revisited* to "The Tell-Tale Heart." Though she'd read Poe's story in a high school English class, she remembered nothing about it except the ending. Now, reading it by candlelight in an isolated house with a murderer, fear crept over her. Poe told the tale of a perfect crime, a motiveless murder, which would have remained unsolved except for the culprit's guilt-induced confession. Emmett's murderer might have committed a perfect crime and probably wouldn't confess because of a guilty conscience.

Her phone chimed. She read Gunnar's text: Roads still icy. Let you know when safe to drive. Love, G.

She texted him her thanks. Then she sent another, lengthier text to tell him that Usher's dog died about the time Emmett Flint did and that they both might have eaten food laced with meds at the Usher house.

Gunnar responded immediately. **Stop snooping, dangerous.**

She promised she would give up snooping. An easy promise. No one in this house of secrets and lies would tell her what she wanted to know.

She picked up *Poe Revisited* again and turned to Rick Usher's "The Tall-Tale Heart." In his modern version of Poe's story, an organ recipient received a heart that beat erratically when he didn't tell the truth. It fluttered when he told social fibs and pounded when he lied for personal gain. Val anticipated the ending. The man would be tempted to tell a big lie that would doom him. The slow-moving story and Granddad's rhythmic snoring combined to lull her to sleep.

She awoke with a start when her phone chimed at six fifteen. Hard to believe she'd slept all night in the chair. She read the text Gunnar had just sent. The roads, though wet, were clear of ice. He was parked outside the Usher house. He would caravan with her and Granddad back to town whenever they were ready to leave. She texted back that they'd be out in ten minutes.

She shook Granddad awake. "Sorry to get you up so early. The roads are good. If I go straight to the café, I can open on time."

"I can't wait to go home to my own bed. I didn't sleep a wink all night."

She coughed to cover a laugh. While he stripped the bed, she called Irene to let her know she didn't need her to open the café. Then Val crept into the laundry room and changed into her now dry clothes, leaving Madison's cashmere outfit neatly folded on the washing machine.

As soon as she closed the door on the Usher house, her spirits lifted. They soared when Gunnar enveloped her in a hug. Thanks to the large umbrella he'd brought, she and Granddad got to their cars with barely a drop of rain falling on them. Once they were on the road, with Granddad in the lead, her next, and Gunnar bringing up the rear in his Miata, she was almost ready to laugh off the fears she'd had at the house. Almost.

Val left the caravan, taking the road to the racket and fitness club, while Granddad and Gunnar continued on to Bayport. More than the usual number of customers came to the café for breakfast. Many had already signed the petition Monique had circulated opposing the café's replacement by a sportswear boutique. Some had even e-mailed the manager and the club owner to argue against the change.

In a free moment Val phoned her cousin and thanked her for the petition drive.

"I recruited everyone on our tennis team to help," Monique said. "They each spent an hour at the club gathering signatures from people taking fitness classes and using the exercise equipment. We're going to do it again today."

"I'm not sure the petition drive will save the café, but I really appreciate it." Val thought of a question her cousin, an avid shopper, might be able to answer. "Yesterday I talked to a woman who won't wear anything but designer clothes. Is there a store in Bayport that carries clothing like that?"

"If she doesn't mind gently used clothes, she

could try Then and Now on Lavender Lane. The shop carries high-end clothes, from vintage to the latest fashions," Monique said. "Tell me why you asked me to age the photos of those men."

Two groups of café customers had arrived while Val was talking to her cousin. "It's a long story, and I have to get back to work. I'll explain the next time I see you."

If Madison wanted champagne clothes on a beer budget, Then and Now would be the place to go. Had she gone there after the rehearsal on Saturday and lied about it because buying secondhand clothes embarrassed her? Val put a visit to Then and Now on her to-do list for this afternoon. Then she could judge for herself if the finicky Madison would even venture into that secondhand shop.

Gunnar arrived at the café after the breakfast crowd had dwindled and before the lunch rush started. He'd had a few hours to catch up on the sleep he'd missed last night while monitoring the weather and checking for ice on the route to the Usher house.

Val poured coffee for both of them and gave him some breakfast bread pudding. She told him what Clancy had said about the rare edition of *Tamerlane*. "Emmett was convinced Usher had stolen that book and asked Clancy to look for it in Usher's study."

Gunnar shrugged. "Emmett automatically believed the worst about everybody."

"And everybody believed the worst about him. Clancy assumed Emmett wanted to steal the book and tried to dissuade him by saying it was recognizable as stolen property and had no resale—"

Gunnar held up his hand as if to stop traffic. "Emmett was a nasty man, but not a common thief. He wouldn't get satisfaction from reaching into your pocket. Instead, he'd have coerced you into giving him what he wanted. Power mattered to him as much as money."

That analysis of Emmett's character made sense to Val. "He asked Madison to look for *Tamerlane* on Rick's shelves and take a picture of it. He wanted photographic proof that Rick Usher possessed a stolen first edition. Then Emmett could threaten to go public with that photo unless Usher buckled to his demands."

"Demands for what?"

"Emmett wanted permission to create a show based on Usher's life and books. Usher previously turned him down, but Emmett persisted. He went to the house on Saturday made up to look like Usher so he could perform a scene from the show. I think he wanted a photo of that stolen book to pressure Rick Usher into approving the show."

"But Emmett didn't have the photo. Therefore, he couldn't exert any pressure."

Val doubted he'd give up so easily. "Emmett had other ways to get what he wanted. He couldn't prove Usher was gravely ill and unable to write, but that didn't stop him from spreading those rumors online. To counter them, Rosana booked public appearances for her husband. But if Emmett spread rumors about a theft that occurred decades ago, how could she disprove them? She had a motive to murder him because, even without proof, he could sully her husband's reputation by planting the book-theft story online."

"That's a thin motive for murder. Emmett had no proof of the theft, and you have no proof he threatened the Ushers. But I heard him threaten Madison. She lied about it to the police."

Val understood his zeal for proving Madison guilty and would have agreed with him if it weren't for the dog's death. "I think Usher's dog and Emmett consumed an overdose of beta blockers at the Usher house. Madison didn't get back to the house until after Emmett left, so she couldn't have slipped the pills into his lunch. Rosana or Clancy could have done that, whichever of them dished up Emmett's meal."

"The dog's death could have been a coincidence. For the sake of argument, assume Madison crushed meds into Emmett's burrito that morning, in the break room at the theater. Then she lied to make me look guilty. If the police dismiss the case against me as weak, she needs more suspects in the wings. Did she try to throw suspicion on the other people at the Usher house?"

Val sipped her coffee and reviewed what Madison had said last night. "Trying to throw suspicion on others might explain her unusual chattiness. She made sure I knew Emmett had been at the house for lunch. By the way, what kind of car did he drive?"

"A black midsize sedan." Gunnar closed his eyes as if conjuring an image of it. "Probably a Toyota, but I can't swear to it."

Unless Madison was more of a car buff than the average female, she probably couldn't swear to it either. "Madison said she recognized Emmett's car near the Usher house. A black sedan doesn't strike me as memorable enough to recognize."

"His car was plastered with Poe bumper stickers."

"Ah. Those would make the car distinctive." Those bumper stickers might have also attracted the attention of other Poe enthusiasts, like Simone and her son, Raven.

The night Val had spent in the dark at the Usher house, cut off from the world, had focused her suspicions on the people who lived there and made her forget about Raven as a possible murder suspect. But if tests showed the dog hadn't died from an overdose of beta blockers, there was no reason to limit the suspects to the Usher household. Raven had access to meds at the pharmacy where he worked and possibly resented Rick Usher's neglect of him. Yet, even with all her practice at jumping to conclusions, Val had trouble imagining how Raven would have had a chance to slip beta blockers into Emmett's food. During the few hours when the actor could have been mistaken for Rick Usher, he'd driven from the rehearsal to the Usher house, eaten lunch there, and then driven to the outlet mall. That accounted for most of his time.

Two women came into the café and claimed Val's attention. As she made smoothies for them, the café filled with more customers, and Gunnar left.

* * *

Val went to the Bayport Police Department headquarters on her way home from the café. She told the chief everything she and Granddad had learned at the Usher house.

The chief winced at the idea of exhuming the dog. "We don't have cause to do that yet. For the last few days we've been asking the public for information about Emmett Flint's whereabouts on Saturday afternoon. Nobody at the Usher house came forward, but now you've given us enough reason to question the lot of them about his visit there. I'll call your granddaddy and find out exactly where he saw that bug in Usher's study. Both of you gotta step back now. We'll handle it from here."

"I'm supposed to cook dinner there tomorrow night," she said.

"Check with me first. Even if I okay it, they might not want you there. We won't tell them who tipped us off."

"They'll figure it out." And Rosana might not pay her for last night's dinner.

Aside from that, Val didn't mind losing the Usher catering gig. She looked forward to focusing on the café and forgetting about Emmett Flint, but she couldn't do that as long as Gunnar was a suspect. He wouldn't be a suspect if Madison had told the truth about his fight with Emmett.

As Val left police headquarters, she reviewed what Madison had told her the night before. Though forthcoming about Emmett, Madison had stonewalled and lied about where she'd gone after the rehearsal. Because she'd shopped at a secondhand shop or because she'd done something else she wanted to hide?

Val drove to Lavender Lane, parked half a block from Then and Now, and stuffed her distinctive curly hair under a knit cap before going into the shop.

Unlike most secondhand stores Val had seen, this one wasn't crammed full of clothes. It had more open space than racks. Attractive outfits hung face out from hooks on the walls. Jewelry and accessories complemented the clothes on display. Yes, Madison might shop here.

A slim fortyish woman in designer jeans approached Val and asked if she had any questions.

"This is my first time here, so I'm not sure where to look."

"Welcome. I'm Holly, one of the owners, and I'll be glad to help you. We're putting out spring clothes in the front here. We still have a few winter things available along the wall to the right, and some of those are greatly reduced."

Val wouldn't mind checking out the reduced clothes. Maybe another time. Today she wanted to give the impression of having lots of money to spend. She browsed in a rack near the store entrance.

Two women pushing strollers came into the shop and drew the owner's attention away from Val. After Holly cooed over the babies, she asked the young women if she could help them.

"We're interested in your vintage clothes," one of them said. "I've been here before so I know where you keep them." She and her friend pushed their strollers toward the back of the shop.

"Are you looking for anything in particular?" Holly asked Val.

"A dress or a pants outfit for a special dinner date. A friend suggested I come here. Maybe you know her. She's about my age, slender with really long brown hair. She sometimes wears it in a braid."

"Oh, yes. She's a good customer." Holly nudged Val toward a rack with elegant short dresses on it. "She buys a lot here, and she's brought us fabulous vintage clothes to sell on consignment."

Maybe the vintage clothes had belonged to Madison's mother or grandmother. Keep Holly talking, Val told herself, and wait for a chance to ask nonchalantly if Madison had visited the shop on Saturday. "Between the vintage stuff and the latest fashions, you have a really unique business. It sounds as if it's going well. I moved back to Bayport about a year ago. How long have you been in this location?"

"Not a lot longer than that. My partner would like to open a different type of shop. I'm looking for someone to buy into this one. If you're interested . . . ?"

"It's not a good fit for me." Val saw a way to bring Madison back into the conversation. "But that friend I mentioned might be interested. She's really into clothes."

"I've already asked her." Holly looked at the sales tag on a dress. "Time to mark this one down." She took it over to the counter.

One of the young women who'd gone to the back in search of vintage clothes approached her. "Excuse me. Last Friday I saw some dresses here from the 1920s or 30s. I didn't have time to try them on then. I was going to do that today, but they're gone. Did they all get sold?"

"No, the woman who consigned them took them back on Saturday. She'd expected them to sell over the holidays. If there's one in particular you wanted, I could ask the next time she comes in if she'd bring it back."

"The mint green silky one with cap sleeves and a long scarf."

An image of a dress like that popped into Val's mind. The actress playing the divorced wife in the Treadwell Players' production last fall had worn a clingy green dress just like it. Gunnar had talked about the disappearance of costumes after the show ended.

She slipped out of the shop, convinced that Madison had swiped the vintage dresses used in the show, consigned them for sale, and come back on Saturday to reclaim them. Was that theft the secret Emmett had threatened to reveal unless she did what he wanted? If it came out that she'd stolen the costumes, the Treadwell Players wouldn't want her around any longer and Rosana Usher might fire her. Madison, though, could neutralize the threat Emmett posed by sneaking the costumes back to suggest they'd been mislaid not stolen.

Yes, she'd been dishonest, but she'd found a way to get around Emmett without resorting to murder. And if she had put a deadly dose of beta blockers in his burrito at the rehearsal, she wouldn't have had a reason to retrieve the clothes from the shop.

Besides, how would she, or anyone else except a doctor, know how much a deadly dose was?

Val climbed into her car. As she'd learned from a previous murder, arsenic was fatal in tiny amounts, but the same wasn't true of medicines. She whipped out her phone, opened a browser, and searched for the standard dosage of those drugs. It varied widely for each type of drug, and pills came in different strengths.

She tucked her phone away and drove home. How could the murderer have calculated how many pills to give Emmett? Crush too many into the food, and the texture, if not the taste, would change. Then the victim might stop eating before swallowing a lethal dose. Overkill in this instance didn't guarantee a kill. Neither did too few pills. Emmett's killer had either researched fatal dosages or made a lucky guess. Research suggested premeditation. A chill crept over her as another scenario popped into her head. His killer might have tried out the murder method on someone else first.

Val was still pondering the possibility of another victim when she went inside the house.

Granddad sat at the dining room table writing checks. He looked up. "What's new?"

Plenty. Except for their brief conversation in the Ushers' driveway and their whispered chat in the bathroom at the Usher house, she'd barely had a chance to talk to him since yesterday. She still hadn't told him about her visit with Simone. "I'll start with yesterday's news. I found Usher's son. His name is Raven, and he looks like Edgar Allan Poe."

"Very funny." Granddad went back to writing checks.

"I wasn't jok—" She broke off as her phone rang.

Chief Yardley was calling her. "I'm at the Usher house," he said. "There's no one here. Do you know where they went?"

"They were planning to do something this evening, but I'm surprised they're gone already. It's barely past three o'clock. I'll see if my grandfather knows." She covered the mouthpiece. "Granddad, did the Ushers say anything about their plans for today?"

"Not to me." He stroked his beard. "I know it's a special day. Last night, while we were sitting in front of the fire after dinner, Rosana poured us all a nip of cognac. Usher proposed a toast to Edgar Allan Poe on the eve of his birthday."

Poe's birthday. A toast. Cognac. Usher's concern about today's weather. Val could guess where the birthday party would be. "They went to Poe's grave in Baltimore, Chief."

Chapter 26

"What?" Chief Yardley's single word sounded like a bark over the phone. "All of them went to Poe's grave?"

Val remembered Rosana's words—*One evening a year, Madison. . . . You have an essential role.* "They're taking part in an annual ritual there. Rick Usher will do what the legendary toaster did at Poe's grave every year for decades on this day. Raise a bottle of cognac in a toast, drink from it, and leave the bottle behind. I don't know what role the others in the Usher household will play."

But she was convinced one of them was a murderer. The question she'd asked herself earlier echoed in her mind—*Could Emmett's killer have tried out the murder method on someone else first?* What if it was the other way around? Emmett might have been the test case, not the primary target. If so, this year's toast at Poe's grave would have a new ingredient—a fatal overdose.

"I'm not going all the way to Baltimore for a toast

to a dead writer," the chief said. "I'll talk to those four tomorrow."

"One of them may not be alive tomorrow." Val couldn't waver and expect help from the chief. "If we don't get to Poe's grave fast, Rick Usher will die. I know where, when, and how it will happen—Poe's tomb, this evening, with an overdose of beta blockers in the cognac."

Granddad's jaw dropped. He jumped out of his chair. "I'll drive. I know how to get to the cemetery." He crossed the sitting room to the hall.

She followed him and kept talking on the phone. "Emmett's killer will commit another murder unless we stop it. And you may not be able to prove it wasn't an accident." She ignored the chief's torrent of questions while she put on sturdy walking shoes, exchanged her parka for a down jacket, and grabbed a black pashmina shawl for extra warmth.

She interrupted him. "It'll take you longer to get to Baltimore from the Usher house than it will take us, Chief. We're leaving now." She rushed out of the house.

"You two stay at home," he shouted as she walked toward Granddad's Buick. "Officer Wheeler's driving me back to Bayport now. You have until I get there to convince me that you're right. Do that, and I'll alert the Baltimore PD of possible trouble in the cemetery."

Val climbed into the passenger seat as Granddad started up his car, a sound the chief could surely hear through the phone. "If the Baltimore police close the graveyard, you won't be able to catch the murderer in the act. The killer's next try might happen behind closed doors. This evening's attempt will occur out in the open. We'll see you there."

The chief sighed. "Tell me who you suspect and what evidence you have."

Val could handle the who and why, but the police would have to get the evidence. Knowing that Granddad would want to add his two cents, she pressed the speaker button on her phone. "Five clues point to the killer—the dog, the dish, the book, the bug, and the blogs. Number one, the dog's death limits who could have committed Emmett's murder to the people in the Usher house."

"Only if you have proof the dog and Emmett died from the same cause," the chief said.

And if the police would dig up Cicero, they might get the proof, Val thought.

"I just remembered something," Granddad chimed in. "Usher told me he used to give Cicero leftovers because Rosana only fed him dog food. When everyone else was having dessert or coffee in the dining room, Usher would sneak into the kitchen and scrape whatever was still on the plates into the dog's dish. He could have done that on Saturday, even though he didn't eat lunch with the rest of them. Emmett's leftovers went into Cicero's dish on Saturday. That's why the dog died."

Val gave Granddad a thumbs-up. He'd given her a lead into her next point. "Now we come to the second clue, the dish. How did the killer get the pills into Emmett's food and no one else's? In the Usher house meals are served restaurant style, plated in the kitchen and brought to the table. In the absence of a chef or caterer, Rosana nukes the food, Madison plates and serves, and Clancy cleans up after the meal. But Madison wasn't there for lunch when Emmett was. Either Rosana or Clancy put the food on Emmett's dish and placed it in front of him."

Granddad grimaced. "Each one will say the other one did it. It's a toss-up." He accelerated as the car in front of them turned off. "What's the third clue, Val? The book? The one Usher was looking for?"

"Right. Emmett asked Madison and Clancy to look for a rare book he was convinced Rick Usher had stolen. If one of them told the Ushers that Emmett was looking for proof of theft or if Emmett himself mentioned the book on Saturday, Rosana would eliminate the threat to her husband's reputation. She's dedicated her life to Rick Usher. But there's another—"

"Wait a minute," the chief said. "You claimed Rick Usher would be the next victim. If his wife committed a murder to save his reputation, why would she turn around and murder him?"

"The bug!" Granddad jerked on the wheel, swerved onto the shoulder, and then steered back onto the asphalt. "It could have happened like this. A couple of days after she murders to protect her husband, she listens to the recording from the bug she planted in her husband's study. She hears him tell me he doesn't trust her to be his literary executor. He says he wants to find his son and asks me to arrange for a lawyer behind her back. After all those years of loyalty to him, Rosana figures he's going to change his will in someone else's favor. There's her motive."

Val had reservations about Granddad's theory. "I'd be surprised if Rosana could set up a computer to access the recordings. She relies on Madison to do the most basic things on a computer. Whoever planted the bug, Chief, should have the recordings downloaded on a computer somewhere in the house." All he needed was a search warrant.

The chief grunted. "Planting a bug doesn't prove anyone's a murderer. You haven't convinced me yet. What else have you got?"

"Online rumors that Rick Usher was too ill to write anymore. Several blogs posted that information in late spring and summer of last year. Gunnar's techie friend traced them all back to Emmett, who used false identities online. He claimed Usher didn't write the books that appeared under his name. Emmett promoted the lies on Facebook and Twitter. Why would he do that? What benefit did he get?"

"Telling lies online is its own reward for lots of folks," the chief said. "They get their kicks from it."

He had a point, Val admitted to herself. "Except for that online campaign against Rick Usher, Emmett didn't engage in blogging or social media, according to Gunnar's computer expert. Someone must have helped him set up the fake online trails and told him where and what to post."

"Madison spends all her time online." Granddad frowned. "Clancy could have done it too. People their age grew up with computers."

The chief cut in, saying, "I need facts, not speculation."

Val noticed congestion ahead and hoped it

wouldn't delay them too much. "If Rick Usher's fans believe that someone else is writing his books for him, Clancy is the likeliest person who would have written them. He's been Usher's only coauthor for the last few years and would be the obvious writer to take over his series. Emmett's online campaign started about the time he met with Rick Usher. Emmett wanted Usher's permission to create a show based on his works. Clancy arranged a meeting between them, possibly in return for Emmett spreading rumors online."

"They exchanged favors." Granddad steered into the faster-moving left lane. "Why did Clancy need Emmett to spread those rumors when he could have done it himself under fake identities?"

The chief said, "He must have known he'd leave a digital footprint. Why would Clancy kill the man who did a favor for him?"

"Emmett made demands on Madison, threatening to reveal a secret he knew about her. That's how he treated people. He probably threatened to tell the Ushers who was behind those online rumors unless Clancy buckled to his demands. I don't know what those demands were, but Clancy got rid of the man who had a hold over him."

By now Granddad was speeding along Route 50. "He's sitting pretty with the Ushers now. He's making money from the books he writes with Rick. I don't understand why you expect Clancy to kill Rick Usher."

"The Ushers pay him a flat fee for his work, lower than the going rate. He doesn't share in the success of the books he writes." Val glanced at her watch.

They were making good time, but would they get to the cemetery soon enough? "Assuming Clancy's the one who bugged the study, he heard Rick Usher scorn him as a writer and a literary executor. He also learned Usher wanted to contact both his son and a lawyer. Clancy had to act quickly, before Usher designated his son or someone else as the executor."

Granddad's face lit up. "He figured he'd be out on his ear before long."

"What would Clancy get out of being the literary executor, Val?" Chief Yardley said.

"The right to negotiate contracts for Rick Usher's intellectual property and take a big fee. He could also resurrect unfinished manuscripts, finish them, and make royalties on them. He could write new books with Usher's popular characters in them and collect royalties he could otherwise only dream of."

Granddad slowed down for traffic. "You can't rule out Rosana. The book is her motive. The blogs are his. Still a toss-up."

Val had no doubt about Clancy's guilt. But she could use uncertainty about the culprit as an argument for the chief to go to Poe's grave. "Both Rosana and Clancy will be at the cemetery. The question is which of them will hand Usher a bottle of cognac laced with beta blockers. If you're there, Chief, you can prevent a second murder and solve the first one."

"I'll talk to the Baltimore PD." The chief hung up.

Whether or not he showed up at the cemetery, Val and Granddad would be there. She researched their destination on her smart phone during the rest of the ninety-minute drive to the city. The cemetery, dating from the late eighteenth century, wrapped around the First Presbyterian Church. The burial ground and the Gothic church, now converted into an event venue, belonged to the University of Maryland. Its law school and its medical facilities loomed over the historic property. Visitors were welcome in the burial grounds until dusk, when the gates were locked.

The sun was setting by the time Granddad parked in a garage a block from the cemetery. He estimated they'd have half an hour until dusk. Val spotted a row of motorcycles in the garage, two of them the same make and size as the one Simone's son drove.

She and Granddad hurried along Fayette Street toward the cemetery. With the sun down, the temperature had plummeted and the wind increased. Granddad put up the hood of his parka and Val wrapped the shawl around her head and neck. They paused outside the iron gates to the burial ground.

He pointed to a marble monument about seven feet high just inside the gates. "There's where Poe is buried."

Even from outside the gates, Val could clearly see a bust of Poe set into the monument's façade. She'd envisioned Poe resting in a quieter spot, rather than close to a busy intersection. Though people hurried along the sidewalk, no one was visiting Poe's grave, even on his birthday. "Where is everybody? I didn't expect us to be the only ones here." She felt queasy. Could she have been wrong about where the Ushers were going tonight and about an impending murder attempt?

"I'll bet they're at the other Poe grave."

"What? Poe has two graves? Did they bury part of him in one spot and the rest elsewhere?" That scenario belonged in a Rick Usher horror story.

"His original gravesite is back behind the church." Granddad cocked his head toward the church. "A couple of decades after Poe's death, folks took up a collection to erect a monument and moved him here. Then they put up a headstone where he was first buried."

"Doubles everywhere. Two Poe graves. Two Usher impersonators." And soon, two murder victims, unless they prevented it. Val's stomach clenched. "Is there a gate closer to the other grave?"

Granddad shook his head. "We gotta go between the raised tombs and the burial vaults to get there. You ready?"

Val surveyed the brick path with Poe's tomb on the right and a tall obelisk on the left. High tombs and vaults lined the path as it continued toward the back of the graveyard. A daunting path for a claustrophobic. Val took a deep breath and noticed movement near the church ten yards to the left. Two couples faced a woman in a long, black coat with a fur-trimmed hood. The woman, who looked like a tour guide, gestured toward the church's tower. Val caught a glimpse of her face. Madison was pretending to be a guide, probably to keep visitors from going to Poe's gravesite behind the church.

She clutched Granddad's sleeve. "Madison's near the church steps. She isn't looking this way now. Hurry and hide behind the obelisk."

Val dashed after him. The lower part of the stone pillar was broad enough to conceal both of them from the view of anyone near the church. She peeked around the obelisk to check if Madison was coming closer. No, her back was to them.

"All clear?" Granddad said.

"Go for it." She waited until he was past the point where he could be seen from the church steps. Then she sprinted after him.

"This path will take us to Poe's grave," he said.

Two teenage girls hurried toward them from the rear of the graveyard. "You'd better turn around. We just saw the ghost of Edgar Allan Poe," one of them panted.

"Thanks. We'll risk it," Val said.

The girls ran around them and toward the cemetery gate. Maybe they'd seen the Poe look-alike, Usher's son.

The path curved to the left around the church. Val slowed down when she spotted a man twenty feet ahead of them. His black clothes made him hard to see in the dimming light. He cut off the brick path and made his way between the raised slabs and tombstones punctuating the grounds. Viewing him from the side, Val glimpsed a white scarf knotted at his throat, his dark moustache, and his longish hair. Raven Wingard.

"He looks like Edgar Allan Poe," Granddad whispered. "That's the ghost those girls saw."

"No, that's Usher's son. I told you he looked like Poe."

Raven was swinging a bottle in his hand as he slipped between two burial vaults.

"He's taking a different way to Poe's grave," Granddad said.

Val hurried after Raven and followed him into a narrow path between two rows of vaults. Granddad kept pace with her. She lost sight of Raven as the path ended in a clearing. A man wearing black, but without a white scarf, stood before a tombstone, his back to them. Even without seeing his face, Val knew he had to be Rick Usher. She'd expected someone else to accompany him and hand him a bottle of cognac, watching as he touched it to his lips. Then, in the nick of time, either the police or she and Granddad would intervene.

It wasn't playing out that way. In the fading light Rick Usher stood alone before the tomb. *Where were Rosana, Madison, and Clancy? And where was Raven?*

Val scanned the graveyard. Several vaults were taller than she was, though most men would have to crouch to stay hidden.

Rick Usher raised a bottle high in a toast.

As she waited for him to give an eloquent toast, he lowered the bottle and drank from it.

"Stop!" Val yelled. She rushed forward and saw a figure in black creeping out from behind a vault to her right.

Someone rammed into her from the left, knocked

the wind out of her, and sent her sprawling. She tried to break her fall with her hand. Her left wrist twisted under her. She rolled onto her back and flexed her wrist. Pain shot up her arm.

Granddad bent over her. "Val! Are you okay?"

"Yes. Hurry. Grab Usher's bottle."

She sat up, her head swimming, and scrambled unsteadily to her feet. As she focused, she saw Clancy grappling with Raven.

"Get out of my way!" Raven dropped his bottle. It landed on soft ground and tipped over. He lunged at Clancy, who dodged.

Rick Usher watched them aghast and backed up toward Poe's tombstone. Granddad seized the bottle from Rick's hand. Rosana rushed toward her husband.

Clancy and Raven circled each other, their fists raised.

Raven held up his open hands in a surrender gesture. "Truce? Okay?"

"Okay." Clancy started toward Poe's grave and stooped to pick up the bottle Raven had dropped. He whirled around and smashed it over Raven's head. Glass flew in all directions.

Raven staggered, holding his head. Clancy advanced on him with the jagged edge of the bottle.

"Clancy! Stop it!" Rosana yelled.

Val feared another murder. She ripped off her shawl, rushed up behind Clancy, and threw it over his head. Raven stumbled.

"*Police! Don't move!*"

Two uniformed police officers stood at the periphery of the graveyard with Chief Yardley.

Only one person budged after the officer bellowed his command. Rick Usher slumped down, hugging Poe's gravestone.

Chapter 27

Although standing still, Val felt as if she were spinning because of the activity all around her. One Baltimore police officer bent over Rick Usher.

The other officer told everyone again not to move. He helped Usher's son up, led him to a raised grave slab, and sat him down. Raven held his blood-soaked white scarf to his head.

Rosana wrung her hands. "Rick always planned to die here at Poe's grave," she wailed.

The officer checking him looked up at her. "He's breathing, ma'am. We've called 911. The university hospital's a block away. He'll get the best possible care there."

Clancy stood motionless with Val's black shawl over his head until Chief Yardley approached him and asked him to identify himself. The chief pulled the shawl from his head and handed him off to two officers who'd just arrived as reinforcements.

The chief took Val and Granddad aside to find out what had happened. He then spoke to the officer in charge, who took custody of the cognac bottle Granddad had taken from Rick Usher. The chief told Val and Granddad to walk to the emergency room at the university hospital, have a doctor look at Val's wrist, and wait there for him. The Baltimore police would need statements from them.

Val got her shawl back before a guard conducted her and Granddad through the dark cemetery to the gate. On the way, they passed the arriving EMTs.

Madison in her fur-trimmed black coat stood on the sidewalk outside the gate. "What's happening in there, Val?"

"Rick fell unconscious after drinking a toast to Poe."

Madison's hand flew to her mouth. "Oh, no! Will he be okay?"

Granddad patted her shoulder. "There's a first-rate hospital down the street. He didn't need CPR, and he's breathing on his own."

But for how long? Val could tell from Granddad's grim face that he shared her worry.

Madison stared at him with teary eyes. "I don't understand why you're here. Did Rick invite you?"

"We knew where he'd be," Val said quickly to keep Granddad from going into a long and winding tale. "Toasting Poe on this day is an annual ritual for him, isn't it?"

Madison nodded and wiped away a tear. "For the past few years he's been visiting Poe's grave at the end of the day on January nineteenth. He never attracted as much attention as the middle-of-the-night visitor last seen in 2009."

Val crossed her arm. "And no one sees Rick either, thanks to you. You're the gatekeeper for his tribute to Poe. How do you keep people away from the grave when he toasts Poe?"

"I give impromptu tours of other parts of the cemetery. If people reject my offer or slip by me, I call Rosana. She intercepts them closer to the grave or hustles Rick away."

"What's Clancy's job?" Granddad said.

"Cleanup. Once Rick leaves, Clancy removes the cognac and roses so no one knows anyone's been there. No publicity. No crowd waiting for him next year." Madison's voice broke. "I hope Rick can come next year."

Sirens announced the arrival of ambulances.

Granddad pointed down the street. "Val and I are going to that hospital. That's where they'll take Rick. Do you want to come with us?"

Madison bit her lip. "I'll wait here. Rosana may need me to move the car to the hospital garage or do other things."

Val walked arm-in-arm with Granddad to the hospital. "I don't know if the police have the evidence to arrest Clancy for trying to kill Rick Usher. But attacking Raven in front of witnesses should be enough for them to take him into custody."

"The jagged glass could have cut that young man's artery. They ought to get him for assault with a deadly weapon."

"They ought to get him for Emmett's murder too." Val was sure that her deductions wouldn't prove Clancy guilty beyond a reasonable doubt. She only hoped the police found the evidence to justify arresting him for murder.

They went in the main entrance of the hospital

and got directions to the emergency room. They walked down a corridor, past a food court and a café, and through another longer corridor. Eventually they arrived at the elevator that would take them to the emergency room on the lower level. By then, Val's wrist felt only slightly sore. If it still bothered her tomorrow, she'd see a doctor in Bayport. She and Granddad sat in the waiting room.

Val called Gunnar and left him a long voice message, summarizing what had happened at the cemetery. Meanwhile, Chief Yardley arrived and Granddad got up to speak to him.

As she tucked her phone away, Granddad returned. "Rick and Raven came by ambulance and are getting treatment. The Baltimore police are questioning Clancy. The chief is going to talk to Madison and then he'll go back to the treatment area to interview Rosana and the young man, if they're up to it. I told him we'd be in the café upstairs. You need to put ice on your wrist, and we can both use some food."

They'd finished eating by the time the chief came into the café with a Baltimore police officer.

"Any word on Rick Usher's condition, Chief?" Val said.

"His blood pressure was very low when they brought him in. I told the doctors he might have overdosed on beta blockers. He's responding to treatment now, and they're hopeful he'll make it."

Chief Yardley turned to the officer. "I'm going to get something to eat. You want anything?"

The officer declined. While he interviewed Val

and Granddad, the chief returned with a tray full of food and gobbled down a burger and fries.

Once the officer left, Val asked the chief how Raven was doing.

"The doctors were stitching up his wound the last time I checked. He's dazed and may have a concussion."

"Is he Rick Usher's son?" Granddad said.

"That's what he believes." The chief sipped coffee. "So does his mother. She'd told him Rick Usher might be at Poe's grave today. The young man hung around the cemetery most of the day, hoping to meet his father."

Granddad smiled. "Some folks at the cemetery took him for Poe's ghost."

"Clancy said he took Raven for a maniac who would harm Usher." The chief filled his fork with lemon meringue pie. "That was his explanation for starting the fight."

"His real reason," Val said, "was to make sure Rick Usher kept drinking the cognac laced with meds. Raven would have distracted his father. Clancy tried to scare off Raven and, when that didn't work, he freaked out. His murder plan was doomed."

Granddad patted her arm. "Because we were there to stop it. What took the police so long?"

"Burglaries, traffic accidents, a shooting. An elderly man visiting a grave didn't have a high priority." The chief washed down his pie with coffee. "I wish you two had stayed home, but based on what you told the officer, they'll be able to charge Clancy. That'll give us time to get a search warrant."

* * *

A few days after the Poe birthday party at the cemetery, Val heard the results of that search from the chief. She shared them with Gunnar, when he stopped by the house for a light dinner before his dress rehearsal.

During the search of Clancy's room, the police found a vial of propranolol, a beta blocker given to PTSD sufferers and prescribed for his brother. Rick Usher took a different type of beta blocker to treat his high blood pressure. The medical examiner ordered toxicology tests that could distinguish the type of beta blocker in Emmett's stomach and in Rick Usher's cognac.

A police computer expert restored the deleted files on Clancy's computer. Among them were the audio files downloaded from the bug in Usher's study and e-mails between Clancy and Emmett. The messages proved that Clancy engineered the social media blitz about Rick Usher's poor health. Emmett's final message included a threat to tell the Ushers who was behind the online rumors unless Clancy convinced them to endorse Emmett's Rick Usher play.

While she was talking, Gunnar finished a hearty bowl of vegetable soup. "So Clancy killed the man blackmailing him. He might have gotten away with it if he'd flushed the remaining pills away and tossed his hard drive into the Chesapeake."

"He never expected anyone to search his things. Emmett Flint and Rick Usher would both look as if they'd died from natural causes. Clancy had the misfortune that Emmett's sister kicked up a fuss and demanded the police investigate his death."

"With the world full of Emmett-haters, they had no shortage of suspects." Gunnar reached for Val's hand across the table. "I owe you and your grandfather a huge thanks. If you'd gotten hurt trying to help me—"

"This is the only casualty, and it's not serious." She held up her wrist wrapped in an elastic bandage. "By the way, I didn't tell Granddad about the café contract not being renewed, and now I don't need to. Monique's petition convinced the club owner to renew my contract. He told the manager to shelve the idea of selling clothes at the club."

Gunnar's face lit up with the huge smile Val loved. "Fantastic news! Will you still hire Irene?"

"I'll give it a try." Val set her soup bowl aside and picked up her salad fork. "I'm looking forward to the challenge of growing the café business."

He leaned across the table. "If you're too busy to get away around Valentine's Day, we can celebrate your birthday here and postpone that trip."

She hadn't expected him to suggest a postponement, but it didn't bother her. They'd known each other for only half a year. They weren't ready to take their relationship to the next level, as Bethany had urged. Better to move at a slow but steady pace. "Let's plan to celebrate here."

"Sounds good." He speared the last of the lettuce in his salad. "Tell me about the book Usher was looking for. Did it have anything to do with what happened to him or Emmett?"

"Not directly, but what Clancy said about it made

me suspect him. He never uttered Emmett's name until Madison forced him to admit Emmett had eaten lunch at the house on Saturday. After that, Clancy couldn't shut up about Emmett and his idea that Rick had stolen the book."

"Too much information."

"Exactly, and he had a purpose. Once it got out that Emmett had eaten at the Usher house before he died, investigators might come to the house. Clancy played up the Ushers' motive for killing Emmett—fear that he'd blackmail them over the stolen book."

"Did Rick Usher steal that first edition from the university library?"

Val wouldn't accuse anyone of theft without proof. "Let's just say he behaved like a man who thought he had that book. He started looking for it after Emmett's visit."

Gunnar glanced at his watch and stood up. "I've run out of time. Thanks for feeding me."

She walked him to the door and hugged him. "Break a leg, Big Daddy."

As he drove away, Granddad arrived, returning from a visit to the hospital in Baltimore. "Rick's out of intensive care and feeling better."

"I'm relieved to hear that. Come to the kitchen for some soup."

While she ladled up his soup, he took a beer from the fridge. "I spent some time with Rick when Rosana met friends for lunch. I asked if I should set him up with a lawyer after all. Not now, he said. He'd wanted a lawyer to handle an anonymous donation of a book to a library, but he couldn't find the book. Until it turns up, he doesn't need a lawyer." Granddad opened his beer. "You were wrong about the reason he wanted a lawyer. It had nothing to do with changing his will."

"And everything to do with a stolen first edition of *Tamerlane.*" She brought Granddad's soup to the table. "Did he say anything else about that book?"

"He bought it at an estate sale years ago. He knew a book like that had been taken from a library, but didn't believe he'd bought the stolen copy."

"Or he didn't want to believe that. The book's return might have been what he needed to put right before he died."

Granddad blew on his soup. "But where's the book? Did someone steal it from *him*?"

She shrugged. "I wonder if he's seen it since they moved here from Baltimore. When people relocate, things get lost or hauled to a secondhand shop."

While Granddad ate his soup, she told him what she'd learned from the chief about the investigation.

Granddad broke off a hunk of French bread. "Sounds like they're sewing up the case against Clancy. Did they find the whole house bugged?"

Val shook her head. "You and I were excessively concerned about bugs. Only Rick's study had a bug in it."

"Why did Clancy bug it?"

"He had access to that room, and everyone went there to talk to Rick. I guess Clancy was so insecure that he needed to know what they were saying about him."

"Sometimes it's better not to know. I talked to Rosana while Rick was napping at the hospital. She was going to put Clancy in charge of the books and copyrights once Rick passed on. Clancy could have gotten what he wanted in due time by waiting."

"He might have waited, if he hadn't bugged the study and heard Rick belittle him. Clancy wanted more than control of Rick's works. He craved recognition for his writing. Rick paid him badly and didn't give him credit for his work. The last straw was when he made fun of Clancy's writing in front of you." Val recalled the first sentence of "The Cask of Amontillado" and paraphrased it. "*A thousand injuries I had borne as best I could, but when he ventured upon insult, I vowed revenge.* That's how the murderer in a Poe story put it. Clancy's motive was similar."

Granddad sopped up the last of his soup with bread. "Speaking of Poe, Raven showed up here when you were at the café this morning. Simone told him where I lived. He thought I might know how Rick was doing. Raven told me he's wanted to see his father for years. He moved to this area just because Rick was here. He used to follow Rick when the Ushers lived in Baltimore, hoping for a chance to talk to him."

"I'll bet he was the man Rick thought was stalking him though neither his wife nor Madison believed the stalker existed."

"Raven didn't mean any harm. He was really happy when I told him Rick wanted to meet him too." Granddad took his empty bowl to the sink.

"At the hospital today Rosana kept thanking me—and you—for saving Rick's life. I told her Raven deserved the thanks. He got there ahead of us, distracted his father from drinking more cognac, and fought off Clancy. You and I would have had trouble doing that. Rosana insisted on thanking him in person. I called Raven and told him to come to the hospital. To make a long story short, he got to see his father."

Val stared at her grandfather, amazed that he'd given someone else credit instead of claiming it himself. When had he changed? "Granddad, you really are a problem solver, like your business card says."

He pulled a card from his wallet and plunked it down in front of her. "It also says I'm a sleuth."

She tipped an imaginary hat to him. "If it weren't for your instincts about the Usher house, Clancy would have gotten away with murder." Of course, Granddad's first instinct had been that everyone in the house was covering up Rick Usher's death.

"I solved another mystery. Before I went to the hospital today, I did a lot of research on the so-called Poe toaster. Until now, no one has identified the mysterious man who visited Poe's grave in the middle of the night."

Until now? "You've figured out who the Poe toaster was?" Val tried to keep the skepticism out of her voice.

"Not the original one, the one who took over in 1990s. The last year the toaster slipped into the cemetery at night was 2009. That was also the last year the Ushers lived in Baltimore."

"Are you saying Rick Usher was the Poe toaster?"

Granddad nodded. "By 2009 he was getting less spry. The crowd trying to capture the toaster was bigger than ever before. When no one took over the tradition of toasting Poe in the wee hours, Rick changed the time of his ritual and toasted Poe at dusk instead of at night."

"That's as good a theory as any about the Poe toaster's identity." None of them had any basis in fact. "But you can't prove Rick Usher was the mysterious toaster."

Granddad waggled his finger. "Mark my words. He'll name a successor. If you and Gunnar stake out the graveyard after midnight next January nineteenth, I'll bet you see Raven toasting Poe. Will that be proof enough for you?"

Val paused before answering. Holding a midnight vigil at a graveyard in January would prove only one thing—that she'd lost her mind. "Who needs proof? I accept your brilliant theory."

Acknowledgments

Like every other writer of mysteries, I owe a debt to Edgar Allan Poe, who pioneered the modern detective story. Everything I wrote about Poe's life, works, and death in *The Tell-Tale Tarte* is true. While Rick Usher is a fictional character, the elusive Poe toaster is not. As far as anyone knows, the toaster paid his last nighttime visit to Poe's grave in the early hours of January 19th, 2009. The Poe performer in *The Tell-Tale Tarte* is not based on any current or past actors who bring Poe's writing to life. The stolen first edition of Poe's *Tamerlane,* mentioned in *The Tell-Tale Tarte,* remains missing, along with the other writings and artifacts taken from the archives at the University of Virginia.

For details about Poe's life, death, and reputation, I relied on *Poe-Land* by J. W. Ocker, *Edgar Allan Poe* by Madelyn Klein Anderson, and the online resources provided by the Edgar Allan Poe Society of Baltimore. I received helpful information about the effects and detection of prescription drug overdoses from D. P. Lyle, M.D., and from pharmacist and toxicologist Luci Zahray, known to the mystery community as the Poison Lady. I thank both of them for sharing their expertise.

Thank you to my critique partners, mystery writers Carolyn Mulford and Helen Schwartz. Always generous with their time, they brainstormed with me, gave my book a careful chapter-by-chapter reading, and offered helpful suggestions at our weekly meetings. I'd also like to thank Paul Corrigan, Toni Corrigan, Susan Fay, Cathy Ondis Solberg, and Elliot Wicks for giving me feedback on the book during its final stage. I'm especially grateful to Mike Corrigan for his support through the whole process of writing this book, for reading and commenting on the book, and for visiting Poe's grave with me on a gloomy day to take countless pictures amid the tombstones. For a change, Mike, you didn't have to assume the role of either victim or murderer in my enactment of the crime. Maybe next time.

I'm grateful to my agent, John Talbot, to my editor, John Scognamiglio, and to the production, marketing, and sales teams at Kensington Books who helped bring *The Tell-Tale Tarte* to readers.

Finally, to the many readers who enjoy detective and mystery fiction: Thank you for keeping Edgar Allan Poe's spirit alive.

The Codger Cook's Recipes

E-Z BEAN DIP

This three-ingredient dip takes three minutes to make. You only need one measuring cup because you use the same amount of each ingredient. Double or triple the recipe for a crowd.

½ cup of packed-down grated cheddar cheese
½ cup of refried beans
½ cup of salsa, spicy or not depending on your tastes

Mix the three ingredients in a microwave-safe bowl. Microwave on high for one minute and stir the dip. Microwave on high for another thirty seconds and stir again. Repeat, if necessary, until the dip is the consistency you like.

Serve the dip warm with tortilla chips.

Serves 4–6.

E-Z GUACAMOLE

This three-ingredient dip also takes only three minutes to make. Double, triple, or quadruple the recipe for a crowd.

1 medium Haas avocado
1 tablespoon lime juice
3 tablespoons salsa, as spicy as you like it

Mash the avocado with a fork. Squirt lime juice on it. Mix in the salsa.

Try the dip. Add more lime juice or salsa to your taste.

Serve the dip with tortilla chips.

Serves four.

ORANGE-GLAZED CORNISH HENS

For this recipe, use marmalade made with sugar. It can be the low-sugar type, but not marmalade made with corn syrup or artificial sweeteners.

4 tablespoons orange marmalade
1 tablespoon + 1 teaspoon balsamic vinegar
1 tablespoon dried thyme
2 Cornish hens approximately 1.5 pounds each
Vegetable cooking spray
[Orange slices, optional]

Preheat the oven to 350 degrees.

Combine the marmalade, the vinegar, and the thyme in a microwavable cup. Microwave the mixture for 1 minute at half-power. Stir to mix the ingredients. Microwave for 30 seconds at half-power. Repeat the 30-second microwaving until the mixture is soft enough to brush on the hens. Set it aside and keep it warm.

Rinse the hens under cold water and pat them dry. Split them in half lengthwise. Coat a rack with vegetable cooking spray and put it in a shallow roasting pan lined with parchment paper. Place the hens on the rack, breast side up. Brush them with half the glaze mixture.

Bake at 350 degrees for 25 minutes. Brush the hens with the remaining marmalade mix, and then bake an additional 20 minutes.

If you have hens of a different size, bake larger ones longer and smaller ones for less time.

Serve with an optional garnish of orange slices.

Serves 4.

CHESAPEAKE BAY PEEL-AND-EAT SHRIMP

Eating Chesapeake Bay specialties often means getting your hands dirty. Hard-shell crabs make the most mess. Peel-and-eat shrimp are a close second. But they're quick and easy to fix because the person who eats the shrimp does the peeling, not the cook.

- 1 cup cider vinegar
- 1 cup water or flat beer
- 3 tablespoons Old Bay seasoning
- 1 pound of large shrimp (30–40 count per pound)

Combine a cup of vinegar, water, and Old Bay seasoning. Old Bay is the most common Chesapeake Bay seasoning found in supermarkets, but other companies make it too.

Bring the mix to a boil in a large pot. Add the shrimp, stir, and cover the pot. Once the water boils again, cook for two minutes and drain the shrimp. Cook longer if you use larger shrimp, but be careful not to overcook because the shrimp will lose their taste and become tough.

Serve the shrimp with a cocktail sauce, either store-bought or homemade. An easy sauce has three ingredients: ketchup, lemon juice, and horseradish, in whatever proportions taste good to you.

Serves 3–4.

WARM CHOCOLATE TART

A tart (in English) or a tarte (in French) is a pastry dish without a top crust.

½ cup heavy cream
⅓ cup 2% milk or whole milk
8 ounces semisweet chocolate
2 large eggs
1 9-inch ready-made shortbread pie crust (or a prebaked homemade sweet crust)

Preheat the oven to 350 degrees.

Heat the cream and milk on high heat in a saucepan until the mixture boils. Remove it from the heat, add the chocolate, and stir until the chocolate is melted.

Beat the two eggs in a bowl and whisk in the chocolate mixture little by little. When the ingredients are smooth, pour them into the crust.

Bake the tart in the oven for 25–30 minutes until the custard is set.

Serve warm with ice cream or a dollop of whipped cream. Refrigerate any leftover tart.

Serves 8.

Adapted from a recipe by Jacques Haeringer for Auberge Chez Francois in Great Falls, Virginia.

TARTE TATIN

Just because a recipe has five ingredients doesn't mean it's easy or quick to make. This tarte takes practice and a lot of courage at the last step when you turn a hot skillet upside-down and hope the tarte ends up on a plate.

It's best to cut the apples 1–3 days before making the tarte to dry them out. Otherwise, you may end up with too much juice in the tarte. Put the cut apples in a lightly covered bowl in the refrigerator. If you don't have time to let the apples dry out, put a piece of foil under the skillet when it goes in the oven to catch any drips.

6–8 large apples, peeled, cored, and quartered (A mix of Granny Smith and Honeycrisp apples works well.)
6 tablespoons (¾ stick) softened unsalted butter
2/3 cup sugar
1 frozen puff pastry sheet
Equipment: a seasoned 10-inch cast iron skillet

Preheat the oven to 400 degrees when ready to cook.

Slice the bottom off each apple to give it a flat base. Peel and quarter the apples lengthwise and remove the cores. See the note above the ingredients about storing the apples in the refrigerator for at least one day before cooking.

Spread the butter on the bottom and sides of a seasoned 10-inch cast-iron pan and sprinkle the sugar evenly on the bottom. Arrange the apples vertically in the skillet, standing them on the flat end, in concentric circles. Pack the pieces close together so they support one another. Apples that stick up higher than the pan rim will shrink down as they're cooked.

Prepare the pastry while the apples are cooking. Follow the directions for defrosting the puff pastry. Then roll it out on a floured surface until it is 1/8 inch thick. Put a 10-inch plate upside-down on the pastry and use a sharp knife to cut out a circle the size of the skillet's top.

There are three stages to making this tarte Tatin:

1. Cook the apples over medium high heat, 15–25 minutes until the juice is bubbling and a deep golden or light brown color.
2. Put the skillet in the oven and bake the apples for 20 minutes at 400 degrees.
3. Remove the pan from the oven, lay the pastry circle over the apples, and tuck it around the apples. Bake the tarte at 400 degrees until the pastry is browned, approximately 20 minutes. Check it after 15 minutes to make sure it doesn't get too dark. You want the crust to be a nice golden brown. If it still looks pale after 20 minutes in the oven, bake it a few more minutes.

Move the skillet to a rack and cool it at least 10 minutes and up to 30 minutes. Put a cutting board or platter over the skillet. Use potholders to hold the skillet tightly against the board or platter. Turn the skillet upside-down. If apples stick to the skillet, add them to the top of the tarte.

If the tarte stands longer than 30 minutes after being baked, heat it over low heat for 1–2 minutes before turning the skillet over.

Cut the tarte in wedges and serve warm with vanilla ice cream or whipped cream, or just eat it plain.

Serves 8.

Adapted from a recipe for "Foolproof Tarte Tatin" by Julia Moskin, *The New York Times*, October 22, 2014.